MW01634639

MARIE

MARIE

A Novel about the Life of
MADAME TUSSAUD

Dorrit Willumsen

Translated from the Danish
by Patricia Crampton

THE BODLEY HEAD

LONDON

The Publishers wish to acknowledge with gratitude
the support of the Danish Ministry of Cultural Affairs.

British Library Cataloguing
in Publication Data
Willumsen, Dorrit
Marie: a novel about the life of Madame Tussaud
I. Title
839.8'1374[F]   PT8175.W5
ISBN 0 370 30880 8

Printed in Great Britain for
The Bodley Head Ltd
30 Bedford Square, London WC1B 3RP
by The Bath Press, Avon
First published by Vindrose Publishers, Copenhagen 1983
First published in Great Britain 1986

Marie is undoubtedly a modern woman as well as an historical personality, but ever since a visit to Madame Tussaud's gave me the idea for this book in 1979, I have been trying at intervals to find out about her own time. I am indebted to Egon Friedell's *kulturhistorie 2*, Casanova's memoirs, Voltaire's letters and household accounts (extracts from letters to his niece and to Frederick II of Prussia appear in the chapter on Voltaire), Stefan Zweig: *Marie Antoinette*; Stanley Loomis: *The Fatal Friendship*; Beaumarchais: *Le Mariage de Figaro*; Axel Petri: *Den forsvundne franske Tronfølger*; R. Broby-Johansen: *Krop og klaer*; and above all to Anita Leslie and Pauline Chapman: *Madame Tussaud, Waxworker Extraordinary*.

My warmest thanks to Pauline Chapman and Michael Herbert, whose archives and interest in the novel have helped me so much.

Dorrit Willumsen

CHAPTER ONE
Departure

Bern 1767

The yellow roses bowed their heads. The dark paintbrushes of the poplar trees washed out the sky. The rain shut everything in, like clothes in a packing case.

Marie Grosholtz stood on tiptoe, her nose and forehead pressed against the glass. On a sunny day she could have seen the white mountain peaks, but today she could see no further than the well. One finger traced a raindrop sliding down the pane.

The black puppy whined and nuzzled close to her, but she could not play today for she must not crumple her dress. She had already said goodbye, but the puppy would not understand. She pushed it away with her foot but it jumped up at her, its claws dragging a thread from her sleeve. 'Oh, *dog!*' There was a dry clack of paws on the tiled floor, the puppy flattened itself down and Marie smoothed the china-blue material with a reproachful look in her eye.

'My new dress, just when we're leaving! When you leave, it means you've gone. Gone, like the balls and sticks and stones you're no good at finding. Gone, like the ten kilogrammes Grandmamma has lost because she's so sad and now her cheeks are all loose and soft.'

Marie put her arms round the dog's neck and pressed her face into its thick, shaggy coat, but it wriggled loose, its wagging tail slapping her cheeks.

'Silly dog, you don't understand! You don't even know what

is inside the carriages you're always attacking. People leaving, people rolling away. You just try to bite the wheels.

'You must stay indoors today. I do not want you to see me going, I do not want you to bark or bite my wheels. I am five years old, too big to cry, but not grown-up enough to swoon!

'Perhaps we shall never reach Paris, perhaps we'll be set upon by robbers and murdered! Or the carriage will overturn. I heard them speak of it in whispers when I listened at the door.'

'The child,' Grandmamma had said, as if she were about to lose another five kilogrammes.

'You must stay here,' said Grandpapa.

'Scum and filth . . . whores and smallpox!' — that was Uncle Frantz's voice.

Mother's voice was as sharp as her embroidery scissors, cutting through all the rest.

'Leaving,' she said, and 'Curtius', and 'Paris'.

The words hung in the air.

If my father had lived it would not have been necessary. I could just have gone on living here and playing and we should have had our own house.

Perhaps he is not truly dead? It may be something they say because it sounds so sorrowful and grand. One day he will come riding down from the mountains, his uniform and harness shining, his horse stepping daintily like a lady in silk shoes. He will ride in through the town gate, past the fountain and right up to our well. My mother will go out and their faces will be like snow in sunshine.

No, not snow, my mother's skin is soft as honey, but honey belongs in the kitchen with Grandmamma and the maids and my mother is a lady. Her skin is like the white steam that settles on the windows when we wash.

No lice or fleas bite her, her cleanness makes them faint away. Her lace handkerchiefs are finer than frost flowers. When we go walking together I always want to curtsey. What if we ran to the mountains — no, she never runs. She embroiders, needle and silver thimble flying through the air. The thin threads turn into flowers, always flowers, even in winter when the panes are frosted over and we seem to be enclosed in a great, white egg. The cold makes everything silent; only the stove roars, to hatch us out.

My mother's lips are red; perhaps she bites them. Otherwise she is pale and refined and has headaches. After every blood-letting — the blood runs from her wrist into a little bowl — she is paler than ever. Her face is as white as porcelain, her eyelashes thick and heavy. If I could only look like her I would gladly have a headache all the time, and the blood-letting, too, though blood makes me feel sick. If I could just learn to swoon instead of vomiting! If you hold your breath — oh, if only I could manage to hold my breath!

How will my father find us, if we move to Paris? I don't want to go at all. Supposing I say that I don't want to go?

'Marie, Marie!' Her mother's voice. Stooping swiftly to kiss the puppy on the nose with a fervour that made it yelp, she smoothed her dress and slipped her hands into her muff. She lifted her knees as she walked, in order to admire her new white boots and stockings, but at the sound of voices in the passageway she began to take tiny steps, straightened her back and pressed her elbows to her sides.

Her grandmother tied the ribbons of her travelling hat under her chin so tightly that tears rose in her throat. She and her mother moved from one embrace to the next, Grandmother, Grandfather, two uncles, two aunts, five female and three male cousins, all endangering her new hat. The sour smell of damp fur from kissing the dog clung to her lips and nose.

The taste of salt at the corners of her mouth came only when the coachman lifted her into the carriage and slammed the door. She licked up the tears, waving to the cousins running after the carriage and to the older people whose hands moved up and down very slowly, like puppets just before coming to a stop.

Then she dried her face and rolled her handkerchief into a hard little ball. It was a snowball, melting and trickling up her sleeve. She looked up at her mother, who suddenly smiled, a rather fierce little smile, showing her teeth like the puppy when it did not want to run with a stick. Marie would have liked to touch her, but did not because her mother's slender figure filled her with the same awe as the statues of the Holy Virgin, or the big china doll she had been given for Christmas and never dared to play with.

Now Grandmamma was sure to give it to her cousins and one day they would drop it on the red-tiled floor. It would turn into a thousand white splinters, while they bawled and the darkness inside the doll's head became light.

Marie straightened up and looked out of the window at the black and shining road ahead. She could see the coachman's heavy blue cape and the horses' tossing tails. She was off to Paris, over the mountains, and one day perhaps she would marry a prince, or at least a count.

She wanted to return in a carriage with golden escutcheons and footmen in white stockings. With a casual gesture she would fling gold coins to the crowd and distribute costly gifts to those she favoured. Her wardrobe would fill the whole of Bern and only the dog would be allowed to jump up at her. It would have grown old and wise and would recognize her at once. She would give it a basket with silk cushions, and put a golden collar on it — no, her waist would be so tiny that she must not bend, so the footman would do it. And he would lift the dog onto a stool for her to pat. She would never take off her gloves and her hair would be like the finest meringue, which crumbles when you set your teeth in it. Her cousins would kneel to her by day and dream of licking her hair by night, when she wanted only to sleep or have a headache. In the morning she would stick a black beauty spot on her cheek, just under her eye when she was happy and at the corner of her mouth on days when she did not care to smile.

Marie leaned her head back, forgetting her hat, and closed her eyes in order to picture herself as a lady in pink and china-blue silk, and more fragrantly scented than any garden or puppy in the rain. She would never walk but would always be carried or driven. The shoes on her little feet would be made of silk, embroidered with white pearls.

She could almost picture the whole scene, when the carriage suddenly stopped and a thin man with a stubble of red beard climbed in and sat down opposite her mother, and another man in dark clothes with plump, scarred cheeks sat in the seat opposite herself. Marie let her gaze travel between the two faces, unable quite to decide if they were robbers, or whether it was the stubble or the scars that frightened her most. Her mother gazed out of the window as if it were suddenly imperative to remember every single field, every single house, the goats' yellow eyes and the big, barking dogs. She hid a yawn behind her fan. Or perhaps it was a smile, or else she was trying to protect herself from the red-bearded man's breath, which was as sweet and warm as stewing fruit.

The air and the pitching of the carriage made Marie sleepy. Her eyes closed and in her sleep she saw her mother's sudden smile, white teeth between full red lips, the smile of a woman who never suffered from headaches. And the roads, the earth, the mountains all parted and bared their teeth. The sun itself revealed a greedy grin.

She was suddenly awakened when the carriage came to an abrupt halt. The scarred man lifted Marie down while she herself took great care not to brush his cheek. She stood, swaying, until her mother took her hand and they went into the inn, where the heat and the smell of cooking slowed their movements.

The red, gleaming face of the innkeeper's wife and her starched skirts pitched and rolled like a ship laden with food. She ladled great sweeping dollops onto the plates. Marie and her mother fed safely on roast turkey, with milk for Marie, while her mother sipped at the slightly sparkling apple wine which made her eyes moist.

With the cheese the red-bearded man came over and offered her mother a carafe of red wine, strong and sweet-smelling, like his breath, but her mother put a cautionary hand over her glass.

Later the innkeeper's wife took them up to a room, the lock of which was broken. The astonished Marie saw her mother push a chair against the door.

'Why?'

But her mother shook her head, splashing jasmine scent on her neck and wrists and round the bed.

For the first time Marie saw her mother's body without the great airy structure of her whale-bone corsets, her stomach and breasts white and heavy, her waist as slim as a girl's, striped and dented by the corsets. Marie closed her eyes as if she had been struck and turned away.

But the bed was as soft and deep as a nest, rolling their two bodies towards the middle, where the warm, heavy smell of her mother gave Marie a momentary longing for the puppy which she usually smuggled into bed with her. Then her mother began to talk, in a voice which was bright and eager with expectation.

'We're going to Paris. Everything will be different. Your Uncle Curtius lives in Paris. I shall never wear dark clothes again, or be shut in by mountains and rose hedges. Never again that weight behind my eyes when the Föhn wind blows. He wrote to say we would be welcome. He's rich. I shall never again live with the memory of my loss, although I don't really know what it is that I have lost.

'I waited too much and too long. Even as a child I was waiting for that knight in shining armour who would come and make everything different. As a sixteen-year-old I was ready to burst with expectation, ready to fly through the air and yield myself to the slightest puff of wind. I embroidered the gardens, the horses and hounds which were to be my future, but I never embroidered the knight's face . . . he might be anybody.

'One day he stepped into my expectations — that Swiss guard, young and brilliant in his uniform. I admired his cape, his gloves, his boots, his buckles, glittering like some great exotic insect. I did not see that the uniform was a chrysalis of premature death. For my bridal gift we bought a house in Strasbourg, and we had bright gold brocade on our chairs.

'My mother grieved over the wedding.

'"Your happy girlhood days are over," she said.

'I had no idea what she meant — perhaps it was my sixteen-year-old impatience, like sitting in a swing, longing to let go and fly towards the horizon, while still clutching the ropes and laughing or shrieking with fear.

'That constant, unsatisfied expectation: the dreams you transform into silken flowers turning towards the light. Or the days when all you feel is indifference, faintness and languor. The doctor's probe wakes you up, the blood runs sweet and sickly into the bowl. No, I did not understand her.

'We moved to the house in Strasbourg, moving for five whole days among the sun-gold chairs and cooing like doves. From time to time I remembered to tell the maid what to make for dinner and I embroidered as if I could make him happy that way. Always the same dogs, always the same flower-buds, peacocks and swallows.

'After that I saw him only when he came on leave. I was jealous of the laughter, the friends, the horses, the adventures, the tight, smart uniform and the boots which gave him his light, swinging gait.

'He arrived full of laughter and aggression, always with stories to tell. When I had something to say the words flickered like shadows round a thin flame. I spoke French badly and he would stare at me as if doubtful that I had any idea of what I wanted to say.

'I let the maid take me for walks along the canals. I saw the cathedral rising like a slender mountain peak, and I wanted to shout, just to know if there were any echoes in that town, or if my cry would rise straight up to heaven like the cathedral spire.

'As a rule I ate in the kitchen with the maid, a slim, dark girl. When she spoke or smiled there was a sudden correspondence between her fine little upper lip and the full lower lip. When she was silent the lower lip seemed to bear her cares and the upper one her smile.

'She was always talking about her sweetheart and whether, or rather when they would have enough money to get married. She was always counting the days, although in other respects she was no good at sums, not where the household accounts were concerned. She talked about medicines that could prevent pregnancy and her eyes were envious and admiring when she looked at me, who did not have to make those calculations when he strode in, shining in his uniform, with his abrupt embraces which made me think of horses.

'After three months I was pregnant. I continued to tight-lace myself, but not quite as tightly as before. I had no one from whom to conceal my condition nor anyone I could impress with my rapid pregnancy. I knew no one but Louise the maid.

'I walked among the sun-gold chairs in light morning dresses, but with a heaviness in my blood, in my fingertips and behind my eyes, as if the dreams of the unborn were buzzing in my head, making me faint and unwell in a new way. I wrote to my mother about my condition and she sent me a silver cross and a pair of tiny stockings saying that I should come home as soon as possible and give birth under satisfactory conditions.

'Louise chattered and was happy. Now we would both have someone to entertain us while we waited, she said. I pulled the rings off my fingers — but my wedding ring was so tight that it would not move. And although I feared the birth I looked forward to the day when it would all be over, when he would have leave and come home and I would lie, slender and weak, in the white lace peignoir, incapable of all but the fleeting kisses and caresses I associated with being in love.

'But two months before your birth came the news of his death. Suddenly he had become a hero and they had put a silver plate in his temple to cover the wound. His skin was very cold and smooth, seeming to reject my kiss in his disappointment. At seventeen I was a widow, my bright clothes fading in the cupboard. Only those I gave to Louise were bleached by the sun and spotted with wine from Alsace. The golden chairs were covered with white dustsheets, as if my surroundings too must die. Naturally I went home and gave birth, without expectation, but also without any real fear. When they saw my indifference they interpreted it as my longing for a boy. But in fact I had no hopes at all.

'The heavy, dark skirts dragged me down with a weight which was not yet a part of my body, and I began to look forward to the day when I could sink down under a fine, smoothly polished stone. I embroidered, or had headaches, and for the first two years I believe you scarcely existed for me. I felt only disappointment at being home again. Sometimes I felt that Louise had gained much more from life than I. All her fear and trembling, all the exaggerated expressions, tears and sudden laughter were concentrated on her body cycle. She would certainly be happy one day, when her sweetheart was ready.

'I crept up to the loft to look at my trousseau, all packed away again. I lifted the stiff dushsheets off the chairs to observe the activities of moth and woodworm. It never occurred to me to use this furniture in the drawing-room. The light dresses in their soft pastel colours could be kept for you, said Grandmother, and I accepted everything she said. She seemed so pleased to have us back, as if my marriage had been merely a brief, unsuitable journey.

'My brothers began to bring friends home, pale students and rich merchants whose eyes sought mine. Dogs' eyes that clung to my movements, while I wore my clothes like armour. And I defiantly tied my corset laces to the bedpost in order to lace myself tighter than ever before.

'In the end they gave up, whispering that my grief had been too great. I could hear them in the evenings, when I was undressing, and I breathed on the looking-glass and rubbed it until it shone. I looked into my own eyes until I almost drowned in their pupils, and saw a haughty sharpness in my face. My bones seemed to be showing their own pure form, before the features collapsed. And so I waited for another five years.

'Never wait, Marie. Never expect anything at all.'

At that moment the door was forced open, the chair crashed to the floor and the red-haired man almost fell into the room.

Her mother snatched up the wash bowl and hurled it at him. Broken china showered on the floor. The man got up, panting, and clutching his forehead, where a little blood trickled out between his fingers.

'*Pardon, madame*, a mistake.'

Her mother slammed the door behind him and pushed the chair back against it, returning to bed on flat, sure feet.

Thunder in the mountains, and after a few minutes the steady patter of rain drops against the windows. The rain enclosed them.

CHAPTER TWO

Up Hill and Down Dale

France, and the countryside spread before them like the pages of a picture book. Marie searched in vain for mountains. The swallows were flying high, the roadside ditches edged with roses and wild orchids.

Her hair sticky with heat, Marie took off her travelling hat and her mother removed her fur collar, stretched and yawned openly. The only other passenger was a thirteen-year-old boy, sitting opposite them. His lips were pressed together and in his shyness he did not dare to meet their eyes. His hair was cut so short that it was like a soft black brush and his cheekbones stood out like wings.

Marie sucked in her cheeks to make her face look narrow, admiring the boy's thinness and his thick eyelashes. She pretended that he was a prince in disguise, until she remembered that his mother had worn a shabby shawl and had had to pay for his journey in advance because he had no luggage.

Suddenly the coach stopped at a house almost hidden under honeysuckle and ivy. Even from where they sat they could smell the flock of agile brown goats in their fold, while the hens strutted about freely.

A woman in an indigo blue dress came running through the hip-high grass with a carpet bag in her hand. She seemed not to notice when the hem of her dress trailed in the hen muck, or that one white elbow stuck out of her sleeve when she passed her bag up to the coachman and exchanged some words with him in a jerky, incomprehensible dialect. Her red hair stood out in a vigorous frizzy mop round her face, which was as small and white as the goat cheeses she was holding out to the passengers.

Marie's mother stiffened as if the young woman's hair might scorch her, or the smell of goat cling to her clothes, but she accepted one of the little white cheeses in her gloved fingers. The woman dropped two cheeses in the boy's lap and stroked his cheek. Marie sank her teeth into a cheese and tears sprang to her eyes at the sharp, acid taste and the laughter in the woman's clear green eyes, which made her think of witches.

With a jolt the coach moved off again, at a flying pace which made Marie laugh and roll about like a ball. She felt she was falling into the woman's blazing red hair. Then came a splintering, crystalline screech and a long, plaintive whinny.

When she opened her eyes she was lying on top of the boy, who was very pale, his lips compressed, on the point of tears. Her mother was lying like a lost doll, her skirts around her knees, her arms flung protectively across her face. A big, star-shaped hole opened directly onto the road.

The woman picked Marie up and held her close, tears and snot running into the soft indigo blue fabric, which smelled sour and warm. Having cried herself out, she lifted her head, to see her mother standing, erect and elegant, facing the coachman.

'Beg pardon, mistress,' he muttered.

Marie's mother spat a splinter of glass onto the road.

'It might have been worse.'

Marie ran to rest her cheek against the smooth black silk, which had retained its cool, light scent of jasmine.

The horses' whinnies rose to screams of terror as the coachman tried to lift the horse which had stumbled and was still lying in a mound of red-brown, slippery skin, its nostrils flaring, its eyes almost shut in pain or obduracy.

It rose at last in one great heave, and allowed itself to be led limping onto the grass. The coachman examined its leg and slowly, swimming through the tall grass, the woman went over and stroked its muzzle.

Marie heard her mother sigh and to offend them still more, the sound horse lifted its tail and dropped a heap of steaming, yellowish dung right at their feet.

With the same slovenly cheerfulness as before, as if neither her flaming red hair nor the white carpet bag of cheese were connected in any way with their accident, the woman fetched a bottle of apple brandy. The coachman drank greedily; the boy's eyes grew bright after a single swallow. Marie's mother shook her head distantly, while Marie tugged at her to come and pet the kid goats.

'No, child, we've had accidents enough. My arm hurts and you have a bruise on your forehead.'

'We shall not get far with one horse, mistress.' The coachman might gaze fatalistically at the overturned coach, but he was already taking their misfortune more lightly.

'No.'

'Can you spend the night here?'

'No.'

'The nearest inn is not good—and we must first raise the coach.'

'Yes,' said the slim, black-clad woman, stepping awkwardly across the horse dung. 'Let us proceed.'

Cursing at her hard, incomprehensible speech, the coachman made the sound horse haul and brace his foursquare body against the coach. The woman, the boy and Marie's mother all pushed, and Marie got holes in her stockings and wagon grease on her fingers as they lifted, groaning, sighing and squealing. With a sudden, miraculous jerk they pulled the coach upright and resumed their places, as if the battered vehicle had become their safe and rightful home. With the wind blowing through the broken pane and goat muck on their boots and stockings they drove on, even after darkness had fallen, becoming more and more wakeful in the chill, star-bright night.

The smell told them at once that 'The Clean Glass' was indeed not good, but it was full of people. Some slept, lolling over the tables, others were drinking and slicing off sausage and cheese, while a little black monkey leaped from lap to lap.

The innkeeper seated them in one corner, his leather apron swinging under Marie's nose as he poured out soup, wine and water. Her mother took tiny mouthfuls, as if her shy, reserved way of holding the spoon might remove her from the place altogether. The boy was silent, but little Marie was enchanted by the monkey's sudden leaps, the customers' loud voices and bold movements and the shrill colours and daring cut of their clothes which seemed to reveal rather than cover their bodies.

One was a very young girl, almost a child, her small breasts visible under the white blouse, one elbow propped nonchalantly on a table, each muted gesture hinting at a half-involuntary caress. There were deep dimples in her cheeks, her hair was black and shining, her eyes drowsy with wine and she seemed scarcely aware that her feet were resting, not on the floor but on the lap of a well-dressed elderly man. Her red silk skirt scarcely covered her knees and his hands stroked their way from her ankles up under the red skirt, while he gazed at her with melancholy eyes. Marie thought the girl was the most charming creature she had ever seen and she too would have liked to touch the legs, as slender and delicate as a young deer's. How she longed for a red skirt and a pair of thin white stockings which did not have to be kept whole!

'Stop staring, child, it is ill-bred.'

Marie, trying hard to obey her mother, looked down at her soup, where beads of fat sketched a shining pattern among the sad cabbage shreds.

'That's a fairground entertainer,' her mother whispered. 'A tightrope dancer, perhaps.'

'Could I be one too?'

'Only over my dead body!'

But neither the bursting bubbles of fat nor her mother's stiff injunctions could keep Marie's eyes from the pretty girl. Two men were playing ball with the bread and the monkey bit into the ripe peaches, the juice running down his chin. No one protested when he dipped his little black hands in the wine glasses. And ever more sorrowfully, with eyes softer than velvet, the well-dressed elderly gentleman caressed the girl's small feet.

Very quietly Marie slipped off her boots and tried to stretch one ankle in a graceful arch. She pressed her toes on the floor until they hurt, already, in her imagination, floating in embroidered slippers along a thin rope.

'People of that sort,' muttered her mother, 'do not even have anywhere to live.'

'Do we?'

'When we are in Paris — we shall stay in Paris until we die.'
'I would like to travel.'
'Travel,' said her mother with a sigh. 'That is not for us.'
'Show me your hand, child, I'll tell you if you will travel!'
Marie turned her head and saw a woman so short and so broad that she resembled nothing more than a bundle of coloured shawls. Her face was old, but her hair was dark and smooth and a little black moustache gave her an animal-like air, at once innocent and exotic.

Marie had once seen a book about sea-lions and otters. She stretched out her hand at once.
'You will travel — across the water.'
'Leave her be, I beg you.' Marie's mother pulled her hand away.
'I see sorrow and fame.'
'She is only five!' Her mother's voice shook.
But Marie beamed with excitement. Fame!
'I'm doing it for nothing, lady. Usually I only see misfortune for those who do not pay! Shall I read your hand, lad?'
'No, thank you.' The boy had both hands behind his back. 'I know my future — I am for the seminary.'
'With those eyelashes?'
With laughter still in her voice, the woman leaned towards Marie.
'You've a queer hand, sweetheart . . . there is a hole in your lifeline.'
Madame Grosholtz stood up and carried her daughter off to the room allotted to them. The smell which came out to meet them was sickly and acrid, but when she tried to open a window she found the hasp was broken. They got into bed without undressing and the smell that struck them there was as dizzyingly oppressive as if they had opened a bottle of musk. They lay on their backs between the sheets of 'The Clean Glass', which had obviously absorbed countless travellers' sweat, urine, fever, exhaustion and dreams.

Soon afterwards the boy stole in and rolled up on the floor like a cat. At first he cried softly and miserably into his sleeve but after a while there was a sound as of crunching broken glass, or sugar lumps.

'Mother,' whispered Marie, 'make him stop!'

'He's grinding his teeth — think of something else.'

Marie let her thoughts float far away from the little future priest and the bedbugs' march.

She was standing in the fairground, on fire with excitement. The sun was shining, the eyes of the crowd fixed on her. She wore snow-white stockings and a skirt of some charming, light stuff in red — no, better a tender pink against her skin.

Light as an angel, she almost flew up a narrow, swaying ladder and everyone gasped at the sight of her tiny feet in their embroidered silver shoes. Smiling, she trod the tightrope on tiptoe, supported by their admiring eyes, and when she looked down it was to see her own picture and her name on the billboards.

The men would gaze at her with melancholy eyes and she would be both elegant and gentle, but she would never marry, for she would travel from one fairground to the next, to hover and to dance.

But suddenly she was falling, in total darkness, and then came the sound of crashing onto a heap of broken stones. Perhaps she had cut herself, for there was a putrid smell and her body hurt. She stretched out her hands and brushed her mother's face.

Together they discovered that the wretched bed had collapsed beneath them. They spent the rest of the night on the floor, but Marie thought again of her fame, by comparison with which wrecked beds and coaches were but indifferent trifles.

At five in the morning they drank scalding hot chocolate while the coachman waited with fresh horses and a light open carriage. The countryside flew by, swathed in the grey morning mist, and after one last rest they were driving into Paris.

Marie's eyes were everywhere. The houses closed about them like grey cliffs, to whose shelter people sprang from the carriage wheels. They seemed to be driving through mysterious ravines and the voices that reached them were hard and sharp as the morning cries of birds.

A young housemaid dashed a bucket of refuse over the street, the gleam of a lemon among the garbage, but the sight of an old woman carrying a basket of green vegetables and a little bunch of yellow roses made Marie snivel with homesickness.

Suddenly the carriage stopped in front of one of those dizzyingly high houses and once again Marie was lifted down with the luggage. Her mother embraced a gentleman with powdered hair and a fine pearl-grey taffeta suit, and when he stooped towards Marie his cheeks prickled against hers until, not knowing whether to laugh or cry, she curtseyed deeply to hide her face.

The table was laid for three in a room whose walls were almost covered with pictures. Opposite Marie's chair hung a painting of a young woman in a light red dress, almost the same colour as her rounded arms. She was leaning over a bearded man lying on a seat among silk and velvet cushions, apparently being assaulted by the woman. Starting eyes, open mouth and outstretched hands attempted to repulse her, but the woman had thrust a short sword under his beard, her face tense with pain and effort, as though his throat were too tough to sever.

'Judith and Holofernes,' Marie read. It was a Bible story, she knew, but the meat stayed in her mouth, and oblivious to the adults' talk she allowed herself to be absorbed into the picture.

She seemed to feel the pile of the velvet and the woman's rustling silks as she stepped into the tent. For an instant she might have wanted to sit on the cushioned seat, but duty, hatred or a promise stopped her. She must have lied to get in; perhaps she was still lying when the blade pierced the man's hot, throbbing flesh, letting out the body's smell and colour, like slaughtering an animal. Marie remembered that Judith had put Holofernes' head in a sack. And she was a famous heroine, in golden sandals.

Marie tried to imagine her homecoming. Judith would walk across the sand — there was always sand in the Bible. She would feel the weight of the head against her back and know that she had done her duty. Perhaps she would narrow her eyes against the blinding sunlight, perhaps tears would run down her cheeks and neck, drying in white, salty streaks. And the sand would fill her sandals, making her footsteps so heavy that she longed to throw away the sack and run. Even by the time the raspberry sorbet arrived Marie had not quite succeeded in picturing Judith's face in the moment when she left the tent. She continued to see only her broad back in the billowing light red material, from the seat where Holofernes lay back without his wild, bearded head.

After supper Curtius showed them his house. The carpets absorbed their footfalls and everywhere there were silk *portières*, mirrors and candelabra, all silent as a church.

An elderly woman with an elegant coiffure was sitting motionless at a table; but perhaps she had heard them, for, ignoring her patience cards, she held out one hand as if expecting them to come to her.

Marie curtseyed deeply, wondering why her mother and Curtius laughed while the woman's face did not change. Perhaps she was ill, for she did not even blink when without a by-your-leave Curtius placed her hand on the table and turned her head to the cards.

'She's made of wax, child — come.'

He pulled out a drawer, from the depths of which rows of round eyes stared upwards, brown, blue and grey, very young and bright, or old, with a fine web of veins.

He placed a pair of green eyes in Marie's hands, where they beamed icily at her, while she seemed to hear the red-haired woman's laughter. The floor moved and the eyes dragged her down into an engulfing darkness. She felt someone lift her up and knew that at last she was old enough for swooning, not vomiting, and from a great distance she could hear her mother and Curtius agreeing that the long journey had been far too much for a child of her age.

CHAPTER THREE

Delightful Children

Nine-year-old Marie and ten-year-old Henriette walked with tiny steps in the shadow of the trees, the withered leaves crackling under their brocade shoes. The slightest unevenness brought the girls to a stop, the fragility of their shoes converted into a little stiffness in their backs.

Marie's cape was pearl-grey, edged with Arctic fox. She was as small and light as a sparrow, with the same dark, lively eyes and a nose that was a little too long.

Henriette's plumpness gave her a seesaw, tottering motion. The shiny, *dos-de-puce* coat accentuated her little pot belly and the doll she was hugging gave her a matronly look. Her lips were lightly parted, but whether in a smile or a sigh, or simply because she was out of breath, no one could tell. Her bright, grey eyes were both purposeful and nonchalant as she turned to check that they were out of the nursemaid's hearing at last.

The girls sat down on a bench and looked at their feet, still not quite touching the ground. Henriette's nursemaid sat at a suitable distance, eyes closed against the sharp autumn sunshine, head bowed drowsily on her breast. Henriette leaned back and undid one coat button, looking momentarily exhausted, but suddenly straightened and rained sharp slaps on her doll's face.

'Do stop,' said Marie, 'you might break it!'

'I am much too old for it anyway — and I do not want my sister to inherit it. And besides, it will not keep its hands over the bedcover when it sleeps — and I have an extra dancing-class again today.'

'Don't you like dancing?'

'I am too quick in the minuet. I have to learn to be slower if I'm to be married.'

'But you're only ten!'

'In my green silk I'm thirteen at least, and I shall be married when I am fourteen, like the Crown Princess. Have you seen the wedding portraits in the windows and newspapers and journals? How lucky she is—'

'The Crown Prince is much too fat.'

'You know nothing about it. He is handsome in his portraits.' Henriette powdered her face so vigorously that she sneezed.

'My uncle made some of the portraits, and they are handsomer than the reality.'

Henriette smiled condescendingly.

'You are not noble, you do not understand these things. She will have hundreds of dresses and piles of diamonds and horses. She will live in Versailles and play around the fountains in summertime and skate and have snowball fights in the winter. If only he is noble and rich, who cares about reality?'

'Who — who must be noble and rich?'

'My husband, of course!'

'Suppose he does not want to have snowball fights?'

'I shall have them all the same.'

'Suppose he is angry?'

'Perhaps he'll kill me, or I'll kill him, or else I shall take a lover. Have you met any noblemen?'

'The Prince of Conti — he's older than my uncle. The Duke of Orléans — he needs two chairs to sit on.'

'Where have you met them?'

'At my uncle's house. He makes their likenesses.'

'Well, let us go to your uncle's Waxwork Cabinet, and in the great Hall of Mirrors we shall meet all those noble, handsome, rich people!'

'No, only as wax figures. The poor people are the ones who come to the Hall to see the pink lights and gilded chairs. The real people of rank and fashion go down to the basement, where my uncle exhibits the murderers and great robbers.'

'Will you take me down there?'

'It's horrible — some of them are in prison, others have been executed. The fine ladies look at them and say: "A thief, a murderer, one would never have supposed it!" The men say nothing. They stare into the criminals' eyes, shining as if they were alive, and the blue light makes you freeze. In any case, many of the rich look like criminals and have cruel hands or foul breath.'

'Marie, I believe you will never marry!' Henriette sighed deeply.

'I would prefer to draw.'

'That is because you are bourgeois. I would be desired!'

'What?'

'I shall enter a great hall, my coiffure brushing the chandeliers and all the men will swarm about me like flies round rotten meat. My fan will flutter like doves' wings before my face. And I shall rise late like my mother and sometimes I shall not rise at all. Did you know my mother stays in bed all morning? She rings for her two chambermaids to bring her hot chocolate and help her out of her nightdress. They massage her whole body with almond oil, lifting her arms as if she were made of glass, and she does not open her eyes. They rub her from her throat to her ankles, and from her neck to her heels. Sometimes she groans a little into the pillow, but they do not press hard, for she would pull their hair if they did. Then they shower a snowstorm of powder over her face and hair and bed, tickling her body all over, and when she gets up she is sweet-smelling and shining white. The maids lace her and put on her morning dress and she sits, looking at her face in the glass. Sometimes she is unwell and spends all day between her glass and her bed. On those days she receives flowers and sweets and visits. When I am feverish I have only a pail to vomit in. Marie — try to feel my breasts. When I pull in my stomach I think they are growing ...' Henriette grasped Marie's hand, but stopped in mid-movement as the nursemaid's shadow fell over them. Their walk was over, she announced, and the sedan-chair was waiting.

Without a glance for the bearers the girls jumped into the chair, the nursemaid trotting behind, panting and unsteady on her swollen ankles.

As always, the rocking and swaying made Marie feel faint. She knew that she should not look out, but she could not help it. All the sounds of the city seethed about them, the garbage in the gutters stank; she saw the thin, bare legs of a street urchin and his inquisitive, provocative stare, and a young serving maid emptying a chamberpot, giggling as she splashed the bearers' stockings; sparrows on a bush of glowing hips and an elegant carriage with six black horses, suddenly forcing the bearers to one side. Her head could not hold the rapidly shifting impressions; she was being torn to pieces.

With a covert movement Henriette drew the curtains and leaned towards Marie in the semi-darkness.

'Have you any more sweets?' Her whisper did not reach the profane ears of the nurse and the bearers.

Marie nodded and took the bag from her muff.

'Give it me. I'm to have no supper.'

'Why?'

'For punishment, because I stole. I stole from Maman's toilette — all the things that can help me grow up!"

'Henriette—'

'Today I shall take her belladonna.'

'But, but it's dangerous, Henriette — fatal—'

'Why should children not be fatal? It stings, and your eyes are like a fallen angel's. I shall make the dancing master so dizzy he forgets to keep time.'

'Is he young?'

'No, old. He says I have puppy fat and prods me in the back with a fork to make me hold myself properly.'

'Henriette, do you think fallen angels dance?'

Marie felt Henriette's soft, aristocratic lips on hers.

'You're supposed to open your mouth, little idiot. You kiss like a boy!'

But Marie was not to learn how to kiss, for at that moment the bearers set down the chair at Curtius' house. The children hastily exchanged a kiss on the cheek like grown ladies. Marie dismounted, but had scarcely touched the handle before the serving girl was opening the door and helping her off with her cape, quickly and silently, as if she were a stiff little doll.

From the salon she could hear that Uncle Curtius had visitors.

She practised a few curtseys, straight-backed, her knees pointing outwards, but invisible beneath her skirt.

'Oh, Marie—' whispered her mother as with a perfect curtsey she slipped soundlessly past the adults — 'You have been running again — your cheeks are quite red.'

Marie sat down guiltily in the corner with her drawing board.

Her mother's gold thimble glinted in a beam of light as she drew a blue silk thread in and out of a pattern in graceful curves.

Curtius and his guest were sipping wine from tall, cut glasses. The visitor was a thick-set elderly man in the uniform of the Royal Guard and Marie bowed her head, blushing, in order not to disturb them with the slightest glance. Almost of themselves her hands sketched patterns and faces while she listened to the guest's voice.

'The Crown Prince's official wedding was magnificent. The whole garden was illuminated, the fountains like running gold. Two thousand candles were alight between the three hundred and six mirrors in the Hall of Mirrors. I heard figures which sounded like pure astronomy, but the Hall itself was a universe, its beauty was simply not of this world. You cannot imagine it without having been there.

'In the midst of all that splendour sat the Crown Prince and Crown Princess, dressed in white, which simply emphasized the contrast between them.

'She sat on her chair, small, slim and upright, glancing across at him now and then as if expecting him to speak to her, as any other man would have done. But the whole situation obviously made him uneasy. He blinked his eyes a little, as if he were seeing everything through water, and his body sagged more and more inside the brocade which did not quite disguise his stomach.

'The guests talked, laughed, danced, ate and drank. Only those two were silent. The King was seen to whisper something to the Crown Prince, probably trying to get the fool to pay a little attention to his poor bride. Perhaps her feet were moving under the white dress, which revealed her slender arms and very small breasts. Her hair shone golden through the powder. She watched the dancers with attentive, curious eyes, but if anyone met them she looked down at once, as if ashamed. Nevertheless she went on smiling, a little artificial smile she must have learned, to distract attention from her heavy Hapsburg underlip. But she did not need it. Everyone there wanted to touch this child.

'When they played the minuet the Crown Prince could hold back no longer; he rose and bowed to her, and had they not been of royal blood everyone would have laughed aloud at such an ill-matched couple. She kept time, dancing so lightly, so delicately that she seemed to float. And she watched him most wonderingly, as he rolled along like a ship at sea. He fixed his eyes on a distant point on the wall, as if hoping the mirrors might suddenly slide aside and offer him a hiding-place, but they simply reflected the light and the white glitter of brocade. In three hundred and six mirrors the Crown Prince and Princess danced, silent as marionettes, each to his own time.

'Shortly after the dance he sat down to eat. Footmen filled his glass with the heavy red Burgundy as if to reward his efforts. His bride did not touch a morsel of food, but sipped champagne for the sake of appearances. Her smooth eyelids were heavy with boredom and for a moment her head dropped like a fresh, forbidden fruit among the dishes.

'She was awakened at once, and those of the highest rank led the bridal pair to the bedroom. I followed, being fortunate enough to be on guard that night.

'Obedient as two well-bred children, they allowed themselves to be undressed. The bridegroom had difficulty in donning his nightshirt, clearly embarrassed by the number of people and the light falling on his fat, smooth body. The girl fidgeted like a young deer.

'The heavy embroidered curtains of the four-poster were drawn round the newly-weds like a wall of roses. Everyone waited, but there was no sound from the bed. They could hear the candles flickering, a door slamming far away and a puff of wind which crossed the room and made the long ostrich feathers flutter in the ladies' coiffures, but from the bed, not the smallest squeak, neither a sigh nor a gentle creaking.

'The guests waited for five or perhaps ten minutes before losing patience. A hand tugged sharply at a silk cord and the curtains flew apart. The crowd pushed and shoved for a view.

'The Crown Prince lay with closed eyes, perhaps genuinely asleep, but his bride looked up with quite indescribable astonishment. Defenceless, oyster-grey eyes shone up at the painted faces as if from the bottom of the sea, until with a little, frightened gasp she pulled the quilt up over her nose.

'Next morning there were no spots on the linen; the bed was almost undisturbed, and now, after nearly two months, everyone is laughing at them and laying bets on the coming of the spots.

'The best-informed is the Spanish Ambassador, who is in direct touch with the chambermaids and the footmen, but to his knowledge the act has not yet taken place.

'The doctors have advised the Crown Prince to eat well — as if that were necessary! And the women are busying themselves with the girl. They have set her to some sewing, but she would rather play. She is a delightful child.'

And as if suddenly reminded of Marie's presence the two men rose and came to look at her drawings.

They saw two profiles, one plump, the other slender, almost sharp; and two bodies, one lumbering, the other fragile. They faced each other, incompatible, but linked by the minuet which lifted their arms in a defensive, helpless gesture.

They were standing one on either side of a magnificent four-poster, one cringing with embarrassment, the other atremble with shyness, naked and at the mercy of a crowd of elegantly dressed onlookers, who had apparently stripped them and were now avidly ogling their every movement.

'Heavens!' murmured the guest. 'How does a little girl like this come to think of such a thing?'

'Child,' said her mother, 'do you have to draw people with no clothes on?'

'Not a bad beginning.' Curtius nodded approval and followed his guest out.

Marie watched her uncle go, hoping he would let her join him in the workshop. She loved to see him make a face appealing or repulsive simply by drawing a line in the soft wax.

Into her mind came the conjurer pulling long blue ribbons out of his mouth, and the smart circus horses dancing the minuet. Every time she heard music she saw them in her mind's eye, decorated with flowers and feathers, prancing on their back legs. Their coats were so bright that she wanted to press her face against them to feel the warmth and the quiver of finely-tuned muscles. A prickle of happiness reached right out to her fingertips.

CHAPTER FOUR
Voltaire

Mademoiselle Marie Grosholtz drew the curtains quickly and a sharp light fell into her girlish room, where the other furniture looked so very fragile and knick-knacky by comparison with the great writing-desk placed under the window.

She bobbed unobtrusively to the old gentleman who had apparently just got up, but who was completely engrossed in the papers and books that almost covered his desk. She poured a little coffee into his cup, took a cup herself and sat so that she could look up into the clear, slightly mocking eyes.

'Monsieur Voltaire—' she said, watching his hand with its distinct blue veins, and perhaps expecting it to carry the steaming coffee to his lips while he gave his simultaneously welcoming and malicious smile, as she continued.

'There is something I wish to ask you. In *Candide* you have a regiment of soldiers locked up with a similar number of women of easy virtue. When they are starving, you have the soldiers slicing off one half of the women's backsides, on which they dine, thereafter winning a very important battle. You say nothing of the women. Did they eat with the soldiers? Was it their lovers who ate these half-portions, or were they all mixed together in one great cauldron? Do you not regard it as a crime to eat human flesh?'

The old gentleman looked affectionately at her and she bowed her head to concentrate fully on his reply.

'No, Mademoiselle, that is mere prejudice. The crime is not to eat meat, but to commit murder. Once I had the honour of meeting four savages from Mississippi, then displayed at Fontainebleau. One of them, a woman, appeared very gentle to me and I asked if she had ever eaten the flesh of her enemies and if so had she enjoyed it. She answered in the affirmative, as if it were the most natural thing in the world. But when I asked if she had ever *killed* anyone she turned away, shaking with fear at the very thought of that dreadful offence, and it was evident that she had precisely the same feelings and ideas about right and wrong as you and I.'

The seventeen-year-old Marie rose to her feet, her movements a little impatient, her hands at her back rather than at her sides, as if to ensure that her bottom was intact. It was clear that she was not fully satisfied, as she went over to the old gentleman, flicked some fluff off the oyster-coloured brocade coat and removed his wig, so that his smooth, bald pate reflected the light.

She took a modelling tool and stroked in the wrinkles and veins on his temples as if tuning a fine instrument. Cautiously she began to remove the colour from lips and cheeks so that the face looked older and a certain transparency began to suffuse the whole figure. Without the ornately curled wig there was also something childlike that made her smile, recalling to mind how her heart had rushed to her throat the first time the maid informed her that M. Voltaire had arrived.

At first she had been almost relieved when he sent his apologies in short, clear notes written in his small, precise hand.

'Unfortunately obliged to travel to Versailles to work.'

'Prevented by rheumatic pains.'

'Expecting a visit from my niece.'

'Prevented because my health and I are, alas, divorced for ever.'

'Absolutely must work.'

She turned over the letters, remembering his face, hands and figure, quick and agile as a lizard and always aware.

Accustomed to posing, he controlled his facial expression, disclosing out of modesty or miserliness only the part of his personality he wanted her to use.

She tried to remember the meagre glimpses of a vulnerable face, a fleeting view of the net of fine wrinkles drawn taut and sharp, as if he were caught in it, struggling to get out. Perhaps pain was responsible. She remembered one suddenly alarming, sharp glance and his fingers scribbling a hasty note.

But these were not yet in her portrait. The figure facing her was a slender, delicate man, with clear, vigilant eyes and a little smile playing at the corners of his mouth. She had not yet found the expression for sensitivity and pain, nor could one yet see that this was a man whose residence was a place of pilgrimage and whose horses were kissed in the street, if she could believe her newspaper.

His profile, fit to be stamped on a coin, was actually on the front page, and beside it his return through Paris after the first performance of his new play was described as a triumphal procession.

She was trying to picture the old man in glory, moved and yet perhaps a little reserved in the face of the stream of humanity pressing so closely round the carriage that the coachman had to hold in the horses, which must have quivered with fear while that shouting, jubilant mass of people kissed their coats or patted their noses. She frowned a little at the thought of the smell of horse and the oddity of kissing an animal.

'Well, you're dreaming over my portrait, and you've removed my wig, too!'

Mademoiselle Marie Grosholtz rose before her living model and moved like a puppet in a choreography full of confusion and apologies.

'I did not think you would come—'

'Today it is all I can do. I have not slept for two nights.'

'Have you been indisposed?'

'No — frightened of the *première représentation*. I am never afraid for my books, you see. If a book is condemned and re-jected I simply deny all knowledge of it. I say that there is a complete stranger inside me who has written this base and foolish work!'

'Yes, but the truth?' The girl bit her lip, for he seemed to be teasing her and was perhaps not really interested in his portrait.

'What use is truth if one cannot tell it because one is dead? No, I see nothing practical in a martyr's death, but I do fear a fiasco.

'You see, as a young man I was almost breathless with excitement over buying a ticket for one of the cheapest seats. I was impressed by the importance of the ticket lady when she passed it to me between two fingers. She guarded the gateway to happiness itself, and perhaps she had seated me behind a pillar.

'But even the pillars, the stairs and curtains — all were ravishing, and I dreamed of one day sitting in a box and treading the red carpets with the long, sovereign stride of the master. My stride has probably altered a little, but on the first night I always feel dizzy with desire and hope and I have a sense of responsibility, indeed even guilt towards the director, the leading actors, the juvenile lead, the woman who sells the tickets and the man who raises and lowers the curtain.

'Of course one cannot embarrass others with such emotions and the night before the *première représentation* I read about my own life. That is to say, I look through my household accounts.

'Every day I keep a strict account of what I earn on my estates and what I spend: wages for my permanent staff and day-labourers and my personal expenses. I have looked through the last eighteen years, in which my revenues and my consumption have shown a smooth and steady increase. It was in every respect a well-ordered life story I was reading, but I myself took up so little space.

'Thousands of ducks and pigeons have apparently flown from my hands, new-laid eggs have been sold, I see the butcher's heavy hand on the receipt for the sum I have paid him to convert my cows and calves into saleable meat.

'I see that I have paid the needy, priests and actors, washerwomen and a little gardener's daughter whom I scarcely remember — at all events I do not remember if I appreciated her work. But the presentation of a sauce I do appreciate, and when I see that I have rewarded my good sauce cook who is also able to serve so attractively, it seems to me that the money is well spent. But the cook's wages, the truffles, lemons and well-matured wines that I have felt so profligate in buying, all these mean extremely little compared with the pains I have taken simply to maintain my window frames. However necessary window frames may be, they have never given me either an emotion or an idea; they arouse neither delight nor repugnance.

'When I was a child words held a magical power which made me shiver and soar. Such words as bubonic plague, gangrene, stillborn made me shudder, with a painful thrill that ran through my body as if the words had actually infected me. I attached far greater significance to them than I attach to the doctor today. Other words filled me with desire: that warm little word *mocca* made my nose tickle pleasurably although I had not yet tasted coffee. Words were more serious than any games. They penetrated my being and sometimes dictated my humour for a whole day. Later I learned to use them, taming and compelling the words to express my beliefs and my doubts. But the accounts said nothing of all that; on the contrary, I felt an insuperable distance between the child living in the magic of language and the property owner keeping his accounts with an almost too decorative, slightly rightward sloping script in which the single variation was the moving pen.'

'Why weren't you satisfied with your plays and books?'

The young girl seemed to want to fix him more with her direct, clear glance than with her question, her hands working calmly on as he talked.

'I was not born rich, you see, and I wanted all the rest as well. I wanted the fine house, the shaggy little ponies, the woods and fields. Yes, even the sheep and the shepherds whom I pay, but more especially the chintz, the fine Egyptian cotton, the lavender water, the violet oil, the linen, as cool and white as freshly fallen snow, the muslins, satins and silks, the fine rustling taffeta, the perfumed soap and the delicate, Chinese porcelain. And I acquired them all. I see from my accounts that I have visited the tailor and the wig-maker times without number. The fine stuffs hang on the scrawny scaffolding they call my body, whose shape you are now being kind enough to perpetuate. Now even my chamberpot is made of Chinese porcelain, but it gives me no sensual pleasure, no more than my toothpicks and eyeglasses, or the flint I purchase for my guns although I loathe hunting.

'I had a really good cabinet-maker and I do not begrudge him the sums I have paid him. His mirror frames and spindly, well-shaped chairlegs always fill me with pleasure. Sometimes I am almost jealous of those wooden legs which never fall short of perfection, whereas I have to pad mine out in order to wear a fine stocking.

'Even physically I fill less and less of everything that surrounds me, all those horses, carriages, washerwomen, cattle, cherries and flowers. If my coffee consumption were measured, and I must surely have drunk more of that dark, concentrated liquid than anyone in this country, it would be nothing by comparison with my household's consumption of salt. Those little, necessary grains have been absorbed into my organism almost without my noticing, but coffee, which makes me sleepless and gives me colic, I cannot bear to forego. It is like those light, happy love affairs, which mean nothing beside my late and hopeless love for my niece.

'She and her sisters lost their father early and I undertook their financial support. I saw little enough of them, but I heard that this young girl was reading Locke. I fell in love with that: the picture of that intelligent child, reading philosophy instead of love stories. Then I saw to their education and marriage portions, but only after she became a widow did I essay some invitations. I ensured access for her to all that might divert that dear, perfect being, the festivals at Versailles and every theatrical opening night. I confess that when I reserved a box for her and her friends or her sisters, I was also seeking to shine and appear important; and when she did not come I ascribed it to grief or regard for her reputation. A young widow's reputation is as white and fragrant as soap — you can wash in it and the foam stings your eyes.

'For only a short time did I enjoy the happiness of living under the same roof with her, and so transported was I that I quite failed to observe that her joy was not equally complete. But she never said so directly and so I continue to hope that we may one day be reunited. I propose excursions to beautiful, recreative places, theatre visits and suppers, and I call her my heart and soul, although she prefers to meet me at the lawyer's office.

'What can it comfort me when the Prussian King writes that if he comes to Paris he has not the slightest intention of going to Court but only of visiting me, as long as that young, philosophically-minded lady avoids my company? Sometimes she makes sickness her excuse: rheumatic pains or colic, precisely my own disorders. Now that I am sick I feel that we are united despite it all, in a sad, ascetic way, and I do not complain. But when she writes that she is ailing I cannot understand how nature can bear to torment such a charming creature, and I long to kiss her hands, but must be content with little letters, which I have solemnly promised to burn.

'I would do anything for her! When she was learning Italian I too learned that operatic language and strung my sentences together in breathless outbursts of love and heart-searing sighs. I had hoped that Italian correspondence would become a love duet, but instead she sent me the manuscript for a comedy, as if it were my destiny that those I love most prefer to bind themselves to me with thin pen strokes on white paper.

'The King of Prussia sent me chests full of poems which I took in like laundry to be ironed and pressed, but I received her little comedy with tenderness and anticipation, like a length of exotic silk. With her everything would be perfect, my life's winter bright and clear, if only that inspired angel would share it with me! All my other accounts add up without the smallest inaccuracy, but she is the error that leads out into eternity, or the little irregularity in a perfect window that opens into the blue immensities of space.'

Mademoiselle Marie Grosholtz saw him tuck away a medallion bearing the portrait of a rather buxom young woman, with clear brown eyes and pretty, evidently soft hands. Then, turning back to her work, she made the few scratches in the soft wax that finally revealed the delicate, quivering life in the sitter's face.

For a moment she rested her palms on the thin shoulders under the oyster-coloured coat, smiling tenderly into her portrait's eyes, unaware that her subject was on his feet. With a little nod M. Voltaire left the room, just as the girl shyly kissed the thin, waxen lips.

She ran to the window to watch his departing carriage, perhaps to wave, but he had already gone. Instead, she saw a handsome young man passing by, slender and elegantly clothed in ice-blue velvet, with eyeglasses to match and to all appearances not a single one of his white powdered hairs out of place.

The young girl most immodestly flattened her long nose against the window to watch him, unaware that Curtius had entered the room and was appreciatively examining the Voltaire portrait, his eyes moving from it to his niece's slender frame.

He joined her at the window and followed her gaze.

'Uncle,' her voice was high and eager, 'I would like to model him . . . he is so handsome.'

'Robespierre — he lives nearby. It's no use wasting time and effort on him, he's nothing!'

Marie Grosholtz sighed, standing arms akimbo in a matronly way unbecoming to the little figurine she resembled.

'If he were to become—'

'Calm down, child! Tomorrow we make an excursion to Versailles, to watch the royal meal.'

'Are we going to model it in wax?'

The words and her rather disdainful laughter hung in the air, but the blood shot into her cheeks when Curtius looked grave and thoughtful.

'That is an excellent idea — I shall write the request at once.'

Unable to say that she had not spoken seriously, she stared wonderingly at her uncle's resolute profile, sharp-nosed and heavy-browed, as he left the room with his firm, dignified step, his stomach pushing his waistcoat out before him. But his hands were fine and narrow, and when he was excited he moved them as if they took the place of a fan. Had she not felt such deep respect for him, Marie would have collapsed with laughter over his finger movements at that moment. But instead she bowed her head, picturing Versailles: the park with the cascading golden fountains and the long avenues. She remembered once dreaming that she was walking up rose-pink marble steps, red-veined and bright as living flesh.

CHAPTER FIVE
Gold and Mirrors

Versailles 1780

All that meat! Ox, lamb, capon, pheasant, pigeon — tons of bloody bodies being jointed, the stench and the irritating buzz of flies. Those cauldrons of steaming soup, preserves, compôtes, candied fruit; the tarts and the mountains of fruit sorbet, decorated with curly white meringue — all for the royal table.

And then the scurrying, shoving, squabbling, munching and tearing at the meat! The cook tore off the turkey legs with his bare hands and arranged them on a bed of golden chestnuts, licking his fingers, blowing his nose on the floor, scolding and stamping with all the pressure. The gravy! The truffles!

The footmen stood waiting, their nostrils vibrating like thoroughbreds'. The youngest coughed his tubercular cough over the silver dish and reached for a cake. No, afterwards, afterwards! The cook slapped his hand away like a fly.

The footmen marched along the corridors, grave as if the white bone in the roast ox were the shining shin bone of a saint; punctilious as if one false step would send the pheasants flying off the dishes and into the looking-glass walls; tense as if to draw breath would be a crime, they bore the salmon sleeping peacefully on a bed of yellow egg yolks, surrounded by shellfish gleaming like Japanese warriors in red lacquered armour.

They passed well-dressed men and women bowing to the weight of the dishes and the meat the King would consume. They walked along corridors as long as streets, while flies buzzed over the meat and settled on their hands and cheeks, and they did not move a muscle to be rid of them. They climbed the gleaming marble steps, and at last entered the hall, where with graceful movements cold meat and congealed sauce were served on royal plates.

Marie Grosholtz leaned out over the balcony railing to catch in rapid sketches the expressions of the King and Queen. There was muttering and pushing all around her, awe-struck admiring sighs and splutters of sarcastic laughter, the rustle of women's dresses, wigs musty with dust and perfume. Some opened snuffboxes of gold, silver and tortoiseshell; some used smelling salts or ate sweets — after all, they did need something while they watched the sumptuous royal repast.

The King smiled and bent short-sightedly over the plates. He raised the wine glass to his lips and tasted the Burgundy with his tongue, his stout body comfortably folded into the chair, his stomach protruding between his parted knees. His hands were dirty and the Queen looked a little disapproving, but he seemed not to notice. He stretched himself and took huge mouthfuls, nodding across to his sister Elizabeth as she chewed her food precisely thirty-seven times.

Queen Marie Antoinette did not trouble either to unfold her napkin or to remove her gloves. Obviously loath to involve the onlookers in her digestive processes, she swallowed a tiny scrap of meat with the expression of one stifling a scream. She looked across at her little daughter, eating nicely, elbows close to her sides.

Marie Grosholtz sketched the Queen's dress in almond green and white, clinging and frothing round the girlish quiver of her movements, with that tension under the skin which might burst through the finely-powdered surface at any moment. The mirrors reflected her beauty as she motioned to the footman to pour some water, as if the smallest drop of wine would make her break down in hysterical tears or laughter.

The sketching was interrupted by two women who pushed past Marie.

'Look, she does not even remove her gloves. Is that meant to be refined?'

'Refined — she is only an Austrian!'
'She has little appetite.'
'No, if it were another everything would be served.'
Crinolines raised, almost hopping to move quickly in their high shoes, the women pushed past the young artist. There was a swinging of skirts and stays, a susurrus of silk. Marie heard the women's spiteful laughter and saw the Queen dip her spoon into the middle of the blood-red cherry sorbet with an injured expression.

Long after the royal family were gone and the dishes carried away, Marie Grosholtz remained, assembling her impressions.

A biscuit crunched between the Queen's small white teeth, the hasty meal, almost deliberately disappointing the onlookers who observed her nervous, delicate movements day after day, as if their lightness were a faulty choreography. Perhaps they wanted her meals to settle on her in a safe, billowing layer of fat, protective as a glove; but she was in too much of a hurry. No flies were allowed to settle on her plate.

The wax figure could not portray those hasty movements and Marie Grosholtz was already surveying her sketches critically, trying even now to decide on an expression. Not that reserved one, not the questing one, not that disapproving glance at the King's hands, for in Curtius' gallery His Majesty's hands must be soigné, strong and pleasing.

Everything must be made simpler, but more perfect, with space on the table for only a few dishes, a smoking-hot joint, salmon resting prettily under a green dressing. There would be no room for more, because this table would have to be considerably smaller than the table she saw when she leaned over the railing. The whole of Curtius' Waxwork Cabinet could fit into this hall! She would have to leave out the footmen, the late King's elderly daughters and the distinguished guests: only the chief characters would interest Curtius' customers, the King, the Queen, Princess Elizabeth and the little boy. She would have to concentrate all the majesty and splendour of the hall on that one little group.

As Marie gathered up her papers to leave, she was stopped by a small figure, a young girl with blue eyes, blond hair and an enviably clear, fine complexion. 'But her nose is as long as mine,' thought Marie Grosholtz, smiling. Then it struck her that she was smiling at a royal Bourbon nose and she curtseyed deeply to the King's sister.

'I have been admiring your work. I wanted to ask you to instruct me. I too paint and model, but no more than adequately.'

Marie Grosholtz smiled again, but the girl continued in her grave, distinct voice:

'If you move here to Versailles your work will be much easier. You can be a secretary to my welfare work.'

Still in her curtsey, Marie Grosholtz hugged her sketches to her like a shield and regretted that she knew nothing of figures.

'My welfare work is from my own resources — there are no accounts. Come!'

And the regal little figure led her by concealed passages and stairs into the park, past the fountains and out into the avenue, where the red and yellow leaves of autumn were falling on the dazzling marble bodies of the statues.

'You see—' The King's sister averted her eyes from Venus, who had already bared her breasts and with an undulating gesture, fortunately arrested halfway, was probably about to expose her sex as well. '— I need someone to talk to. I see no one but my brother and my sister-in-law and a few dogs. Otherwise I keep myself to myself. Most people here are either malicious or corrupt, possibly both!'

She shot a sudden look of hatred at a young lady walking down the avenue as languorously as if she could barely support the weight of her dress and jewels.

'Naturally my welfare work gives me some pleasure, but it is difficult to make real contact with people who constantly kneel to one. And naturally I could marry — I love children — but looking as I do, I could scarcely retain the affection of a man of my own rank for long.'

Marie Grosholtz's cheeks flooded with red. She thought of telling the King's sister that she had pretty eyes, but remembered that this was a compliment especially reserved for ugly women. Nor did this regal little person seem in need of comfort as she strode with assurance across a yard containing a few buildings which looked rather like workshops.

Marie Grosholtz wondered if the King's pious sister was a little mad as she unhesitatingly threw open the door of a smithy and nodded to a powerful young smith who shamelessly went straight on with his work, his leather apron curving over his stomach as he bowed over the forge, sparks showering from his hammer.

Marie Grosholtz tried to suppress a cough, but it was quite unnecessary: the hammer blows stifled the cautious little sound. Flakes of soot began to spatter the drawing she was holding protectively against her dress and she wondered anxiously if the King's sister was so interested in the young smith and his handiwork that politeness would force her to stay there in all that noise and smoke until her face and hair were blackened too.

At last the impudent young man looked up, but only to push his glasses onto the bridge of his nose. He drew breath for a moment, the sweat running down his neck and cheeks and spreading in round patches under the sleeves of a shirt which had apparently once been white. He gave the girls a friendly nod and the King's sister smiled back affectionately before turning to her astonished companion.

'Perhaps you would agree that my brother and I are a little misplaced?'

Mademoiselle Marie Grosholtz suddenly recognized the mighty smith as her King. Her mouth opened but she could think of nothing to say.

There was no need for her to feel awkward, however, for the hammer blows would also have drowned her voice. The noise followed the girls almost all the way back to the palace, sometimes in time with their footsteps.

Marie Grosholtz was allotted a room beside the Princess's and whenever she remembered this proximity she held her breath, afraid of causing an unnecessary disturbance.

It was a pretty room, with cool blue silk hangings and silver looking-glasses. The two chairs were so spindly that she scarcely dared to sit down. She saw the room as a fine glass watch and moved about restlessly, her nerves ticking away under her thin skin.

There were flowers on her table, roses with smooth leaves, so perfectly shaped that they might just as well have been made of wax or porcelain. A bright, almost searing red merged into a transparent yellow. These were not flowers she had asked for or picked, nor were they a gift; quite unconnected with words or feelings, there they stood, simply in order that the vase should not be left empty.

She left the room with short, hasty steps, free as she was to go anywhere. But she could not yet find her way about or move with the necessary certainty, so time and again she was stopped by the guards and her heart would thud as she gave an account of her status as artistic instructress and secretary to the King's sister.

Thinking she had passed a woman in the passage, she turned towards the hurrying figure, only to meet her own bewildered eyes in yet another mirror . . . had she even curtseyed to herself?

Soon afterwards she saw another young woman coming towards her. 'If only she were a little taller,' thought Marie. 'If only her lips were roguish, rather than as woebegone as a lost child's!' She smiled, and discovered again that the little lost lady was herself. Mirrors: their blue irony made her dizzy. The distant, shifting images affected her, making her afraid of opening the wrong door and finding herself suddenly in a blaze of light, facing an audience and not knowing her rôle.

With beating heart she fled back to her room and opened the smelling salts. Perched on the edge of a beautiful, comfortless chair, she made another start on her letter.

My dear Uncle and Mother,

I have a feeling that this position will completely change my life, and it is not a happy feeling. I have made many sketches already, but I am far from satisfied, there is so much to disturb one.

Whenever I look at the walls I see Vigée-Lebrun's portraits of the royal family. They are so impressive: the splendour, the red velvet, the heavy gold jewellery and the faces expressing an almost celestial dignity. That is not what I want to make.

My problems do not arise from want of interest on their Majesties' part. The Queen asked if I would make a model that could act the part at the royal dining-table and perhaps also a pretty, obedient figure the courtiers could dress in the morning and put to bed at night. I smiled, but felt dispirited. She did not have much time.

The King sat for me yesterday while he read. His small, round glasses spoiled the balance of his large, full features and I therefore tried to concentrate on his hands and body, but I could not ignore his face. He was completely absorbed in his book and seemed suddenly so sensitive and alive, almost handsome. I thought he was reading a romance of love and war. But it was a weighty historical work that moved him so much.

Perhaps I rob my models of their humanity by locking them into a single expression. Even choosing a firm look and a confident smile suddenly seems a betrayal.

Perhaps it is simply not easy being so close to one's models. All those changing expressions and situations do but disturb one at the moment, images constantly replacing one another. Even my own body and face can sometimes bring me to despair.

My dear Uncle, perhaps it is impossible to make a brilliant and truthful tableau of that royal mealtime, which those involved so heartily detest?

Marie crumpled the letter and rose to her feet. Going to the window she pushed the roses aside to look out.

'What one wants, one can do,' she murmured, tapping her cheeks lightly to encourage a hint of colour and good cheer. She tore the letter to shreds and picked up a fresh sheet of paper.

My dear Uncle and my dear Mother,
Simply to tell you that I am very happy. The King's sister shows me great friendship and trust. She is a hard-

working pupil, with a preference for modelling flowers, madonnas and fruit.

I have already made many sketches and impressions. I was a little uncertain when I laid plaster over the royal faces and those highborn nostrils breathed in air through two little straws. It goes without saying that I took great pains. Only the King's brother, the Comte de Provence, displayed the drollest fear of choking His face is almost as pale as wax too, with full, heavy features and eyes placed too close to his long, thin nose. He has tiny, perfect ears and silken hair. I look forward to being at home again and showing you how far I have come. I believe that Louis XVI and Marie Antoinette must be the happiest, handsomest and most perfect couple in the world!

Your most affectionate
Marie

A litter of white puppies were playing in the grass, biting each other's ears and Princess Elizabeth gently poked her fingers between the tiny teeth until the puppies loosened their grip.

Two ladies were swinging, their skirts unfolding like great, bright blooms, while the Comte d'Artois leaned back a little to enjoy the sight of their legs and laps, rhythmically swaying. They swung higher and higher and clung laughing to each other, like two swooning amorini.

A sunbeam crossed the Princess's arm and Marie went indoors to fetch her parasol. She opened the door to the garden room and stopped.

A woman was kneeling on the floor, her skirts thrown over her head. Only her hands emerged to grasp her wig, adorned with pink ribbons and roses. Above that mound of skirts, rosettes and ribbons and between two legs in snow-white stockings knelt the Comte de Provence, with a distant expression in his brown eyes and his ten polished nails braced against the woman's bottom. From inside the skirts came a sharp little sound, like a cry of surprise, and the ornate wig tumbled to the floor.

Marie looked down into the Count's eyes, which swam in a
face she had already modelled in wax. She felt his fingers in the
hollows of her knees and stumbled like a horse that suddenly
plants a hoof in a hole. His hands were round her ankles, as if
feeling for a fracture, and then on her breasts. His lips were thin
fish, moving under the skin, and she heard the sound of her own
voice suddenly contracting into flounces, laces, ribbons and
sighs like torn silk. The fish stiffened under her skin and she
struck down hard on the waxen face.

The woman, who had replaced her wig, regarded her with the
mild indifference of a doll.

Marie fled back to the garden, hearing the laughter from the
swing like a snapped necklace of little beads which scattered at
her feet so that she almost stumbled.

The Comte d'Artois took her arm in jest.

'Don't look so frightened — you're shaking like a March
hare!'

Marie sat down with her back to the swing and Elizabeth
kissed her on the lips.

My dear Uncle and Mother,

Princess Elizabeth has her own little country place and
we are there almost daily. Today she was visited by her
two brothers, who paid me great attention. The King and
Queen were unfortunately not present, and I did no work.
The Princess's little white dog has had puppies resembling
rats with big eyes, but everyone finds them captivating. I
yearn for meatballs and cabbage cooked with nutmeg!

Your most affectionate
Marie

The Queen. It is not her features that are particularly difficult,
nor her costume: she looks magnificent in the green riding habit
and the hat with the white ostrich feather. But the horse — is
there room for the horse in the Waxwork Cabinet?

Or does she lean over the balcony, a rush of love and admiration coming up to meet her like a great wave, washing her

white and shining? She smiles so that the people see her little white teeth; but people want to see through her skin into her very soul, as one looks into a transparent sweetdrop, or as Elizabeth believes God sees.

Have we room for all those people looking up at her? All those eyes that decide her movements?

Voltaire is dead and buried in unconsecrated ground. My Uncle told me, showing me a little wax sculpture he had made just after hearing the news. The portrait's expression is almost immodest, the face, hands, whole body taut, as if all the longing, pain and hope of the moment of death were forcing their way out. The eyes and mouth open to the dark, the feet swaddled like two defenceless infants. Pain has broken him. There is neither peace nor submission in his death, only a last, sharp, defiant question.

The figure shocked me. I looked at my Uncle's strong face and well tended hands. I had never before thought of death in connection with him or my mother, or even myself for that matter.

Elizabeth and I eat heartily. She orders the footmen to bring huge plates of roast meat, fish, game and gateaux to her room. She tastes everything eagerly, apparently without realizing that her charming, virginal features will gradually subside into the solidity of a double chin.

These heavy meals are her little secret deception. She stuffs herself so that in public she can be satisfied with very little and the onlookers wonder loudly that a meal which could scarcely keep a canary alive could make the Princess so chubby and her skin so fine and smooth.

As soon as she has fulfilled her official duties, we shroud ourselves in great fur-lined capes to visit the old women at the Home. Elizabeth gives them fuel and clothes for the winter. Today they will have meat broth and a single glass of wine.

Their old faces remind me of plucked fowl and each time I am ashamed at finding it so difficult to behave naturally with these feeble, sick and often under-nourished women. Perhaps their obsequiousness, in particular, makes me feel foolish.

Matron receives us, promptly falling to her knees. Her sudden collapse alarms me — is she sick? — but Elizabeth stoops calmly and makes her look at us. Boundless gratitude pours from the black-clad woman's lips. I crouch a little to be at the Princess's level and as she bends lower over Matron I am obliged to do the same, until in the end we are all kneeling in the passage, exchanging courtesies. At last Elizabeth rises, I rise, we brush down our skirts. Matron clambers panting to her feet, an ecstatic expression on her face.

The old women's thanks are less well formulated, but they bow their heads and fold their hands as if to turn in upon themselves for sheer bashfulness. White faces against earth-coloured and grey dresses, a winter landscape of bodies, soon to sink under ground. Only here and there the glint of a worn ring or a cross. And their smell rises to meet us, bitter as the hard stalks of chrysanthemums when the leaves are dry and the petals droop with a faintly feverish tinge.

In the carriage again, Elizabeth pats my hand encouragingly. 'Now we must visit the children — that is altogether different!' She leans back against the cushions with her blazing rings and all her solid flesh.

Even before the carriage stops we hear the children's falsetto voices rising in anticipation. Their Matron also curtseys to the floor, and since it is not entirely clean I am loath to crawl about again.

Fortunately her thanks, though lucid, are less effusive. She leads us swiftly to a room where in honour of the occasion the little savages are tamed with cake. Some thirty boys stare at us with open curiosity, the two-year-olds speechless with excitement, the thirteen-year-olds fixing us with narrowed eyes, suddenly gleaming with aggression or desire.

Elizabeth is quite at home, talking to the bigger ones and patting the little ones on hair cropped so short that their eyes are as prominent as fledglings'. Our smooth, well-nourished faces are an offence to the children, almost all blemished by pock marks, flea-bites, falls, blows and ulcers round their lips. Their neglected state exudes from them; it cannot be suppressed by pats and sweetmeats.

Suddenly a little dark boy bores his head into my stomach

and wraps himself in the fur of my cape, absorbing its warmth. I
feel his stiff, skinny body relaxing, but one of the girls from the
Home grabs him and pulls him away.

'Why did you do that?' she asks.

'Wanted to feel if she was made of glass,' he whispers.

I laugh to show that I am neither offended nor afraid of
catching lice. My laughter tinkles against the walls and the
Princess turns to laugh with me, but I shake my head. My
laughter is like a bell outside me, ringing on and on despite the
boy's big, beseeching eyes, and I might equally well run from
the room or burst into tears.

But Elizabeth and I move on to visit the girls, who have
licked the cake crumbs from their lips and are now bowed over
their sewing.

The Princess's hand almost covers their heads as she pats the
tightly plaited hair. The girls' sweaty little hands begin to shake
and flutter like sparrows about to take off and fly up into her
great, unshakeable calm.

When Elizabeth moves the ostrich feathers bob on her curls
as if some marvellous, exotic bird had chosen her head for its
nesting place. The little girls follow the movements with wide,
wondering eyes. For a moment I fear that they will suddenly
rush towards us, tearing at our finery, our hair and clothes,
adorning themselves with all our lace and feathers; for in all
that excessive humility there is a sensual and savage desire for
the caress of silk against their bodies and the warmth of fur or
velvet, and I feel a simultaneous guilt and weakness which
makes my movements stiff, as if I must be always on my guard.

But the lovable Princess, my benefactress and pupil, has no
such sentiments. At home her nail slides up and down a length
of heavy homespun as she remembers the emaciated child who
will be so glad of a warm, hard-wearing coat. In the goodness of
her heart she makes the coat so thick and heavy that it will
weigh the child down, a coat for sleigh rides in the Siberian
wastes, not for play.

Elizabeth, with her prayer book and wreath of roses. She
prays for the sick, her pious hands shaping a little image of the
withered leg or broken arm to help the patron saint of the sick

to grasp her meaning. Saints love perfection and the Princess takes great pains. She asks me to instruct her, to make the little rose-red arms and legs more effective, and they become plump and smooth, angels' limbs, with no trace of sickness or affliction. Even when the Princess prays for a ninety-year-old, in her sight his spindly, gouty sticks become a pair of charming baby's legs with dimpled knees. She models in the same exalted, rather stubborn way as she prays or sings. No doubt ever seems to enter her mind.

Now at last I know why the Queen's portrait gives me so many problems and why she likes to be alone. She is with child and suffers much from it.

Her distress is apparent most especially at mealtimes. The fork chinks suddenly against her teeth and she looks round as if seeking help, but there seems to be no one to understand her nausea and her swooning fits. Her cheeks have grown hollow and she has dark shadows under her eyes; I cannot possibly immortalize her so.

Elizabeth likes to talk to me about her sister-in-law, for it is obvious that she holds her very dear. At times her descriptions fill my head with pictures which serve as preparation for my work. I am astonished that Elizabeth, the youngest, describes the Queen as a wild or errant child.

'Maria Antonia,' says Elizabeth loftily, 'she was only fourteen when she came here.'

I, who am twenty, conceal a smile, for it is barely two months since Elizabeth's sixteenth birthday. The Princess, my gentle, precocious pupil, continues.

'She had promised her mother, the Austrian Empress, to be an angel, but she missed her dogs. If only she had had just one Austrian dog, it would have protected her, or at the very least have consoled her and kept her company on the journey. Now she must submit calmly and with dignity to everything.

'That slender child was already legally married to the Crown Prince of France, for in Vienna she had stood before the altar, holding her own brother by the hand and vowing to be true to him, while she tried to imagine the husband she was really taking in marriage. She knew only that he spoke French and that his face in the locket was broad and sleek.

'Her own brother was more handsome. His arm across her shoulders burned through her dress, as he pressed her suddenly against the wall and kissed her so that their teeth scraped together. She wanted to bite. She wanted to run through the parks and woods, as they had when they were carefree children, and at the same time she longed to be in France at once and to meet her husband, with his smooth cheeks and prominent eyes. She groaned, because her brother was crushing her against the porch wall and she was afraid that her mother or the Archbishop might come in.

'Next day she left, with her mother's admonitions in her ears. Sitting in the heavily upholstered carriage, she concentrated on being an angel, but one who was more tightly laced every day. Her legs went to sleep, her hands were restless and she contemplated jumping out of the carriage, running across the fields and escaping. But angels do not escape, they do what God ordains, and God and her mother had ordained both the marriage and the journey.

'At the frontier her Austrian servants, Austrian dressmakers and hairdressers kissed her hands and handed her over to French servants, dressmakers and hairdressers.

'Her new dresses were shorter, stiffer and more difficult to wear. She had constantly to smooth the clouds of lace as they tightened her corset until her immature breasts stood out and she could scarcely draw breath. She did not understand their language, she felt like a child in their hands as they forced her into ever tighter waists and smoothed and straightened as if her every movement were at fault. They powdered her hair until it was like a white cloud in the glass, as if she were really becoming an angel, and perhaps the strange buzzing in her legs came from the thin air of Heaven.

'On the day when she was to meet her bridegroom she threw herself in the dust, in all her glory, at his grandfather's feet. She did not know which of them she was to marry, and once again her only desire was to escape, but she was already imprisoned in the complexities of their language and the stiffly switching skirts.

'They patted her hair with soft, scented hands, and this time her marriage ceremony took place in the hall which the mirrors turned into a world apart.

'The frothy white skirt was kilted up over her petticoat, but when she protested she was informed that this was the French fashion and she was merely ignorant.

'The powder made her quite transparent, this child-bride with white flowers in her décolletage, as if her breasts were a little burial place. The cool weight of pearls was in her ears, round her wrists and on her shoes and she had to sit quite still on the low stool so that no one should see up her legs under the white foam of skirt about her hips.

'My brother, her bridegroom, entered the hall, also dressed all in white and perhaps she did not notice him brushing a tear from the corner of his eye, because they were arranging her skirts so that her ankles and feet in the little pearl-embroidered shoes would be visible. She was looking down at the locket bearing his portrait.

'When at last he stood before her, smiling like a hooked fish, she knew that they were supposed to dance, and rose a little too swiftly — she loved the minuet! Her arms had the right gravity, her feet the right lightness, her knees were regal. She breathed in almost soundlessly as she made her curtsey, knowing that she was perfect, even if my brother stumbled so that there was nearly a scandal.

'Immediately after the dance he led her to the table, if one could call it leading. With bowed head and rolling gait he drew his bride behind him and began to eat at once, the grease running down his chin. My grandfather whispered that he should converse and I tried to make signs to him, but he brushed his face as if to wipe something away and said one always slept well after a good dinner, and it had been a strenuous day.

'She ate nothing. Outside, the rain extinguished the fireworks, but the champagne corks went on popping. The wine trickled down over our tongues and rose again in our cheeks. She laughed a desperate laugh as if she were being tickled under the skin, right out to her little mother-of-pearl painted nails. She appeared wide awake and alert until the moment when her head sank down on the tablecloth.

'We lifted her up and she opened her eyes as she was carried in under the thick, flower-embroidered brocade canopy which smelt of smoke, scent and snuff. The linen was still damp with holy water, but she was tucked in under a stuffy eiderdown that made her feel sick.

'At eight o'clock next morning she was awakened by two faces peering into the bed, one old, one young, one stern, one merry. Her eyes travelled from one to the other as her two future ladies-in-waiting pulled back the curtains and lifted the eiderdown off her. The light hurt her eyes and she hung on their arms while they sprinkled water on her hands and splashed her face with a lightly stinging perfume. They laced, coiffed and painted her, apparently oblivious to all the people coming into the room.

'First an elderly woman in black threw herself on the floor to beg a dowry for her daughter. They were noble, but poor, she said, and the young bride nodded sympathetically. Then came a young woman whose husband had suddenly died, leaving her in need. Confused and ashamed that she had no money, the fourteen-year-old rummaged in her jewel-box and gave the woman a little diamond bracelet. The woman kissed the hem of her petticoat and left.

'Her hair was combed while her headache worsened and a good-looking young footman came in and read some involved verses which his master had written about the wedding. She did not recognize it: 'The flower-decked bride whose slumber was a gift to the people.' Only then did she remember that she had fallen asleep between the ice and the champagne and had woken briefly when the fireworks had made her think war had broken out. She smiled at the footman, relieved that she had apparently not caused offence.

'While the two women laced her a cardinal walked in and courteously invited her to confess her sins. Gasping for breath, she mentioned one or two at random, but as soon as he had withdrawn she asked the older lady-in-waiting if she could not talk to her husband instead of all these chance arrivals.

'The woman was deeply shocked: the Crown Prince was engaged in his morning toilette, she said and it would be improper to disturb him now.

'They began to rouge her cheeks while a fair, clumsy girl asked for employment in the kitchen, to be followed immediately by a plump milliner, bearing sketches and fabric samples pinned down like butterflies.

'The young Crown Princess was still half-naked when a polite jeweller asked her to try on one or two diamond rings, which she liked and was allowed to keep in return for setting her name to a piece of paper.

'A boy tried to sell her a little white dog with a delightfully bulging coat and merrily cocked ears. The boy clicked his fingers and the dog rose on its spindly hind legs and tripped across the floor in something like a minuet. The Crown Princess wanted to give him her signature as well, but the boy would only accept money. Close to tears, she asked him to wait, while the sound of the dog's little claws scratched and scrabbled over the floor and into her brains.

'It was late in the morning when she met her husband in the little blue chamber. He too appeared tired and despondent and she hastened to say that she did not wish to rise before ten and that she herself wanted to decide when she would speak to people she did not know.

'"Yes, but—" he said humbly, "we do not belong to ourselves — our lives belong to the people."

'However, he was kind enough to explain that immediately after her morning toilette she could move into a smaller room and go to sleep again; he himself never slept in the great four-poster. Moreoever it was required, for fear of assassins, that he should sleep with a snoring guard, to whom he was ceremoniously tied every evening.

'She laughed aloud, but he did not even smile, and on his wrist she saw the thin trace of a cord. All the same, in the hope that he was joking she proposed that they should have a pair of lifelike puppets made which could be taken round the palace, while they themselves ate, slept and lived happily in small, secret rooms.

'Amazement spread over his big, dismal face, and she realized that she had already ceased to be an angel.'

Elizabeth sighed and spread the altar cloth she was embroidering

across her knees. She was calculating whether the growing out-
lines of the purple grapes would meet properly: one false stitch
and the whole work would be ruined!

She smoothed the cloth with a protective, satisfied air:

'I would not like to be in my sister-in-law's place!'

Elizabeth herself had asked her brother's permission to
remain unmarried. A fitting match could only be found for her
abroad and she would feel rootless in any other country, yet
somehow the fate she had deliberately avoided seemed to
absorb her, as if she were actually living her sister-in-law's life
and experiencing her problems.

The chief problem, of course, was that huge, irresistible
desire for happiness. Every movement that woman made must
be pleasurable. If she should happen to crush a louse, she
must appear to enjoy it, otherwise the sacrifices of all her
subjects would be in vain. Perhaps that was why it seemed so
insulting to let the sparkling decanters of wine pass by; even to
drink water was by no means guiltless.

Home again. The windows seemed so small, everything
seemed in some way oppressive. We embraced and kissed one
another, my uncle's rather rough cheeks, my mother's which I
suddenly saw as slack and wrinkled.

A chicken was boiling in the kitchen and later appeared on a
dish, the white flesh swelling under the well basted skin. My
mother's heavy Alsatian cooking, the sticky, sweet tart. I
remembered her slim body in the hot bed, she had been so
young then, her voice so bright and full of expectation. Now
she went out only to buy food, to the greengrocer, the butcher
and sometimes to visit the corset-maker or the dressmaker.
There was still a shy expectancy in her movements and even
now that her back was bent, a rather dried-out lightness
remained.

My uncle was not content; although he said nothing directly,
he seemed to feel that I was not doing enough. I promised to
model the Princess Lamballe, preferably asleep, for I was
certain she would entrance everyone. There was something
almost unearthly about her beauty — every time I saw her I

wanted to fall in love, but it seemed to me that I might just as well have fallen in love with a woman as a man.

I kept such feelings to myself, nor did I tell them what I knew of the Queen. I dared not say that for the time being I regarded the royal meal as an impossible subject.

Princess Lamballe's glistening chestnut hair streamed freely over the arm of the sofa. If she stood up it would reach to her hips and she could have wrapped herself in it. Her slender arms were unadorned and her foot, arched towards the floor, had pink-polished nails. The Sleeping Beauty was neither powdered nor laced as she posed with half-open lips and uncovered breasts, as casually as if unconsciously caught in a childlike sleep or a light swoon.

With meticulous fingers Marie fixed long, curling eyelashes in the eyelids of her model, the wax cool against her fingertips, silken-soft as the sleeping Princess's skin.

Marie's eyes moved critically from the slender form on the sofa to the skilfully-worked figure whose dress concealed a graceful, almost imperishable body made of kid, steel and kapok.

The Princess Lamballe's breasts rose and fell; a little throb in her throat betrayed her pulse-beat and the long, mysterious pathways of her veins, her skin and flesh were vulnerable, her stomach a glowing concavity.

But the outstretched wrist, the fingers of the left hand slightly curved as if holding a secret, the lovely lips which never opened to utter criticisms but only to issue lovely little sighs, *bons mots* and kisses — all these the wax figure faithfully reproduced.

Marie shivered suddenly at the sight of this perfect beauty, closed in about herself. She looked across at Elizabeth, who was still embroidering bright blue bunches of grapes on a yellow background. Perhaps only her benefactress's presence prevented Marie from suddenly pulling the brown curls or tweaking out one of the Sleeping Beauty's long, curling lashes. She was seized by a desire to see her jump up, protest, cry out, awake from her briar rose sleep and her certainty that when she opened her beautiful eyes she would always see a prince or a dear little puppy-dog, never a toad or a monster.

Suddenly a rustle at the door made all three young women jump. Princess Lamballe rose to her feet and stood, a little chilled, before the fire. Marie had the uncomfortable feeling that someone must have read her thoughts and it was with some relief that she picked up the sheet of stiff paper which an invisible hand had pushed through the door-jamb into Elizabeth's boudoir.

The King's sister had no sooner opened the paper than her cheeks flooded with red and she rose with unaccustomed abruptness and threw the sheet on the fire.

The small, hissing flames were all too slow to consume a clumsy drawing of two naked girls lovingly entwined, four small, pointed breasts, two dark, sharply-drawn sexual organs, twenty fingers with pointed, claw-like nails, greedily caressing breasts, pudenda and stomachs which suddenly glowed red and opened up in the fire. The faces under the high coiffures were coarsely caricatured. One, with a heavily protruding underlip, resembled the Queen and the other, with its immoderately large, rather cow-like eyes was the Princess Lamballe, whose face and sex had both been provided with moustaches.

'Filth!' Elizabeth spat out.

Princess Lamballe showed no sign of anger or distress. Pushing her hair back from her forehead, she responded to the insult with a little peal of laughter.

'Holy Mother of God!' Marie exclaimed uncharacteristically. Her eyes filled with tears as the sentence continued in her mind: 'My uncle, my mother, what if anyone thought that of me?'

A hand was stroking her hair.

'We never did anything like that! But if it were true — what then?'

With her own, aristocratic mildness, the Princess flicked the insult away like a golden gadfly. She left the room, her movements gracing the air.

'Wicked slander!' said Elizabeth, pushing aside her embroidery, blue and pink silk threads snaking to the floor. The words emerged jerkily, as if she had been shaken to the depths.

'They were just two girls — they rode donkeys and horses and kissed each other on both cheeks when they met. Princess Lamballe was already a widow and Marie Antoinette the Crown Princess and my brother's neglected bride.

'All eyes were on them, especially on her, as she waited and he never came. She waited in the four-poster bed, on the blue silk sofa and in the knobbly beds of the hunting lodge and the pleasure palace, but he deferred the act.

'Later the family and doctors bundled him into her bed. He obeyed anxiously, dutifully, eating heavily in the hope of success, walking, going early to bed or riding and hunting with his hounds. He even fasted, for all the good it did!

'She would watch his hands covertly, both at table and when he was working. He never used ivory or gold but worked with iron and wood and forgot to brush off the shavings. His hands were rough, with work-worn nails. One of his pleasures was filing down keys to make them fit complicated locks.

'In bed his hands moved over her body as if she were an object he had to perfect and polish, but his sex never became erect.

'Sometimes she felt she was watching their bodies from a distance, tiny as puppets, the Court pulling their strings, lifting their arms, parting their legs — but someone or other in that powdered, salacious Court had snipped through the little thread that was supposed to raise his sex, just to laugh at their unhappiness. She burned with longing, and with shame.

'She heard their laughter, the eager whispers that she was barren — once someone even shouted the word after her. She knew they considered him a milksop. Night after night he went early to bed, as if he could sleep himself out of their dilemma. He was beginning to get on her nerves and she would put the clocks forward to avoid his company. It would have been far too embarrassing had she been forced to weep.

'Sometimes she sat up till dawn playing Hazard and he paid her gaming debts gauchely, bashfully. She made friends of both sexes, went to the opera and laughed too often and too loudly. At masked balls her skirts swung round her ankles, but she thought herself hidden behind her mask. She conversed, danced and allowed cavaliers to kiss her hand.

'A ball could keep her excited for weeks, lying in the blue room in the afternoons, her mind churning, fantasizing. She passed on her ideas to the milliner. 'My heart's desire,' 'inmost longing,' 'hidden craving.' Thus she named her dresses. and she bore the scream of silk, the red nervous tremor of velvet, the pride of brocade, the exuberant rush of lace, the silver lamé flashing like rapiers and the tickling caress of swansdown. Every costume was a passionate dream that had pushed its way into the open.

'Afterwards she would lie exhausted, wearing cool shades of ivory and white, as it she were still a young bride, the bitter almond green, the blue and pearl-grey nuances of water. Sometimes in all secrecy she would paint over traces of nightly excesses on her throat and face.'

'And now?' Marie looked enquiringly at Elizabeth, whose hands were clasped in her lap for fear they might tremble.

And to the King's sister the least question was apparently an accusation, for she pursed her lips for a moment before bracing herself to reply:

'My brother underwent a quite insignificant operation, which remedied nature's defect. Since then he and my sister-in-law have been the happiest couple in the world! She always remembers that she is the Queen.'

I do not understand it. I have now been living at the King's sister's side for over a year and I do not know where the time has gone. It oozes out of the clocks.

When I was a child time seemed infinite, because I was waiting and waiting — for what, I did not know. But now every day, every week and every month takes me by surprise. It must be this division of time, chopped up into tiny pieces by walks, talks, meals, fairs and parties. It is an age since I have had an uninterrupted day, smooth and whole, to be shaped according to my will.

But I would not have missed any of it, especially the parties, at which Elizabeth and I were wallflowers. Even as a child I was averse to dancing — oh, I had my dancing lessons, but when a partner approached, with his jug ears and red cheeks, I would run away and hide under a chair. I preferred watching to being led, but as the dancing teacher and my mother and uncle all thought that shyness was responsible, they did not correct me overmuch. If forced I sometimes pinched the boy to make him turn the opposite way, for there was always some face I wanted to observe.

Yesterday my uncle and I had our first serious disagreement. I wanted him to let a cool white light fall on the Princess Lamballe as 'The Sleeping Beauty', but he chose pink. She is inviting in that pink light, people flock round her and sometimes the men's glances are indecent. That primitive, obscene sketch seems to have burned itself into my brain and I cannot get it out.

I did at last succeed in saying that I could not model the Queen until after the birth, and in return my uncle required me to model Benjamin Franklin for the gallery. Of course, I could not refuse, so now I have to travel to and fro several times a week. Fortunately Elizabeth is very understanding.

But why that man in particular? We do not talk much while I work, but I can see that he wishes his portrait to make a pleasant impression. He does not say so directly, he is too modest for that, but his modesty is as obtrusive and deliberate as any other mannerism. His round face is as well-known as the moon's, his thin, unpowdered hair and the challenging simplicity of his costume have already set a fashion. I have seen young gentlemen promenading in brown homespun, with a gnarled stick, as expensive as everything else.

'He is an important man,' said my uncle. 'He has invented a lightning conductor and helped to compose the Declaration of Independence.'

This meant little to me, but I nodded and made the expression in his grey-blue eyes very intelligent and gentle, in fact as boundlessly forbearing as only glass can be.

My mother's eyes were tired and for the first time I realized that she has never really learned French. She was afraid of the gallery, her world was restricted to the kitchen, the parlours and our street, which to me grew daily smaller; one or two shops, cafés, an equestrian circus and Philipstal's magic picture theatre, where I was always admitted free. All this appeared to me almost unreally small, like a child's pocket full of bright, worthless treasures.

Suddenly I felt angry, unreasonably perhaps, with my uncle who had undoubtedly always looked after us materially. But did he really think that after that long and dangerous journey my mother could be content with the confines of his parlour and his kitchen?

Certainly she had never expressed a desire for anything at all; she was as modest and as shy as a hare, but he could have offered her more than mere protection.

The Queen's gait was always smooth and light but now she walks across the short grass slowly, as if it were knotting itself round her ankles and she might fall, or perhaps the roses make her queasy. For preference she isolates herself at the Trianon, her pleasure palace.

Elizabeth believes that she has over-vivid memories of the first pregnancy and childbirth, when all eyes were on her pregnant body, absorbing her every movement, drinking to her nausea from tall cut glasses. With the Crown Prince she would walk past them, not heeding their sniggers and obscene whisperings.

Arm-in-arm the two of them walked past the fountains and all those smooth, marble bodies. She thought that now at last they would speak of love, but he knew nothing of the piquant phrases of the cavaliers or their long, velvety declarations of devotion. He seldom visited the theatre.

Courteously, and as gently as possible, he explained that it was her duty to give birth publicly before representatives of the Court and the people. She smiled, rather surprised and put the thought aside, until she was lying under the heavy, rose-patterned canopy, biting the quilt, while the doctors' sharp instruments, reminders of blood and death, terrified her far more than the pain.

The air was heavy with lavender water, rose-water, musk, tobacco, sweat and the smell of fish from the fishwives' long black skirts. She kept her lips tightly closed, held herself rigid

and thought that she was no longer the Archduchess Maria
Antonia, nor for that matter Marie Antoinette, but a spindly
puppet and they, with their strings, would pull her legs apart
and drag a red scream from her mouth and a little doll from
inside her. Their eyes scooped her out so that she was nothing
but a thin shell, and over by the window she could see her
husband biting his nails.

She begged for air and he had sufficient presence of mind to
open the window a little, though some protested at the draught.
Others climbed on the furniture, the better to see her face and
her sexual organs.

One of the doctors erected a screen, which caused angry
shouts, and the screen fell across the bed with the pressure of
the crowd. She sank into a profoundly painful darkness, desir-
ous only of death, so that she might be alone.

Then she saw them carrying a child away from her and a few
minutes later the cannon began to thunder. After the twenty-
first report she held her breath, but the silence told her that it
was only a girl.

Elizabeth modelled a round little boy baby and supplied him
with such large and well-developed sexual organs that she could
scarcely find room for them between the fat little thighs. She
blushed when I tried to help, and wrapped the figure gently in
the big embroidered altar-cloth. Elizabeth prays every day that
the Queen may give birth to a Crown Prince.

The confinement is close at hand and Elizabeth and I have
reserved time with the Queen's hairdresser. I am nervous of
meeting Monsieur Léonard, who will be aware of all my
weaknesses — a false colour, an awkward movement, a broken
nail. Do my stockings match my shoes, is my jewellery too
modest, my décolletage too deep?

Perhaps he will say: 'Remove that beauty spot — quite
sickening!'

And I shall have to say: 'Your pardon, but it is my own!'

M. Léonard is an artist who finds previously undiscovered
beauty in a cauliflower head, or a woman. His fingers build airy
fortresses of towers and waving plumes. All the doors have to

be made higher for the sake of his coiffures and the ladies kneel in their carriages, their skirts kilted up above their knees. Meeting him is almost as important as being presented at Court.

The Queen is his ideal model. All fashions yield to her, or she makes everything fashionable. His fingertips and her silken hair are exquisitely in touch: he brushes, curls, powders, he arranges the hair under great, airy hats, majestically towering, and in his garden coiffures he excels himself. The Queen's hair locks both careless and charming with a fresh head of cabbage, an open artichoke, seven innocent carrots and a handful of coquettish radishes — so natural that flowers are now considered vulgar.

He contemplates Elizabeth's green dress for a long time before experimentally placing a cabbage stalk behind her left ear.

'No, thank you,' she says firmly, 'it must be something that lasts.'

'As usual,' he nods, and I notice that his legs are too short and the expensive model coat does not fit him particularly well. But his hands are sure and lively as he works on the curl papers in the Princess's hair.

I blush when M. Léonard ties the sheet under my chin, wondering whether he will find me worthy of a basket of fruit, a bed of leeks or a naval battle, and I dare not ask, for my hair is completely in his power.

It is obvious that he does not think me very stylish, yet he accepts my hair, in that he begins by powdering the colour away altogether.

'The darkest colour I can manage at the moment is Lamballe. I'm too nervous for dark women just now,' he adds, almost apologetically.

My face in the mirror nods sympathetically, in a way his want of chivalry reassures me. He uses his gaucheness as a shield, in order to concentrate wholly on my hair, and I feel an agreeable tickling on my nape under his smooth, dry hands.

'In fact, you are fortunate,' he says, 'you take a cast and there it remains. Everything I create walks straight out of the door, only to be ruined, yet I must always produce new ideas. When the coiffure can go no higher I must create a desire for something flat; my whole life is a battle against myself.'

He gives a heart-rending sigh and I am both surprised and flattered that he knows of my work. Forgetting the hot iron he is holding by my temple, I turn towards him — precisely as the first cannon fires. Elizabeth falls to her knees, M. Léonard drops the iron and kneels beside her, pressing his hands to his heart, among all the powder and hair combings.

At the twenty-second crash Elizabeth lets her tears flow, M. Léonard sobs and I, kneeling on the sheet, am thankful for the little burning spot on my temple, for I neither weep nor swoon easily.

After the hundredth gun we all dry our eyes and noses on the sheet and with the curl papers still in her hair Elizabeth runs to the Queen's chambers. Singing and whistling, M. Léonard begins to pile my hair up on my head in hundreds of curls as white as the lambs that graze on the Trianon lawns, airy as froth or meringues. Suddenly I remember that as a child I dreamed of one day looking like this, without realizing that my eyes are too sharp and observant for all that sweetness.

'And how,' I ask, 'how am I to compose myself for sleep?'

'*Ciel*! Do you think I have arranged your hair for you to go to sleep?'

I shake my head apologetically.

In the corridor I meet Elizabeth's eldest lady-in-waiting, who smiles at me as kindly as a flesh-eating plant.

'Sweet,' she says, 'all you need now is to be a little sinful. When are you going to make a likeness of me?'

I almost run down the corridor. If I were to make her likeness, just as she is, with those old painted cheeks and the malicious little curl of the mouth, even if her voice sounds like candied fruit, she would hate me and intrigue against me until the day I die.

Today I saw the Crown Prince, a pretty child, with something elf-like about him. His fragility and his delicately-shaped hands went to my heart, but not because I long to be a mother. Rather I felt that I could never capture his likeness in wax. His mouth is small and pink, with a thin line round the edge, as if nature had planned it larger and suddenly repented.

There was a greasy, spicy smell in the room. Two roast chickens stood on a dish on the bedside table, their legs bulging with fat, much thicker than the baby's. The hard-boiled eggs were bigger than his feet. A terrine of steaming bouillon and two bottles of Burgundy stood where his tiny hands could reach them at any moment.

I asked Elizabeth what purpose all this food was supposed to serve.

'The Crown Prince's night food,' she said. 'It has been served so for three generations.'

The nurse did not wait for us to go before gobbling up the chicken and swilling it down with gulps of Burgundy.

The Crown Prince's young footmen played ball with the eggs.

I knew my uncle would press me for the royal meal tableau.

'The boy must be there too, of course,' he said.

'He's still much too little.'

'Then make him bigger — people want to see him.'

I said that I had been occupied with the festivities for the liberation of the American colonies.

For our all-white costumes, M. Léonard had made great white satin hats decorated with pomegranates. The air was as soft as feathers.

The coloured lamps cast their orange, pink and green light on our faces, transforming us, liberating us to float just a little outside ourselves.

People who scarcely knew each other suddenly behaved like consummate lovers, walking, dancing, vanishing into pavilions or sailing on the canals in little flower-decked boats.

The Queen stepped into a boat with a handsome Swedish officer I had often seen on festive occasions and they sailed away under everyone's eyes. Only on Elizabeth's face did I see a trace of concern, otherwise the night was an artificial, rosy dawn and we did not know if we were stepping into reality or out of it. We were reflected in one another.

For once I danced a great deal, especially with a certain very young man, but we soon became separated and an older, red-cheeked gentleman courteously offered to accompany me wherever I wished to go. He put his arm around my waist and it was charming to look out over the slopes and waterways. His grip tightened and in panic I began to excuse myself on religious grounds — but alas! his had been a priestly family for generations and moreover he felt particularly sinful because he was married, yet all that sin and remorse were no hindrance to his sudden passion.

'What about honour, and faith?' I said, suddenly clutching at the words which Elizabeth utters with such feeling and gravity.

At that moment someone laughed, and my brave, passionate cavalier was so appalled to think he might be the cause that he pulled his cloak right up over his head, and I wanted to tickle him under the chin, for he resembled a peaceful great tortoise. I laughed as well, and far away my laughter echoed back, like an exuberant duet with an invisible partner. My hero was scared out of his wits.

That was how I came to walk home across the park alone. The misty dawn was breaking forth and the lovers were still lying in the grass, the women's skirts spreading like great plucked flowers. The pomegranates burst and fell over their faces like bloody rain.

In the King's chamber the lamp was lit at six o'clock as usual.

Of course I have to fulfil my obligations to my uncle, and today I found precisely the hair I have been seeking for so long: the exact match of the Queen's, both in thickness and in colour, now lies on my table like a skein of golden silk. Every time I see it I am aware of faint odours of soapy water, food scraps and wine dregs. The smell of decay lingers in that beautiful hair, which had lent a moving lustre to the grubby little servant girl.

There was no need for her to tell me she worked in the kitchen, for her dress was still damp over her stomach, her hands broad and swollen.

'My hair—' she mumbled. I stood, transfixed. Did she really wish to help me?'

It was not that, she said, but she had heard that I would pay.

As I put money on the table she snatched a pair of scissors from her pocket and seemingly relieved now the deal was done, began to hack at the lovely hair, the long strands falling on the floor and on her clothes.

I made her sit down and for some reason set a mirror before her and proceeded to comb her hair thoroughly, perhaps to give her an opportunity to repent. But she did not so much as glance at herself.

When I began to cut she seemed to shiver and it was only then that I noticed her wide little face, severely blemished, the right eye covered with infected sores.

Once only did a sob escape her half-open lips; otherwise she displayed no signs of grief. A snub nose and small, white teeth made her resemble an ungainly pug dog. I concentrated on the hair, adding lock after lock to the soft pile which, removed from its owner, shone with a beguiling, honeyed warmth.

The girl stuffed the money into her pocket and to compensate for the loss of her beauty I found a little lace cap, which I arranged as well as I could. I do not know if she smiled, or if it was merely a twitch of those parted lips; but whichever the case I picked up a collar of dark brown fur which does not suit my colouring and fastened it about her neck.

She touched the fur as though fearful that I might reclaim it, but I told her that she had done me a great service.

She rose, the weight of her body surprising us both, as if that radiant hair had borne her up. Perhaps it was only now that she became conscious of her pregnancy.

She stopped at the door.

'Do you need teeth?' She pointed between her lips.

Indeed I do need teeth, but did she really think I would pull them out? In any case, they were too small, a child's teeth. Did that inarticulate little kitchen maid really think me some kind of hyena or jackal?

I urged her out and Elizabeth and I spent the rest of the day at the Trianon.

Here everything is fresh and unadorned, the water clear as crystal in an artificial spring. Japanese carp and goldfish leap in the lake, cows white as snow come at your call, and luke-warm jets of milk fall into bowls of Sèvres porcelain.

At Trianon all the peasants have clean hands and the lambs trip prettily about with blue ribbons round their necks. We walk with our parasols and light canes, for Elizabeth soon becomes breathless and we often stop. But no matter, for within a bare twenty paces you may imagine yourself in China, England, Greece or Austria.

The shrill scream of peacocks rises above the chatter of mandarin ducks. Daffodils, daisies, clover and orchids grow in the grass, the luxuriance of wild roses, honeysuckle and jasmine sets off the ginkgo, the dove tree and the splendid foliage of the fig.

Suddenly, in the midst of the herb garden, we caught sight of M. Léonard, like some exotic bird in green silk breeches. Behind him stood the mulatto footman in flame red, his dazzling smile and graceful, cat-like movements making him appear master rather than man. And the gardener bowed as deeply to one as to the other. Dainty as an old sparrow, he trotted about the beds, handing fresh herbs to the Queen's hairdresser who twisted the leaves expertly, appraising the new, unexpected shapes. Negligent of where he trod, he almost cried when one yellow silk shoe caught his eye. The old man stooped and gently scratched off a little earth with his nails.

'My good man, have you any notion what such a pair of shoes cost?' asked M. Léonard, his voice still quavering.

The gardener's wife came out to view the damage, her hair caught back from round, greasy cheeks with a hairpin, her eyes gleaming with innocent curiosity between narrowed folds.

At that moment two elegant women walked by, one leading a lamb, the other pressing a big broody hen to her breasts. Lettuce and cabbage sprouted provocatively from their coiffures.

'Begging your pardon,' whispered the woman, 'but do they eat them after?'

The hairdresser gazed at her with an innocence to match her own, for he scarcely knew the adornments for what they really were, when they arrived puréed, blanched or finely chopped, or he saw footmen slitting green grapes, removing both pips and skin with a little silver knife.

M. Léonard's vegetables grow on silver dishes and are washed in eau-de-Cologne.

*

70

I understand my uncle less and less. He has mounted the busts
of the Duke of Orléans and Necker in the best positions, where
the gallery light falls softly on their faces. The Duke of Orléans
is no longer seen at Court; he is too busy holding court himself,
they say. His palace opens into an arcade filled with gambling
dens and bars and he himself is uncouth, drinking himself under
the table at every visit to my uncle. Why should we tolerate
him? Elizabeth shall never know that I have sat at table with
him, and with Necker, to whom my uncle seems also to have
taken a sudden fancy. I know that this man of finance has made
repeated attempts to bring order into the State's accounts and
the Queen hates him for his fuss-budget prying into the expenditure. It is in honour of such as these that my mother stands in
the kitchen for hours, creating Swiss and Strasbourg
specialities; but fortunately these two tedious gentlemen are not
an attraction in the gallery. The people wish to see the royal
repast, which Uncle Curtius has modelled on my sketches, and
the dazzling light in our largest salon falls sharply on well-nourished royal countenances.

I should be both glad and relieved, for Elizabeth says that the
Queen is with child again, so I dare not ask her to sit for me.
But every time I see those proud wax figures on the gilded
chairs I feel some unease, for they are defective in a way which
is impossible to correct. Not a colour is too bright, nor a hand
too large: this is something far more significant, but no one
notices. The people come pouring in, the women finger the silk
on the sly, the children gasp with excitement, but at times the
men's eyes betray something close to bitterness or hatred.

The royal party raise laden forks to smiling lips in careless
enjoyment; even the little prince reaches out for the food. If
only it were so! He eats, if possible, even less than his mother —
a morsel of something crisp or sweet — and she looks besee-
chingly at him, urging him at least to taste the large helpings
heaped onto the plates. But the spiced, greasy smell of food in
the nursery seems to have robbed him of his appetite once and
for all. He is a grossly over-protected child, picking only at
delicacies, but his charm and his touching vulnerability delight
everyone. Despite an unhealthy crookedness of the spine, there

is something almost supernaturally ethereal about him, which the wax figures do not show, and one would never know how he suffers from sitting so long at table.

When I left the display I was minded to mention this defect to my uncle, but we had a guest for dinner: Robespierre, the little lawyer I once wished to model, simply for his looks.

He is still handsome, to be sure, his greenish spectacles toning with his coat, his coat with his breeches, stockings and shoes. Not a single shade is misjudged.

He watched me through the soup, the roast and the gâteau. I could not swallow a mouthful. When we retired to the drawing room for coffee my heel caught on the step and as I stumbled he took my arm.

'Regrettable, were such a charming young patriot to break her neck!'

My body stiffened and I felt the hairs on the nape of my neck rising like those of a wild animal. Only the thought that M. Léonard had arranged my coiffure gave me some kind of assurance.

Once more the cannon thunders a hundred times, but the welcome for the second prince is far less heartfelt than I had expected. The child is not to blame; bursting with health, he is truly Elizabeth's dream of an easy, happy, plump baby. But only the family seems to pay him any attention.

Instead, Necker talks to the Queen about her excessive expenditure. She stiffens, offended, when he speaks of the gambling money which she has every reason to believe secret. He lists gifts, pensions, hairdressers' accounts and purchases of jewels, dresses and furs.

The flour used to powder wigs and cheeks forces up bread prices, he says, but as she shakes her unpowdered, golden hair his voice and all his dry talk seem quite unconnected with her erect figure.

'But,' she exclaims, 'if the park grows freely in the modern English style, we have no need of gardeners, and as to the footmen and kitchen staff, we can make do with less than one tenth.'

He is stupefied: dismissals solve no problems, it seems.

'Yes, but how does one economize while employing fifteen thousand people?'

'Only on personal expenditure.'

She frowns. Then, in a sudden fit of enthusiasm:

'We positively do not need all those dishes every day. I am more than content with an egg, fresh milk and salad!'

The King, anxious and distrait until then, looks suddenly terror-struck and enquires if she has been reading Rousseau, or fallen under the influence of some nature movement or other, but she shakes her head. What need of a book for something so simple?

'That is not the way,' says Necker. The King appears relieved, the Queen downcast. 'It is exclusively your personal expenditure on luxuries which must be restricted.'

'Yes, well, for the future I shall wear no jewels and only dresses of white linen.'

'Impossible — you represent the entire French silk industry!'

She bites her lip and gazes at him with eyes at once resigned and innocent.

'What of my hats, then? The large one with the sailing ship — does that belong to the Fleet? And the one with flowers and fruit to the gardening industry? And what does a hat cost, beside a hundred gardeners? Or a little pleasure house, beside this ice-cold palace?'

Necker departs, her eyes still fixed on him, awaiting an answer.

It is clear that each takes the other for an idiot. Once again he tries to raise loans abroad and she gives orders for more salad vegetables to be grown.

Well, I have seen Rousseau in my uncle's gallery — a strong face, a broad back. That man does not live by salad alone!

Time. I am twenty-eight years old today. It is raining, and because it is my birthday I feel responsible for this soft, fine rain which will drive into Elizabeth's face when she goes to Mass. I can imagine her stumpy little figure before me, and am astonished that in the eight years we have been together she has changed from a very young girl to a middle-aged woman. Perhaps she is deliberately making her body into an impregnable fortress of fat; perhaps she cherishes a secret passion, or a dream to be protected? There is no pride or aggression in her movements, only a huge gravity which makes her genuflection in church appear to come from her heart.

Elizabeth's skirt will trail a little in the puddles as she leaves the Mass, for at that moment she is in a state of exaltation or contemplation which renders her completely indifferent to external things. And the rain will fall on that gentle, heavy-featured face, which has become matronly without ever being youthfully feminine.

Walking in the park, I wonder at my continued dislike of the full-bodied white statues which gaze through me, or into themselves. They always make me long for crowded streets, shops, coloured signboards and advertisements; for the smart circus horses or for Philipstal's magic lantern slides, which absorb me into another world where I am still a child.

The park is cold and I return to my room, where I study my face in that elegant mirror which has an atmosphere and a character of its own, far too grand for common sense. It veils my skin, which appears transparent, in a dream of frozen blue. I peer curiously at the reflection, until my long nose bumps the glass. It is still a young girl's face, but just to make sure I feel my cheeks, chin and throat and stroke my body to discover if it has sagged into matronliness unawares.

Beyond the wall Elizabeth sighs, evidently not much helped by today's Mass. As always, she shares her joys with others and keeps her sorrows to herself, but something has changed.

On the stage the Queen stood bathed in golden light, wearing high-heeled blue silk shoes and a simple blue dress. Behind her, the bed with its pink coverings was set slightly askew so that the audience could see the pillows and quilts. Her demeanour displayed her longing for the bed and her beloved, for at that moment the Queen was the young Rosina in Beaumarchais' comedy *The Barber of Seville*, her little hands reaching out towards the window, the pillows — and the

Comte d'Artois, wearing Almaviva's splendid *lait-de-puce* costume.

All the Queen's dignity and concern for her lost slenderness had vanished. Her eyes shone and her movements held a quivering intensity, her voice an eager lift. She despaired, she blushed, her tenderness and love filled the hall to the backmost row, where the handsome Swedish Count was attempting to conceal his emotion.

They clapped when, hot and expectant, she reached towards her elegant brother-in-law, and they clapped even more when the lovers on the stage had each other at last. And the Swedish Count slipped discreetly out into the park.

The Queen was still sparklingly young and full of spirits, sitting opposite the King, wagging her little blue shoe after accepting the clapping and kneeling, kisses and admiration.

'Our next performance will be *The Marriage of Figaro*,' she announced.

'No.'

'But why? Wasn't I good?' Rosina's light twitter was still in her voice.

'It is an immoral piece.'

'Those enchanting rejoinders — I know them all by heart.'

'I forbid both public and private performances. The Count in the play thinks of nothing but deceiving the Countess, a mother is on the point of marrying her son, the legal system, family life, our honour, nothing will be taken seriously. I do not understand what you see in the Countess's role — it must be your headache.'

'I am the chambermaid, Suzanne. Women in my condition do not have headaches.' She was almost singing even now.

'Perhaps it also appeals to you when Figaro says: "If heaven had willed, I might have been a prince." Or: "What have you done for all your privileges, Count, apart from being born"?'

She nodded curtly and wagged her shoe again: 'I see nothing wrong in that.'

At that moment the two elder children came in. As if taking sides, the daughter stood by her father, while the son leaned against his mother.

'Then you do not feel that we have any duties?' Absently the King stroked his daughter's hair. 'In any case, there is no reason to feel sorry for that Beaumarchais — he grows fat, supplying material about us to the gutter press.'

'I am above that kind of thing.' She lightly twitched at her girlish blue dress. 'Why should that prevent one from using the good he does? It is difficult to be an angel all the time.'

'He is a vulgar parasite.'

'Parasite! Do you know that he is sending the receipts from the first two performances to nursing mothers?' she triumphed.

'Nursing mothers—' The King looked thunderstruck. 'Nonetheless, the play shall not be performed — think of our children!'

Her face softened and grew thoughtful, the girlish laughter, the nursing mothers and all Beaumarchais' piquant dialogue forgotten. She was a mature, pretty woman, with fine wrinkles round her eyes.

'Thus,' thought Marie Grosholtz, 'and only thus shall the model be. A family tableau, the spouses attentive and affectionate to each other. No reserve, no disagreement — the rumours of the Queen's nocturnal parties, masquerades and games of hazard, the Swedish Count, none of that shall be in my tableau, only the love and confidence, and the children.'

She almost ran across the park to begin the sketches and there was virtually nothing but the Queen's dress to be changed. Rosina's girlish garb must give way to a modest, woman's gown, perhaps in wine red or gold with a touch of sable.

She slammed the door shut and bent over the paper: soft, motherly features, fine little nose, clear, direct gaze.

Somewhere in the park someone was singing. She bit her lip and tried to concentrate on the Queen's portrait, but the song came clearly to her. She knew it from the streets, and sometimes it had followed her right up the stairs to the wax gallery, but she had never heard it here. Never before.

> King, if you'd enjoy
> Seeing cuckold, seeing whore,
> And a bastard boy—

> Look in your mirror more;
> Look at Queen and Prince ...

She heard a window shut with a crash.

Pictures, pictures, I cannot make them come together. When I walk in the streets the palace seems to be one of Philipstal's illusions, made of mirrors and artificial light. When I enter the palace the streets seem so distant, their stench so inconceivable, that they might as well be on the other side of the world.

Yesterday I took an impression of the Prince's and Princess's little faces. The little girl behaved with adult dignity and calm when I massaged the oil into her cheeks and then left the plaster to dry.

The boy's patience is of another order. He endures discomfort to conceal his crooked back, but less from embarrassment than from consideration for his mother. He leans slightly towards her, standing on his toes to appear taller. He is as light as a feather, an elfin child with the physical defect which he knows will carry him into eternity.

'You will remember me,' he said suddenly, with an expression so tender and dizzying that I can never portray it.

How could I forget?

Then I fixed hair after hair in the fine, domed crown of the Queen's portrait, which will be a perfect likeness.

It is my great good fortune to have come into possession of that hair. I went down to the kitchens to ask after the girl. Not knowing her name, I stood just within the doorway in the hope of catching sight of her among all those busy, closed faces, which almost froze me out although the heat was in fact so oppressive that their sweat dripped into the soup.

I asked a footman if he knew the sullen fair girl, one of whose eyes had probably been destroyed by the pox.

He said he had never noticed her, but a thin young woman said she remembered the kitchen-maid suddenly falling ill, and an older woman drew me on one side and whispered that the girl I sought was dead, perhaps by her own hand. At all events she had been buried in unconsecrated ground.

'Was she a relative of yours?' she asked impudently.

I hurried away and told Elizabeth that I wished to visit my family that evening, but instead I took a walk.

In the street I saw a boy aged perhaps three or four, his legs so thin that they were bowed under the bony little body, his lips covered with sores.

I followed him, speaking in comforting, ingratiating tones, wanting to give him food and money, perhaps to make his portrait, but my wheedling, fawning voice must have frightened him. In any case, instead of replying he walked faster, stopping only once to snatch up a pigeon's egg from the road and pop it in his mouth. The shell cracked between his teeth. Perhaps I should have shouted, screeched like a bird, but he had gone. His movements had no grace, they were rapid and sharp, like knife blades.

I feel as if all about me were thin and fragile as Chinese porcelain which a single awkward movement or injudicious sound would snap like the eggshell between the child's teeth.

I cannot make the pictures fit. The world seems disconnected, the roots torn out. It is like a sudden fear in pale grey plumage, with pink and silken pads, softly clasped about my temples. Perhaps — if I could see it all with an insect's eye, all the images at once, big and clear-cut — perhaps it would all join together again, healed like juicy green stalks, and I would be as light as a blue-winged butterfly, or carrying a gentle death upon my back.

Yesterday, at last, I completed the Queen's portrait, which Elizabeth admired. Neither she nor I attended the first night of *The Marriage of Figaro*.

Carriage after carriage rolled from Versailles to the theatre. From the window we saw Princess Lamballe's carriage, Madame de Polignac and the King's brothers. The golden gates opened and the palace emptied itself of sound and colour. M. Léonard had worked for over twenty-four hours without a break, creating the final coiffures in feverish excitement.

All those who were able to secure a box had done so long before, but most people stood. The flood of inquisitive men and women in gala dress pushed open the doors and flung their money to the floor. Silk was trodden to shreds, pearl strings broken, but no one noticed. Everyone was shoving and kicking in order to see: that first evening alone brought in a fortune.

Milk flows from women's breasts today with Beaumarchais' assistance!

The Crown Prince can no longer stand.

The Queen passed me in the park, her skirts brushing the grass. I curtseyed to this figure whom I scarcely know, in wondering homage to the clear resignation in her eyes, the crystal gaze turned in upon herself.

There was no more trembling, no more voluptuous excitation. She seemed lapped in dread, calm, clear and icy cold, her eyes darkly ringed. She looked up at the little platform where the boy had asked for his bed to be placed while she fulfilled her official duties. No sun as yet.

She passed indifferent fingers through her hair; M. Léonard was waiting with his curling tongs and combs. On this occasion she was to wear white, lilac and silver, and if the sun shone the boy would be able to watch her shining too, a distant little figure in the procession.

Yesterday I was at last able to mount the royal family in the gallery: the King, the Queen, the Princess and the Crown Prince. Everyone says the likeness is striking and I noticed Uncle Curtius admiring the group, but without praising me.

He allowed me to mount the figures on my own and though I did my best not to be disturbed by all those who passed by or stopped to look, I could hear them whispering about the dying Prince. 'Divine punishment,' said one, and I longed to turn and strike him.

Suddenly a man shouted: 'Why doesn't she display them with the great thieves?'

Everyone laughed and once again I controlled myself and concentrated on my work, my hands calm and sure.

When every single hair and silken fold was perfect, I returned to the house, expecting to find my mother bowed over the stove, but the kitchen was empty and smelled different.

From the larder containing sausages and smoked ham came a loathsome, rotten stench. There was a light inside. I flung open the door and almost overturned a scabby little man with a stack of books and a candle. Fortunately my mother had moved the hams.

I screamed and he clapped his hand over my mouth. Had he not been so unappetising I would have bitten him. Instead I ran off to my uncle.

'There's a man, stinking, in the larder!' I cried.

'Yes — yes — your mother will wash the larder later.'

'Who is he? If I may ask.'

'A doctor.'

'He is evidently unable to cure himself.'

'Marat works as a journalist. He must remain in hiding until we have justice in this country.'

'That sewer rat! I shan't set foot here again.'

'You don't know what you're saying. It is my express wish that you return home immediately.'

We ate in silence, yet at least my uncle had enough decency to make Marat eat in the kitchen.

Elizabeth sat facing me with her embroidery. Recently she had spent almost more time in my room than in her own, as if she preferred to be a guest, although I could never really regard myself as a hostess.

I realized how little we had really come to know each other during those eight years. We had walked arm in arm, admired each other's clothes, imprinted a light kiss on each other's cheeks or lips. I felt profoundly attached to her, yet not once had I told her anything of myself.

What should I have said? That my uncle collects mirrors? That could scarcely interest her. That my mother's Strasbourg *cuisine* exudes a penetrating smell of cabbage as far as the exhibition halls? Perhaps.

Elizabeth had never shown by her conduct that she felt superior to me and I do not recall her once exploiting her position. Her royal blood had no special colour or scent when she pricked her finger, but the rituals, the palace, the park, the sycophantic dance of the servants created a distance between us. Completely unawares, we may have been merely figures in a production which I was now obliged to leave.

'Elizabeth,' I said, 'I regret that I must ask your permission to return home. My uncle can no longer spare me.'

'Yes,' she said. 'My brother's only fault is that he is always afraid of doing something wrong.'

For a moment I wondered if she had understood me and when she rose to go to her room I was disappointed that she had not tried with a single word or glance to persuade me to stay.

Soon afterwards she returned and placed three months' wages on the table before me.

'And the chairs,' she said. 'I beg you to take the things you like.'

'What of my successor?'

'There will be no successor.'

She sighed. In the vase were white chrysanthemums, artificially forced into growth, their silken petals and bitter scent spreading an aura of death through the room.

Outside it was spring, the light was clear and sharp, and a chill breeze stirred the curtains. Suddenly I longed for my Uncle Curtius.

CHAPTER SIX
Tableaux

1789–1794

The heavy, gleaming silk curtains hung smoothly down, but Marie's hands were trembling slightly as she packed her modelling tools and her clothes. She avoided looking at herself in the glass, knowing she would see only sorrow and the sharp prick of anger against her uncle, who was suddenly conducting her move like a campaign.

'The bureau,' said Curtius, 'and the chairs — be especially careful with the chairs.' He made the court footmen carry out Elizabeth's gifts as if they had always belonged to his niece.

'This is no place for a young girl,' he said, when the heavily-laden carriage rolled out through the golden gates. 'You should never have been allowed to come here.'

'They are the kindest, the dearest people I have ever known.' Marie's voice was high, almost shrill, when with a sudden, nervous movement Curtius struck her on the mouth. For a moment she glimpsed the coachman, turning to look at her with eyes the chill green of sea waves, his young face pale and scarred.

Marie pressed her hand to her lips and shrank into her corner to avoid so much as brushing her uncle's cape as they travelled. Feigning interest in the chestnut trees, she saw only Curtius' white glove, strained over his knuckles, and the coachman's cold green glance washing over her and turning her to ice.

In Curtius' house she hung her dresses in the wardrobe and set out her modelling tools in the room she had had as a girl. Leaning her forehead against the window pane, she stared down at the

street, the two royal chairs beside her where the gold would catch
the light. Outside she could hear her mother's footsteps, so light
they seemed to be brushing themselves away.

Marie followed the small, dark figure down to the kitchen.

'We shall be seven for dinner,' said her mother, gazing dismally
at three skinny chickens. 'Not even half each.'

'Mother — who is coming?'

'They talk a lot, but I don't know them.'

'But what has happened?'

'The weather,' said her mother, shrugging. 'I think the weather
has changed.'

Once more Marie saw a streak of light at the dining-room door.
Opening it, she bobbed ironically to a sallow little man who had
wrapped a white kerchief about his head.

'You here again?'

'For your sake, and for your children's.'

'I have no children.'

'Naturally you must not give birth in a corrupt society. Wait
until the storm has swept it clean.'

'When?'

'We will speak of that at dinner.' With a smile that was almost
charming he closed the door.

'In such company those three little fowl are more than ample,'
thought Marie, looking across at Marat's hands and skinny wrists.
His sores oozed as he raised the meagre chicken bones to his lips.
'If only he would eat in gloves! He wipes his hands on our napkins
and touches our silver knives and forks. He licks the sauce from
the knife. Uncle Curtius must have forgotten all about good man-
ners and infection. Nothing would induce me to touch the dish he
has held. Perhaps his whole body is covered with sores — thank
heaven I shall never see it!'

Fighting back nausea, she shifted her gaze to Mirabeau's big,
pock-marked face which radiated almost irresistible health and
strength by comparison with the rest of the company. He spoke
with his mouth full, brooking no interruption by Robespierre's
dry, cultivated voice and ignoring the sick little man and the young
painter, David, who in honour of Marie had tried to conceal the
wen on his cheek by turning his brocade collar up over his ears.

For a moment Marie allowed herself to be carried away by the surging enthusiasm in Mirabeau's voice, seeing him as an enormous, invincible sea monster, shouldering all obstacles aside and rushing forward, proud, aggressive and pure. A giant fish, his little parasites no more than a slight itch, driving him on still faster, with a yet more fiercely thrashing tail.

Then she heard her uncle say: 'So you do not think the monarchy can be saved?'

The giant shook his head. 'Only by civil war, but their ideas are too limited. They reckon in hairs' breadths and drops of blood — they are too stupid.'

'Too gentle,' she was about to say, but as she opened her mouth she saw Marat plunge his silver knife into the lean white meat.

'No reason to spare them, or their brood.'

She controlled herself, sitting on between her mother and her uncle and imagining herself one day smoothing snow-white plaster over these four faces and leaving it to harden. She would reproduce each ugly, blemished feature: the scars, the sores, the bitten nails, the pallor, the vice, the bleak perfectionism. She would not miss the tight, malicious furrows by Robespierre's mouth, or David's weak features and the strange, self-willed growth of the cyst.

'I shall lock my mouth with seven seals,' she thought, 'but I must be honest in my work.'

As if reading her thoughts, David gave her an ingratiating smile.

'Will you make my portrait one day, without retouching?'

She shook her head, smiling politely. 'I think you would do it better yourself.'

The spiced pears circulated for a second time, and for the first time in her life Marie withdrew after the dessert.

'We shall meet again.' David's brocade sleeve brushed her modest gown.

Her nod was so slight that it could scarcely be regarded as a promise.

Even by locking her door she could not shut out the distant murmur of voices. She could visualize the four faces quite distinctly and the sharp stab of hatred informed every cell of her skin and every drop of blood behind it.

If she opened her mouth now, she would scream. She would tell them all about Elizabeth's piety and about the royal couple and their children; but they would be the wrong words and Curtius would brush them away with his glove. He was transformed into a dark cloud, a brooding storm that might break at any moment. The whole house was changed, only her mother was her customary mild, silent and unapproachable self.

If only she could sleep! She closed her eyes and sank back into the pillows, but thoughts and images kept rising to the surface.

She remembered the person she had once been: a child, filled with expectation, delighting in her own girlish figure, proud when Curtius praised her drawings. And the assurance that came then, as she went through the great handsome rooms of the gallery, stopping now and again to give some garment a critical, professional tweak.

At last she heard the men taking their leave, their voices slurred with wine:

'My dear friends,' her uncle enthused.

'*Au revoir* — and my regards to your charming niece.' That was the painter's voice. The carriages rolled away.

Without lighting a candle she got up and began to get ready: a simple dress, a pair of boots, the heavy, fur-lined cape, her hat pulled well forward. Now she might easily be an old woman, or even a man. Her jewellery, a purse of gold coins.

She scraped back her hair — 'charming niece'! She must leave this madhouse full of criminals — and a sick man in the larder into the bargain! She would take a hotel room for one night and drive out to Versailles at dawn. The gates would open when she gave her name. She would fling herself into Elizabeth's arms, sobbing, perhaps, like a character in Rousseau's novels. Anything would be better than this accursed house; she would even feel safer in the street.

Suddenly she heard voices and footsteps and wondered for a moment if her tortured nerves had created the clatter of boot heels, the scrape of soles and voices inside her own head. From her window she saw a crowd of people standing outside, some dressed as if for an afternoon walk, others in bedroom slippers, wrapped carelessly in their capes. Torches made their faces shine like snow, but their eyes were dark and wide, their mouths open to the blackness, their teeth gleaming white. They were like some special race which had inhabited the meanest streets of the city, walking its most secret gutters. Their voices came in shrieks, feverish and not to be denied.

'The King is to dismiss Necker — give us his bust and the bust of the Duke of Orléans!'

The shouts soared, battering against the windows.

Marie looked down on the livid faces: wigs set askew in haste, flapping capes, down-at-heel shoes — yet they were mustered like an army.

She saw Curtius come out and speak to the two men in front. Minutes later he brought out the two busts and a roll of the black muslin her mother used for her dresses.

He tore the material across and draped it over the figures. For a moment all was quiet, as the torches cast their vivacious light on the two wax busts, now dressed in long black capes.

With jubilant shouts the mob advanced along the streets, splitting the darkness with their torches and the silence with voices as hoarse and frenetic as seagulls'.

Necker's young bearer marched, stiff and well-disciplined, while an older man lent his jogging gait to the Duke of Orléans. The two wax faces were grave and tense in the flickering light; only a superficial scratch, it seemed, would make them bleed.

Marie crept away from the window and put her boots back in the cupboard.

Like a convent girl, Marie Grosholtz observed the street from her window. The sudden emotion and affection she had sometimes felt, standing in the midst of a crowd with a stranger's breath on her neck, glimpsing a sweetly-curved cheek or a snub-nosed child — all these were gone, and the mere sound of measured footsteps was enough to make her cringe like a frightened animal.

How could a new race of human beings have grown up, in two years, or three? For there was a new species on the streets now, faces and bodies intent, sniffing out their prey. Closing ranks, they would circle it patiently or head straight towards it. Handsome or ugly, their faces were all turned in one direction and there was a strange fire in their eyes. Rain or sweat ran down their cheeks, throats and arms, making their clothes cling to their bodies. A savagely provocative, sharp smell hung about them like a miasma. Their feet did not dance, but simply bore them along, either bedazzled or purposeful.

'It all began *chez moi*,' bragged Curtius. 'Not a drop of blood was spilled before I gave them those two heads, draped in black according to artistic convention. You would think I had made them specially, but no, Necker and the Duke are my good friends and I was hardly over-eager to give them up. I had a suspicion that things would go wrong, and I was right. The older man, carrying the Duke of Orléans, took a bayonet thrust in the stomach and that pretty young fellow carrying Necker was killed. It must have been an extraordinarily lifelike scene when my two wax heads rolled in the street, and since blood was spurting all over them, people thought they were bleeding. My effigies aroused people's excitement. Perhaps we actually crossed the fine line between life and death that night, but not without loss on my part. The Duke was returned to me that very night, intact as they had promised, but Necker was brought to the gallery by the Swiss guard six days later, hair singed off, face smashed — such a lifelike, perfect piece of work, and now it must be completely remade!'

Curtius' hands slid down over the spanking new uniform of a captain in the National Guard which he wore at every opportunity. He looked his guests straight in the eye. He had plenty of time for story-telling: his captaincy did not involve many duties and visitors to the wax gallery were lamentably few.

The wax figures still sat on their chairs and stools, almost human but at the same time so self-assured and impassive that they appeared invulnerable. Women leaned on slender, beribboned shepherds' crooks, caressing a genuine stuffed lamb, their bodies clad in rustling silk and vibrant velvet, their breasts so white and rounded that it was impossible to associate them with either blood or milk — but they were not interesting. Streets and squares require no entrance fee and at the city's centre the guillotine's thin, sharp profile stood out against the sky: a pure, ascetic shape, not unlike the apparatus of trapeze artists and tightrope dancers. Death had become a subtle thrill, momentarily uniting audience and performer.

In flesh and blood those lovely, unreal idols walked up the narrow steps. Perhaps they bowed their heads, perhaps they stared defiantly out at the tattered sky, perhaps the wind disordered their skirts or snatched the kerchiefs from their hair. Here they were different, but the white powder became the universal colour of death, the hectic rouge of their cheeks a final blush. Those who had flirted with passion and dreamed of great dramatic depths were now suddenly allotted tragic roles to play according to their talents. Power and fame seemed to have sucked all life from them, as if their misfortune were no more than a slightly overwrought performance, incapable of arousing heartfelt compassion.

Curtius' former customers walked lightheartedly to this focal point, enjoying with bated breath a new, free entertainment, drinking wine, eating biscuits and nuts, sucking candied sweets, and knitting as if to keep a hold on reality. And every day the same steps, the same plunging blade, the same executioner, and almost the same movements. If you stood a long way back the faces were distant and blurred, the small figures like fairground performers in brilliantly-coloured costumes. And when they bowed their heads it might well have been to acknowledge the applause. Repetition dulled the whole performance, as if the violence and death were merely a play lacking in any variety.

'*Maman* — look at the lady in bits!'

'Yes — hold your tongue and watch.'

'Do they cut the heads off the dead ones too?'

'Do be quiet.'

'Want to go home — my legs are tired.'

'There's nothing happening at home.'

No, nothing would make Marie Grosholtz go there, even though as a small girl she had once met the inventor of that renowned instrument of execution.

She still remembered Doctor Guillotin as an attractive old man with a delicate, mouse face and thin, projecting ears. His voice was meek and low and he had presented her with a large box of candied fruit.

Curtius had not the heart to declare that he did not believe the invention would become so popular as to entitle the doctor to have his profile exhibited, so he invited him to coffee instead. Marie still remembered the delightful old man's description of the device. It would be a neat ending, he said. The new technique of the *guillotine* would make death instantaneous and absolute, almost without suffering. There would be less of those vulgar emotions, the sudden, quite pointless sympathy for the condemned and the shouts of dissatisfaction at executioners who seemed too hesitant or too brutal or who simply made a false stroke. Even when drunk, that hard-pressed character would still be capable of releasing a cord. The technique would turn death into something pure and detached, concerning only God and the condemned person.

'Both the victim's end and the executioner's continued life and work will be eased by this invention,' he said. 'Not to speak of the speed and the practicality of it in the event of mass executions.'

Marie gazed wide-eyed at the sweet old man, imagining something akin to her mother chopping sausages. The candied pear began to cloy in her mouth.

'The child—' said Curtius, and proposed a game of chess.

But Doctor Guillotin was still so enraptured with his invention that Marie saw him pick up the white queen, dip her in his coffee and stir, while apparently pondering a particularly subtle move.

'And this old idiot takes the bread out of our mouths, too,' she thought every time Curtius asked her to open the cash box. 'No, ten wild horses couldn't drag me there.'

But Curtius did ask his niece to accompany him to the Madeleine cemetery, wearing his glittering captain's uniform and long black rain cape, regardless of the weather. Between them they carried a small carpetbag containing a bottle of water, a flask of oil and some powdered plaster. They waited very patiently for the cart full of stiff bodies and severed heads. The driver stopped and greeted Curtius. Marie nodded and turned away.

'It's a job like any other,' said Curtius, his connoisseur's eye discerning at a glance whether or not the cart contained anything of interest.

'Thou shalt not kill — but you may eat meat,' thought Marie, wondering if this was altogether right. Trying to see as little as possible, she handed her uncle the oil flask and mixed powder and water into a smooth, porridgy mess. In hot weather the smell nauseated her, but she tried to ignore it, out of courtesy to the dead, and assisted her uncle in silence, as if plaster were a healing dressing and she herself a trained nurse.

But one day, perhaps inadvertently, Curtius passed her a head she knew. The smell of blood struck at her and as she turned her eyes instinctively from the cleanly chopped throat, the tears welled up and her mouth filled with vomit. Once again she looked into the thin, painted face of Elizabeth's old lady-in-waiting, Jeanne, baring her white porcelain teeth in death. Slowly, as if to accustom her fingers to the work, Marie began to smooth the oil over the cold little face.

Jeanne. You asked me so often to take your likeness, but I refused, because it would mean modelling your seventy-year-old face with all its wrinkles, burst veins and open pores, while you longed to see yourself fresh and blooming once more.

Jeanne — your hair white under the powder, adorned with costly ostrich feathers, your girlish smile which always showed your porcelain front teeth, your little squirrel eyes, alight with malice and coquetry and that artificial blush applied in your looking-glass. All that is left is a tiny, crumpled mask, either bad or 'primitive', as we say of pictures we do not understand from far countries. You used to tease and mock me, calling me 'old maid'. You were always on the lookout, watching for dark circles under someone's eyes, a cut lip, the mark on a shoulder. You recognized a love affair before the lovers themselves, a special vibration in the air, the quiver of an ankle, a hastily opened fan, one flower in a bouquet — you detected all the signs with malicious glee.

Laughter, and your small, coquettish scream when you displayed your still shapely leg on a swing. Jeanne — for the first time your pretty white teeth come into their own, thanks, perhaps, to your silence. Forgive me for the deep furrows tugging at your mouth. Your face is so cold, dreadful in its rigidity — don't let your chattering squirrel's laugh break through the plaster!

*

At home, she helped her uncle as usual to reposition the figures. She saw him arranging the chill blue light over Jeanne's death mask and over two other very young women, one with beautiful, thick eyelashes, the other freshly powdered and elegant, her regular features set off by black silken beauty spots — rather too many, perhaps — the one on her forehead concealing a wart.

Curtius set up a placard at the entrance advertising his latest novelties and the crowds flocked in again to touch the immobile features, imagining they were, in this frozen form, experiencing the execution for the first time.

'Is it so impossible to put oneself in another's place?' thought Marie, feeling guilty at the sight of the hands reaching out towards a nightmare — and their dreams.

She remembered that she herself had once observed death quite calmly and soberly, in another luxuriant late summer at the Trianon where she had sat on the grass with other ladies day after day, enjoying the beautiful, rare fish in the pool.

Carp and comet goldfish played among the reeds, glinting like metal in the sunshine. Then the weight of their eggs would pull them to the bed beneath and some were never seen again. But others returned to the surface, their lines now clear-cut and noble. They seemed haughty, unable to react to birth, as if they knew they were going to die.

With many other women, Marie Grosholtz laughed at the fishes' struggles, loudly admiring their beauty and swift, elegant movements. The gardener gathered up the dead fish so that the air over the pool was always clean, fresh and aromatic with the fragrance of flowers.

Marie bit her lip at the memory and went up to her room. She looked at her modelling tools. The sky was dull, like unpolished silver. She sat down at the charming little spinet her uncle had given her, although she had no special taste for music.

Marie felt alive at Ivry-sur-Seine. Only an hour or two in a hired carriage and they were in another world. 'Our bolthole,' thought Marie. 'Our country place,' said Curtius, although the rather shabby little farmhouse, with its orchard and farmyard, was only rented.

As they approached, the neighbour's dog came running out to meet them and Marie buried her fingers in the thick black coat, feeling that she had come home. She leaned back to look at the sky, and the grass was long and soft, and the humming of the wasps over the fruit trees was a purring joy.

Their treasure at Ivry-sur-Seine was the pig, which they called Mops and kept locked up, to conceal their riches. It could be washed and petted, too, and Marie and her mother would sometimes gaze despondently at the poor unsuspecting creature.

They went out among the redcurrant and gooseberry bushes and ate handfuls of the acid, unripe fruit. The hens pushed against their skirts and when Madame Grosholtz fed them she addressed them like children, with much the same tender sighs as Marie had heard silk-clad ladies lavishing on lambs and cows at the Trianon. If she closed her eyes and breathed deeply, she could imagine herself standing on those soft lawns, surrounded by orchids and narcissi. But not for long. Either the neighbour's goat would complain resentfully and at length, or the pig's tell-tale grunts would call her back to the fruit bushes and the long, tussocky grass.

In this green idyll Marie's mother would suddenly remember old skills, churning butter in a stone crock, picking black and redcurrants while Curtius fell asleep with his papers and political pamphlets spread before him. And the heavy, sweet scents of the afternoon spiced the yeasty dough when they kneaded it on the kitchen table before putting it aside to rise. Their riches seemed infinite on the day when a cat crept in and gave birth in a basket to five piebald kittens. They never tired of watching those soft balls of fur, their first enchanting stumbles across the kitchen floor, their little red tongues which scattered beads of milk all over their shining coats. Even Curtius allowed them to sharpen their claws on the chairs and make climbing expeditions up the curtains. The furnishings at Ivry-sur-Seine were far from valuable and their prosperity was concentrated in the long rows of jars of preserved fruits, raspberries and redcurrants, glowing ruby-red in the sun.

More and more often on those long, slumberous afternoons, Curtius' head would fall forward heavily on his chest and when

Marie saw the nape of his neck her heart contracted with tenderness and fear: he was so shrunken now, so thin and wrinkled. But a moment later he would be picking up one of the handsome white hens, which sat in his hands proudly, twisting and bobbing its little head. At the chopping board it would give one terrified cry and Marie would run into the house to avoid seeing its head being severed and its scaly yellow legs stiffening.

But in the evening she drew the curtains and placed the two five-branched candlesticks on the table, and the three of them ate long and well, drank their wine and relaxed as warmth and satiety suffused their bodies. When they heard footsteps they swallowed the food as if every mouthful were a criminal act; feloniously satisfied and comfortable, they drew closer together — fortunately none of the three had a tendency to fat! Marie looked from her mother to her uncle, wishing she could turn back the clock to the time when Curtius could protect them against anything, when she had admired him and regarded him almost as a god.

'Let us stay here longer — let us stay here for ever,' whispered an inner voice, but the words were never spoken.

As usual, they went early to bed. She put her little silver clock at a distance, so as to be awakened by the sparrows' shrill calls. For a moment she smiled towards the light like a child, longing for the morning to be as endless as the long blue ribbons the conjurer pulled out of his mouth, but her mother was already up. They tucked fruit, vegetables and freshly-killed chickens like contraband under their hats and shawls and took leave of the cats, the hens and the pig. The sharp, slaty morning air was still in their nostrils when the carriage rolled into Paris at six o'clock and they gazed wonderingly at shops opening to sell limp vegetables and grey meat at soaring prices.

At home Curtius locked her into her work. She made sketches and leaned courteously over the new important personages, so flattered to have their portraits exhibited that they did not so much as move a muscle when she smeared the thick yellow oil over their necks and cheeks.

Sometimes she smiled, at the thought of what would happen if she forgot to insert the straws in their nostrils. 'Would that make me a criminal?' she wondered. 'I only seem to like people with the wrong ideas!'

Once or twice she visited Philipstal's picture show. His gallant, velvet-brown glance and the lively movements of his broad hands were the same, but even in that magic world the new masters were strutting about in their laced shoes and flat hats. She closed her eyes until it was time for the landscape pictures. The Alps made her dizzy and she stared distractedly at the snow, imagining what it would be like to freeze into a pointed, crystal-clear icicle. She kneaded her hands to warm them and found herself back on the little wooden bench between wide-eyed, open-mouthed children absorbed in Philipstal's world of light, mirrors and motley threadbare images.

At home in the kitchen her mother splashed white wine into a pan and stirred it solemnly.

'Can I help?'

'You have your work, child — and this is becoming increasingly difficult.'

'What shall we be having?'

'Potato soup, potato puffs, potato cake!'

'But we are used . . .'

'We are used to so much. I have never been a reader, but listen to what I have found in today's paper.'

Her finger with its neatly-cut nail pointed to the front page.

'Citizen, hang your dog and live on potatoes twice a week!'

'But does no one protest?'

'Oh yes, even in the rain!'

The roll of drums and the sound of many feet brought the two women to the window as a procession moved slowly past.

Marie clutched her mother's hand. 'They are women,' she whispered, amazed.

'Hm, yes, perhaps—'

They wore their skirts and shawls like a uniform, advancing nimbly, swaying, dancing, intoxicated, hungry. The rain gushed over them, but still they moved on.

Perhaps they were not all women. Marie saw broad shoulders, muscular arms, hairy hands under ruffled sleeves; coarse skins and powerful jaws barely concealed by lace caps and shawls.

Under one golden wig she thought she recognized the Duke of Orléans with a roasting spit in his beringed hands, but the women surrounding him noticed neither stubble nor rings. Their skirts billowed around their hips, their shawls swept them forward, unassailably touching and deranged, flourishing cooking spoons, kitchen knives and long, flashing tailor's shears.

The mean houses with their fusty basement rooms and yards, the empty pots no longer existed, effaced long since by the drums and the cold, sharp air. Exhaustion transformed them into one race, one unconquerable army advancing towards a dream of warm beds, heaped plates, rooms filled with diamonds and marble shining like wet, exposed flesh.

They were propelled along the long road from Paris to the golden gates of Versailles, shouting for bread, but bread was already something abstract, like a new law or an impossible promise. They were deafened by drum rolls, by feet that dragged and stamped and raised voices that cracked the window panes. In they burst, following their own cries; in, into the fairy-tale palace, up the shining pink marble steps, hands grasping banisters as fragile as white iced cake. Everything was as laughable and light as if they had already won, and when they killed the guard with their swinging shears and butcher's knives it made no difference, for everything had changed and the murder seemed to have been committed long ago.

It was an overwhelming, intoxicating power, which did not come to them like a revelation from heaven; it was not in the rain that fell, stinging and ice-cold on their shoulders. It was inside them, like a fever held in check for many years, like blows waiting in the palms of their hands half their lives and now suddenly released. Their screams came easily and they pressed forward, into the flesh, into the palace, their dream palace where no one should ever live again. Into the narrow golden corridors where none should hide or flee or cheat again.

The next day they drove the royal family into Paris in a slowly rumbling carriage, singing a tender lullaby about the baker, the baker's wife, the baker's son, the flour and the bread.

The smell of the city seeped in through the draughty windows of the Tuileries, where the royal family showed themselves all day long. The gesture was neither grand nor gracious, they simply appeared at the window when it was cold.

Marie Grosholtz went there too, wrapped in many shawls, waiting to catch a glimpse of Elizabeth. Her heart almost stood still when she saw her former benefactress walking across the garden. For a moment she thought their eyes met, but the Princess's were looking inwards, like the eyes of the white statues which had once made her blush.

Then she heard high voices as the two children ran up. Elizabeth too launched into a short, puffing trot, clearly no more than a desperately feigned cheerfulness, as she hopped like a fat little bird trapped in a snare.

At home Marie sat down on the slender, gilded chair, hesitantly testing her pen, as if for a profile that would not quite come off. 'Dear Elizabeth.' 'My beloved mistress.' 'Your Highness.' She did not know if she should stand, for she had never done more than rise, to be standing ready when she heard the Princess's step. Before she could decide, the pen had made a blot. She crumpled the sheet of paper, pulled the curtains across and locked her door.

My father was in the Swiss Guard and very probably a hero, and now my uncle belongs to the National Guard. Once I sought myself in the mirrors of Versailles and took pleasure in making fine figures. Now fate has made me the recorder of death and horror and I am trying to hide, to disappear among my own tableaux, as anonymous as a cobble in the road.

But often something stirs within me, urging me to abandon this cold, passive role, and whatever I do, I feel like a traitor.

Yesterday my uncle gave me some work he thought would please me. You will surely remember the portraits I made in the happy days of your brother and sister-in-law and their children. That group is to be set up at the Trianon, which is now open to everyone. My uncle has at last been given permission by 'the authorities', though I can scarcely tell what 'the authorities' may be.

I drove there with an officer of the National Guard and a woman who had taken part in that fateful procession which brought you to Paris.

We spoke little, and the woman cherished the deepest suspicion of me, yet she told me that on that cold, rainy day she had been courteously received and fed. Otherwise she was still just as hungry.

I shall not weary you with a description of the palace and the park, all so indescribably empty, and yet as if you were only away on holiday. But the woman asked a question that shook me: 'Where's the room full of diamonds?' she kept repeating. I told her that no such room existed, but she had pictured it so clearly that she insisted I lied and the stones had been secretly removed.

It struck me that I have now and then made a lip less heavy, a nose thinner; have I been helping to create ideas about rooms like jewel boxes?

I did my work with a heavy heart, those dead figures making me long for the living. If it would still divert you to model fruit, flowers and the limbs of saints, I will gladly join you. I have heard that the Princess Lamballe has left her exile in England to be with your sister-in-law — but one hears so many things. People are fleeing one after another. Oh that you and your family could do the same! I bury myself in my work, and I say 'bury' quite deliberately. Heads roll from my hands, handsome, cold and smooth, without tears. It is like living in a bad dream. I am silent, as far as possible, surrounded by enemies, even in my uncle's house.

But Marie Grosholtz never finished her letter nor did she decide how she should address the King's sister. She concealed it among her kerchiefs before leaving with her mother and uncle for Ivry-sur-Seine.

Here too there were problems: the lock of the pigsty had been broken and the creature appeared to have followed its new owners without a care. They tracked its small, pointed footprints until they disappeared in the grass and Marie's and her mother's eyes were full of tears at the thought of their dear, unfortunate animal being slaughtered and eaten by strangers.

They were still depressed the following morning when they

returned to the city, where every handbill told them that the
royal family had tried to escape to Austria, but had already been
brought back and put under lock and key.

'Misfortunes never come singly,' said Marie, kicking the
travelling rug.

Curtius sent her a sharp, side-long glance.

'I was thinking of the pig.' Once again she kicked out, reflec-
ting that even the pig was not a proper subject.

But she had little time to consider the vanished pig, for Curtius
put her in charge of the exhibition while he himself went into the
town, and although there were few visitors she could not concentrate on the two newspapers lying beside her cash box.

'King recognized from coin while relieving himself.' Or: 'King
apprehended when he left his carriage to admire the corn.'

Not knowing what to believe, she bit her lip at the thought of
that big, shy man, perhaps unable even to conduct such a private
matter unseen. 'But where would he have learned?' she thought,
hoping that he had in fact been recognized as he stooped to assess
the grain. Her uncle was sure to know; she would ask him as soon
as he came home.

She was sorely disappointed, however, when Curtius appeared later that afternoon, bringing one of his so-called friends
with him. Marie sighed, resigned to a whole evening with this
dreary, pompous man.

Moreover, Curtius seemed in such good form, almost elated,
that he would probably argue and drink coffee far into the night.
She made an unspoken resolve to withdraw immediately after
dessert, pitying her poor mother who would be obliged to
remain bowed over her embroidery, always ready to run for fresh
coffee, a few more little cakes and some preserves, port wine or
perhaps a glass of champagne.

From the way Curtius looked, it would be both preserves and
champagne; he was treating this quite commonplace person,
whose name Marie could not even remember, with almost
subservient friendliness. When he introduced himself his hand
was disagreeably limp, his voice a mumble, as if his name were an
obscenity or an intimacy.

But now he was preening himself under Curtius' flattering

attentions and — oh no! — her uncle was telling him to sit down and make himself comfortable while she took an impression of his face so that his esteemed portrait could be exhibited with the famous.

Marie could scarcely believe her ears. She had imagined that this self-absorbed gentleman might one day wish to pay a considerable sum to have his bust made, just to be able to present it to his mother or his aunt or whoever might conceivably want to have him about. But now he was sitting down and crossing his legs, an almost ritualistic pleasure spreading over his face as she began to massage oil on his forehead and eyelids, and so far round his temples that she made his wig greasy.

'It is simply to prevent the plaster from sticking,' she told him distantly, reluctant to allow this portly young man to take the touch of her fingertips personally.

'It is extraordinarily kind of you, mademoiselle. I know your uncle, but had not yet had the pleasure of your acquaintance.'

'I withdraw when I think it fitting.'

'You can feel quite free with me. Does it disturb you when I talk?'

'Your face is in motion.'

'This is the most wonderful, most moving day of my life — to be immortalized! As for the drive, you will know that M. Barnave and I were selected to conduct and protect the royal family all the long way back from Varennes to Paris.'

Marie's fingers stopped on his chubby cheeks. She poured more oil into her palm — far too much — and massaged it into his nostrils, the corners of his eyes and round the hairline to make him go on, concentrating her movements on forehead and temples, as if these were particularly difficult parts of the man's physiognomy.

'Your uncle said it would make your work easier if you could borrow some of my personal effects. Just say what you need, mademoiselle. My wig — my shirts — my shoes? I am particularly sensitive about my shoes; I have bunions and must purchase shoes of good quality.

'Perhaps you would be interested in the shirt I lent to the King? The poor man was completely soaked with sweat and unfortunately he saturated my shirt as well. It must be laundered before you can have it — I would not have you think that I sweat. Only for those two days and nights when we were shut up in the carriage, it was unavoidable. We were so tightly packed. The King and Queen and their two children and the King's sister, and of course my colleague and myself. Naturally no one had thought of us, but it was evident that the fugitives appreciated our helpfulness and our courage.

'Had it not been for us, they would in all probability have been killed. Eggs, tomatoes, chicken legs and other extremely indelicate articles were not the only missiles thrown at us. From time to time we heard the sound of stones hitting the solid polished sides of the carriage.

'Am I tiring you? You really must say if I am disturbing you in any way?'

'No, please go on. It makes the image more lively.'

'It was an experience to enter the carriage. I had never been so close to any crowned head before. My heart almost turned a somersault — and all that luxury, the tea-set, the toilet fittings and a little selection of good wines — they had thought of everything. The women had neither eaten nor drunk very much, to be sure, but the King — even in his hour of need! Yes, he did sweat. But there was something majestic even in his burning.

'Apart from all the luxury, and then the tragedy that hung over them, they were like an ordinary family returning from a sojourn in the country. I wonder they were recognized at all: that false pass was a clever bit of work, the King's sister could easily have been taken for the well-to-do baroness her papers said she was. The Queen sat erect in her grey governess's dress, the King was just a little broad and clumsy to be taken for a footman, but the children — well, they were like any others.

'The little boy wanted to piss and his father helped him himself — there was actually a chased silver pot among their goods! They were clearly family people and had they travelled in two light carriages they would have slipped past us as easily as anything. In fact, they were so close to their goal that one could but pity them. Now the whole journey had been in vain and they had to travel all the way back into the bargain, and in that intolerable heat, too.

'It was the Queen I pitied least. She conversed with my colleague in any case, discussing politics, and she seemed not unintelligent.

'She committed one act of foolishness, lifting the boy up to the window, perhaps in the belief that his pretty little face might move people. She may even have expected them to cheer him. But there were only howls and insults, words I would not allow to pass my lips. You see, they more than hinted that the King was not the child's father. She wiped away a tear in silence, then sat straight as an actress hissed off stage, having first given way to tears in the wings.

'The flight was probably mainly her plan. Some Swedish Count had ordered the carriage and it was he who drove it out of Paris. And the man who rode ahead to see to fresh horses and so on was none other than her hairdresser; obviously the two men she relied on most, her lover and her hairdresser.

'The Count is at least an officer, but that hair artist, to whom she had also entrusted her jewels — they say he burst into tears when he realized he was going to leave the city. That scrawny little man scrambled onto a long-legged army horse with a perfume bottle in one hand and a map of the route in the other. I do not really understand why he was the one; he's never even been a soldier! But I suppose she wanted to look her best when she slipped across the frontier.'

Marie Grosholtz was still stirring the plaster, adding more water and stirring again, staring at the young man as if trying to absorb and retain every prominent and characteristic feature of his face.

'What of the King's sister?'

The slightly corpulent citizen blushed and almost broke into a sweat.

'Well — she filled me with quite different feelings. You see, she seemed so terribly melancholy and gentle. Perhaps not quite handsome, but as defenceless and touching as a pouter pigeon! Her tired, heavy head brushed my shoulder for an instant. It was clear that I inspired her with confidence and respect, and that's quite a special thing for women. Yes, in another situation I really believe we should have fallen into each other's arms like true lovers.'

'True lovers!' Marie's head buzzed. 'If only he had done something to save her . . . No, she would not have allowed it: Elizabeth's tenderness is on the religious side only. Otherwise, her mind is small and proud.'

She slapped plaster on the enamoured citizen's face with an almost brutal vehemence.

While it was drying, she stared out of the window as the sun sank behind the houses, setting the whole city aglow. 'All that time, in a stuffy carriage — they must have been half dead. And to be caught, so close to their goal!' Her forehead sought the cool of the pane.

At that moment a fearful rattle burst out behind her. She spun round and gave a shriek as she saw the mask crack, revealing the previously ruddy face, now deathly pale, the lips blue.

'Forgive me!' The young man flapped his arms in the air like an overweight angel, the tears·streaming down his cheeks. 'I am simply not accustomed to being immortalized.'

Mademoiselle Grosholtz beat the friendly gentleman hard on the back, realizing with a shock that she had forgotten to insert the straws in his nostrils and had in fact treated him like a death mask.

'It does not matter at all,' she said quickly. 'With your permission I shall begin again.'

'If it really is not too inconvenient, mademoiselle!'

Already sitting still as a good child, his eyes closed, he was quite unaware of her blush. She removed the last fragment of the dried mask and smeared him with oil again.

'But,' she said, inserting the two little straws, 'what happened to the hairdresser?'

'He's probably been executed already, or will be tomorrow. The surprising thing was that when we caught him he was the very image of a soldier. He had hoped to the last that the royal flight would succeed, but he was quite unmoved by his own fate, really quite indifferent. Perhaps he learned something when he was a theatrical hairdresser — the scoundrel!'

'Scoundrel! If the escape had succeeded he would have been a hero.'

'H'm — you may be right.'

Once again she was smoothing the cold plaster over his face,
when he suddenly jumped up with such force that the little bowl
fell to the floor.

'No! He is and remains a criminal! The escape was not meant
to succeed. For a moment I was carried away by your viewpoint.'

He looked uneasily at the slender young lady now stooping
over the fragments and the plaster drying on the floor like a little
white mountain landscape.

'Mademoiselle — quite confidentially, you're not a spy, are
you?'

'No, as you see my work is quite superficial. But I must ask you
to sit a little more quietly.'

Marie Grosholtz often woke at four and sometimes even at three
in the morning and had formed the habit of going down into the
street quite early for fresh air. The morning made her dizzy, like
an over-fresh wine, as she sipped it, assuring herself that everything was normal, she was in the safe street of her childhood and
in a little time the shops would open, though with almost nothing
to offer.

What had become of it all? The fat pigeons, the capons, the
silk, the potatoes, the bread? Even the street lighting no longer
functioned, the ground had swallowed everything and closed
over it, like a cold, bitter crust. The corn no longer grew in the
fields, the hens laid no eggs, the cows gave no milk, and it was
rumoured that wolves ranged the outskirts of the city.

Marie Grosholtz shivered slightly, but quickly suppressed her
fear. One should not believe everything one heard. For one
thing, she lived in the centre, and for another, she was not especially afraid of wolves. What did annoy her was that she had holes
in her gloves. She spread her fingers against the light to see the
damage: the pink skin was so worn that it was falling to pieces, no
matter how carefully she sewed it, and she loved those gloves,
whose colour reminded her of an old doll's hands. Because it was
morning she allowed herself, out there in the street, to play with
her own smooth glove fingers, holes and all. Then she stuffed
them in her pocket, which was still more improper, but she was
quite alone and at peace, almost relaxed, but for that little quiver

in her body because she had slept badly and had not yet eaten or drunk anything at all.

It was therefore from surprise rather than fear that she started at a touch on her arm and found herself looking down at an old woman in torn black fur, and a big black kerchief which she had apparently not taken the time to secure. She had simply put the two ends in her mouth, and was surprised when it slipped down as she began to speak.

'Mademoiselle, do you know anyone in the Swiss Guard?'

'My father . . .' Marie thought of shining mountains and horses and water in great stone cisterns.

'He is dead.'

'Yes.' Marie picked up the kerchief and tied it under the woman's jutting white chin.

'My husband, too. Come.'

She knew that she should snatch back her hand and return to her uncle's safe house, but she followed the little black-clad woman, who must of course be crazed or senile and in any case both hard of hearing and short-sighted.

'Madame—'

But the old woman laid two fingers meaningfully on her lips. 'We may find him. We may be able to help each other.'

With a frail gust of energy she pulled Marie along, through alleyways and passages, gutters and scrap heaps. They reached the Tuileries area and were suddenly in the gardens, where the woman moved as if she were known.

Marie could not withdraw her hand, which seemed welded to that of the little fur-clad figure now moving so fast and with such agility that again and again her kerchief swung backwards against Marie's face.

In the quiet, shady gardens, the two women trod on thick cushions of moss which gave under their feet as if some secret depths were ready to swallow them up. The splashing of the fountains was a strange and ghostly sobbing and the shadow of the walls fell on their shoulders with an almost physical weight.

'Let us go — if the guards were to see us—' Marie could hear her own voice, as humble and resigned as Elizabeth's prayers reaching her through the wall.

Perhaps the woman read the words on her lips, for they could not have reached her ears or interrupted her constant, soundless weeping.

'The whole of the King's guard has been killed.' Her fingers tightened on Marie's hand. 'Look, mademoiselle — even the statues are bleeding.'

Just in front of them stood the Goddess of Justice herself, with bloodstains on the white marble folds of her tunic and the subtle, dreamy smile of a young prostitute.

Marie noticed the same smell as when the cart entered the Madeleine Cemetery and the morning melted into a sticky, crimson image. The old woman opened her fur-covered arms and pointed like a shabby angel of death towards the walls of the palace where the guards lay pierced through and through like toy soldiers abused by children to make their games more real. Only their uniforms shone with a hard enamelled gleam.

Marie tore herself away and stood for a moment, supporting herself against the smooth statue. The word 'traitor' came faintly to her and she saw the small black figure scuttling desperately across the lawns like a bird flying to its nest. Slowly she stroked her hands down her cloak, trying to wipe out the picture.

Unable to find the old woman's hiding place, she stopped at a wrought-iron gate which might not be too high for her. Twice she leaped to catch the iron spikes apparently made to prevent any such activity, and managed at last to swing her right leg over. The spikes sent a sharp pain through her breast and stomach and for a moment she thought she would be impaled between grass and sky for ever. Then she tumbled down on the other side.

It was much too early to look for a sedan chair, and in any case she had no money. Her skirt was torn so high up that she ought not to move her legs. She felt momentarily lost, then began to run across the unfamiliar town through which she had always been driven or carried. Nonetheless, she found the right direction and at the smell of Astley's equestrian circus she knew she was close to home.

She stopped briefly to lick the blood and rust from her hands, dry her forehead and clean her nose on the pink gloves. From the notice board she could see that the horses no longer

danced the minuet. Instead, this was the only circus in the world
which performed a brilliantly dramatic ride called 'Storming the
Bastille'. In free training Mr Astley swung a couple of bloody
heads with a wild, arrogant gesture. Marie remembered that her
uncle had in fact made duplicates of those severed heads, but she
was not particularly surprised. Now she gave a hysterical little
laugh, like a bell tinkling outside herself and she could not stop
laughing at the black notice outside Philipstal's place, announcing that all the magic lantern shows were suspended for the time
being.

She climbed the stairs, holding her torn skirt together with
both hands, and stepped out of it as soon as she reached her
room. Feeling feather-light, she lay down on her bed and closed
her eyes, resolving never to open them again. She pressed her
forehead, hands and breasts hard against the wall, even opening
her lips, as if she could swallow up the stone through the hangings, and disappear.

A little later she opened her eyes after all, to look at her hands
with the cracked nails, so red and torn that she could not appear
without gloves nor, far worse, could she hold a pencil or
modelling tool.

She sniffed at her skin — still no smell of the Madeleine, but it
would come soon. Just now it would not be particularly difficult
to die, it was simply a matter of a very little perseverance.

But at ten o'clock her mother arrived with a cup of chocolate.

'Have you a temperature?'

'Only a headache.'

But it was impossible not to take just a little sip.

'The sweetness will make me vomit,' she thought. 'Soon I shall
get up and turn my whole stomach inside out until the bile
comes.' But she grew warm and tired, no more.

At twelve Curtius arrived with a doctor and Marie turned her
face to the wall to avoid any awkward questions. She felt his
precise, gentle fingers on her wrist and imagined him as a very old
man with a refined, mouse-like face. She heard him suggest
opening a vein in the young lady's foot, in order not to frighten
her with the sight of blood.

Marie could not help drawing her feet up a little and she pursed her lips together so as not to laugh when the doctor stooped slowly over her bed in search of her feet. Then she felt a firm grip on her ankle and the sensation of treading on a wasp. 'A tiny little knife,' she thought as the china bowl scraped briefly against the foot of the bed. She could feel the blood rippling through her like little coral-red waves, right out to her fingertips.

But she could not hold sleep together: it was thin and fragile and kept crumbling away. Her skin smelled slightly sour with sweat.

'Don't you love us any more?' Her mother's voice sounded exactly as if she were offering a guest the last fairy cake.

'I would die for you.' Marie's eyes opened involuntarily.

'These days it is more troublesome to live — and Madame Philipstal is down in the kitchen blubbering.'

'What is the matter?'

'Philipstal is in prison, poor man. An old picture of the King had slipped into his magic show, though he swears it was a mistake. He has a weak stomach as well and your uncle is doing what he can through his connections to get him out. You should get up for a little, if only to please your uncle . . .'

Marie inhaled the fatty, spicy smell of marrow soup which her mother had brought up on a tray, but she did not touch it. She swung her legs out of bed and began to dress, slowly, as if wrapping a thin protective skin round herself which the slightest incautious movement might break. She dispelled the sweat with perfume and brushed her hair, noting that her face was only a little paler than usual.

If she just stayed at home and stopped reading the newspapers everything would seem quite normal. She soon heard that Philipstal was home, that he was eating gruel and drinking milk and putting on the usual number of performances, but she did not visit him. She never went further now than the Madeleine Cemetery with her uncle and more and more rarely to the green sanctuary at Ivry-sur-Seine with him and her mother.

But round about her everything continued: shops opened and shut, conjurers pulled ribbons out of their mouths and at Astley's circus the Bastille fell five times a day. Prison doors opened and shut, a ten-year-old boy was arrested because he had never exhibited any form of patriotism, a girl imprisoned because she had worked for a priest without suspecting that religion had become a kind of crime. Seven men were run in because owing to poor metabolism they were so fat that they could not possibly be real revolutionaries.

One day the beautiful Princess Lamballe was imprisoned but released again on the following day, almost as surprised at her freedom as at her arrest. She was still extraordinarily delicate and refined, her imprisonment having apparently not affected her. Her corset made her hobble a little, lace inhibited her movements, her shoes pricked her slyly and she walked gingerly, light-footed, to avoid the blood and filth of the street.

But suddenly she made a movement expressive of nausea and revulsion, her gloved hand flying to her mouth as if to hold back vomit. Suddenly a spring seemed to have broken in a complicated piece of mechanism.

A young bank clerk sprang forward to knock her hat off, but pushed her over backwards instead, and she was amazed that the street could be so soiled and people so ill-behaved, but there was neither anger nor fear in her lovely eyes. She expected him to help her up, brush the dirt from her costume and ask if she were hurt. Her want of aggression had the effect of mockery, and someone grabbed her hair as if to assure himself that all that sweetness, that innocence and astonishment were really flesh and blood, and medallions, rings, powder boxes, scraps of blue silk and long snowy feathers were scattered over the pavement. People stopped only momentarily at the hot red stream of blood and no one knew who had actually severed head from body, or who had suddenly laid the body open so that liver, heart, intestines and lungs unfolded abruptly, in obscene, glistening colours, with a strong, animal stench.

The bank clerk gathered up the little head almost reverently, feeling the slender nose, the lips that opened as if for a disarming kiss. Every Sunday, week after week, he had gazed at the Sleeping Beauty in the Waxwork Cabinet, lying bathed in light from an invisible sunset, the long, soft hair falling loosely over the arm of the sofa; and one day, quite unseen, he had stroked the fine, cool face and pulled a single hair from a curl. For a moment he had expected her eyes to open, but still she lay there like a needless dream princess encased in her glass casket or her safe, self-sufficient slumbers. And it seemed to him that her breasts rose and fell, the nipples gleaming faintly pink through the lace, her feet as perfect and smooth as silk.

With the certainty of a sleepwalker he now headed straight for Curtius' Waxwork Cabinet, while others seized the body and dragged it along in an obscene funeral cortège. Suddenly, without paying for admission, they were standing in the middle of that great hall with all its famous effigies, and the bank clerk handed the Princess's head to a silent, white-faced young woman, who received it with steady hands, showing no sign of emotion or fear.

Mademoiselle Marie Grosholtz smoothed the plaster mask over the Princess's face. She pictured her still on the Trianon lawns, her blue eyes which saw everything with a child's wonder, her small hands caressing dogs, lambs and tame birds. And when she leaned over the water no one knew if it was to see her reflection or to play with the fish.

The Princess had loved cows and would stroke their foreheads for hours and lose her violet-blue gaze in their mild, dewy eyes. But from the back they terrified her out of her wits with the angularity of their bones, and their tails which could not be tied up with silk ribbons.

She rescued kittens, fledglings, bees, even flies about to drown in wine or milk, while her lips formed kiss after kiss, sigh after sigh, her voice trilled out its small, engaging exclamations or fluttered in sweet, intimate confidences.

No sign of anger: her face expressed an insensate, stubborn and defiant gentleness, as if the Princess's heart and mind were incapable of comprehending hatred.

Marie saw the primitive, indecent sketch before her eyes again, the flames leaping through it, the stomach opening like a glowing hole, and suddenly she was stepping into a bad dream, whose movements she already knew by heart.

Alone again, she worked conscientiously to make the features as lifelike and natural as possible, applying make-up to the long lashes and finely-arched brows. She had to make several attempts before catching the right, chestnut-brown colour of the

hair. If only she could ask M. Léonard, who had helped her
before, if only he had got away, she thought. He had his craft in
his hands and could have made a living anywhere. She looked at
her own palms, which had almost healed by now.

She did not see Curtius later on, when he stood for a long time
before the Princess's portrait.

'She is recovering,' he murmured, impressed. 'This is the first
real piece of work she has achieved since her illness.'

From habit he smoothed the uniform jacket over his stomach.

'Come,' said David, the wen on his cheek glowing through the
powder, his hat askew, his face twitching with excitement. 'Bring
your pencils and plaster.'

Marie had no time to put on hat or cape before he had whisked
her down the stairs and into a carriage.

'Are you kidnapping me?' she asked ironically, leaning back.

'Wait and see — it is a show!'

'Are you inviting me to the theatre in the middle of the day?'

The carriage stopped and she followed him through an entrance where the nameplates had been replaced, if at all, by
dog-eared labels. Two members of the National Guard were
posted in the third room, but they nodded graciously when they
saw David, and opened the door.

Marie thought there was something familiar about the smell of
the rooms and in the kitchen she gasped for air. A white vapour
covered the windows, transparent drops trickling down over
dirty cupboards.

She accompanied David to a big, zinc tub standing for no
apparent reason in the middle of the floor. The water was still
steaming hot and a bitter medicinal scent mingled with the scent
of blood, which had turned the bath so red that it seemed already
to be part of an over-coloured picture.

Without a thought for his clothes David plunged his arm under
the figure in the bath, lifting it as if the body were still alive and
they were to carry it down to the waiting carriage together.

A face rose up through the water, a head wrapped in a white
bandage, now dyed pink, a little face drained of colour, drops
trickling down the nose from the eyelashes. The mouth was

open, the naked body covered with little pink scars and yellowish, weeping sores which suddenly gathered into one gaping hole from which the blood still flowed in a dull stream. His penis was an earthworm, his feet small, his ugliness as open and as defenceless as a flower.

'Killed,' whispered Marie.

'Murdered — the murdered Marat,' said her escort solemnly. 'Take an impression of his face — both you and I will have a use for it.'

As if the familiar movements might calm her, she began to stir the plaster and as she smeared it over his face she seemed only to be making his dressings more complete. She saw his arms floating gently and peacefully on the water and when she cautiously removed the mask it seemed to her that it was his real face that she held in her hands — quite simple, and as light as an eggshell. She stared down into the white, open eyes and felt a moment of dizziness.

'Come, we have by no means finished.' David helped her down the stairs and into the carriage, where he solicitously covered her knees with a soft fur rug. Like two jackals, Marie thought. A tenuous quivering began at the nape of her neck and spread out to her fingertips and down to her knees. She saw that the carriage had stopped before a prison. David stroked her cheek soothingly, but the gesture was much too feeble and hesitant.

'Why are we here?'

'To meet the murderess! Wait until I come for you.'

She stared at the back of the coachman's neck, wondering if she could ask him to turn round and drive her home, or perhaps feign a swoon, but she had a feeling her escort would see through her ruse, and in any case he was back again before she had made up her mind.

'I won't set foot in a prison. I refuse to meet the witch!'

The painter smiled quite blithely as she shrank back in the carriage.

'Come on, you'll like her.'

'She must be insane, and so are you, apparently!'

'You must see her — she's fantastic! They treat her like a

queen. Her skin is so clear that you can see a drop of wine running down her throat.'

'You are making me ill,' hissed Marie, but she picked up her bag of tools and followed him, taking great care where she placed her feet.

Almost deferentially, the guards let them in, to see a young girl of erect, almost haughty bearing, who seemed neither mad nor evil. Marie stole a glance at her hands, which were long and narrow with short clipped nails and which lay in her lap as quietly as two birds in a nest.

'Here is the young lady whose mask you are to take.'

Marie gave a slight, involuntary bow.

'If you have no objection?'

'No,' said the girl, in a clear, rather countrified voice, 'nothing can frighten me now.'

Marie inserted the two straws very carefully in her nostrils and explained how she should breathe to experience the least possible discomfort. There was a faint smile on the girl's lips, as if the straws tickled her — or perhaps she really was looking forward to seeing a cast of her own attractive face.

While the plaster hardened she sat straight as a statue in her red silk dress. Perhaps she had actually dressed up for the murder in Marat's dirty kitchen.

David drew sketch after sketch: one of the Fates, marble-skinned, with flowing locks; a Valkyrie with hair like a smooth golden helmet; the girl's eyes, at once distant and sharp; the light shining on her skin like raindrops.

When Marie removed the plaster mask from her face she did not move a muscle.

'It's done.'

'Yes.'

'Forgive me, but why in the bath?'

'I found him there.'

'But in any case, why?'

'All that man stood for was repugnant to me and my family. I had heard so many people wish him dead without lifting a finger that I decided to sacrifice my life. From that moment I have felt invulnerable. It was all so easy!'

'You hated him?'

'No, not really. The feeling was as sharp as metal, and yet pure and clear.'

'But you could have opposed him politically.'

'Politics are dirty.' The girl looked down at her hands.

'Or written to him—'

'He would simply have ridiculed or vilified me. After all, he had the gift of the gab.'

And to indicate that the audience was now over, she rose and turned her back on them, pressing her forehead to the little barred window.

'Do you think,' whispered Marie when they were sitting in the carriage, 'that one always has the face one deserves?'

'No.' David's hand went to his cheek. 'But I wish I could paint her as a heroine.'

'Won't you do that?'

'Are you mad? If you make a tableau of the murder you must make the dying Marat the hero, or you'll be finished.'

'So what will you do with all those sketches of her?'

'I shall use her in another painting. I may even give her a Greek hairstyle.'

'I shall make it as I see it.'

He observed her birdlike profile, her concentration, as if the image were already in her head.

'Marie, don't you think we're made for each other?'

She cast a shocked glance at the pale little man, with his soaking wet sleeve.

'We are too different.'

'There are explosive substances, even poisons, that cancel each other out.'

She leaned back, thinking of the murderess's pretty face, closed and smooth, as if death were a grain of sand in a pearl.

'But a child—' he went on, with forced irony, 'a combination of you and me. How would that be?'

'I have not considered having children.'

'In a free society women give birth without pain.'

'I know nothing of either law or biology!'

Marie Grosholtz did not trouble to invite her escort in. She sat down at her drawing-board and had her meals brought in, but she scarcely had time to eat.

She thought of the young girl and the clear, flinty mornings and the scents of Ivry-sur-Seine. She remembered the stench and the shock when she first opened the door to the larder and saw that hunted, exhausted creature with a stack of books and a candle, and again and again she pictured the meeting in Marat's dirty kitchen. There he lay, in a hot bath which dulled his pain. The water washed his sores clean and made his body light, no longer weighted down. He felt relaxed, floating in the water, his thoughts airy and subtle and the white vapour surrounded him like a very fine protective tissue.

As in a vision he saw the young woman step in: a Judith, suddenly standing tall and straight before him.

His nostrils quivered like a calf's.

Her eyes were clear and she held his gaze, making him feel small and vulnerable, like a child who has kicked off his bedcovers. She was a cool, sober dream, against which he had no defence. He clasped his hands, and a cold, clear pain drew the life out of him.

Marie worked with pencils, charcoal, chalk, steel, kapok, glove leather, wax, human hair, glass and silk, seeking to reach the soul through the skin as she applied the final colours to the two wax faces.

At last they could be displayed in Curtius' Waxwork Cabinet, she herself helping to veil the light so that a thin vapour seemed to enwrap the two figures.

Money flowed into Curtius' cash box in a golden stream. Every day men, women and children stood spellbound and shuddering round the man in the bath and the tall fair girl, half expecting the little rustle of the silk skirt, the draught of their own quick, warm breath lifting her long blond hair, the slight hunger and the feverish glow of her cheeks to culminate suddenly in one wild, flying gesture.

Robespierre himself stood by the tableau for a long time on a visit to Curtius and out in the street he gave a neat little speech to the passing citizens, telling them to go in and feel what he had felt.

Marie looked at him from the side as he sipped Curtius' best Burgundy, wondering if indeed he felt like the hideous victim or the pretty murderess, but his face expressed no emotion whatever and she was content to welcome the advertisement.

She heard the two men agreeing that Curtius, with his fluent German, would be the right man to send on a short but important mission.

'I dare say my niece can see to the daily running of the exhibition,' she heard her uncle say. The blood rushed to her cheeks with pride and when at that moment David walked in, she gave him a triumphant smile.

'It's nothing to do with you,' he said irritably, 'you can thank her for all your success. You should have seen her driving to the scaffold, the people dancing round the tumbril, shouting and screaming as if they would have liked to proclaim her queen. She stood absolutely straight, her face radiantly white, not even closing her eyes against the rain that plastered that long, blood-red dress of hers to her body.'

'Poor girl,' murmured Marie, involuntarily bowing her head.

'Poor thing.' The painter took a gulp of wine. 'She was magnificent!'

The doll was pulling her arm downwards, the red weight of the tiles becoming part of her body. Outside, the snow was like a white china landscape which might break at any moment. She looked down at her little shoes, knowing that as a punishment she must be alone. The tears were a stone in her throat, a weariness that made the doll slip from her arms, its head cracking against the rust-red tiles. Outside, the landscape shattered, so she could never escape.

Someone was shaking her, but she was wrapped in her heavy, red grief, her lips sealed, unable to open her eyes.

A voice penetrated her sleep: Curtius — Curtius, who had let her in, Curtius angry, shaking her until her head lolled to and fro. But it must be a dream. He had no business here, in her nursery!

Marie opened her eyes, seeing the veins in his temples and his wigless scalp shining.

He was stooping over her, his shirt flapping round his legs. The

morning light was thin and grey, there was not a sound from the
street. She half rose, putting a hand to her mouth.

'Marie!' His voice was soft, brittle. 'They've come for you and
your mother.'

But she was incapable of reacting and the old man had to pull her
out of bed, over to the close-stool and the washstand. The sudden
cool of china against her skin, the smell of the morning urine, as of
hot, nervous animals, the perfumed washing water, fragrant as
spring fields full of daffodils. A jolt at her heart — the Trianon! —
and in the mirror her face as pale and motionless as a doll's.

She noticed her uncle's fingertips, soft and insistent on her skin,
as if modelling the fear into her. But her body was stiff and it was he
who pulled the long lace nightgown up over her head and
dropped it onto the floor, he who laced her corset, not particularly
tightly, but just enough to make her breathe faster, he who pulled
the silk stockings up over her ankles and fastened the garters. With
an old man's stiff-kneed movement he helped her into her shoes,
found skirts and finally a dress of grey linen which fell round her
body like a soft pile of ashes. He fastened a white collar with silk
rosebuds round her neck, giving her a child's tenderness and
innocence.

Marie reached for her rouge and a locket, but he shook his head.

'My hair—' she whispered.

It hung heavy and unkempt on her shoulders and Curtius pulled
the comb through it with a hesitancy in his fingers she had never
before noticed.

There was a crash, a scramble, the door was flung open and two
bright red caps appeared: two men, one with dark stubble on a
long, ravaged face, the other quite young with a pock-marked face
and cool green eyes.

'An odd pair,' the bearded one grinned at Curtius.

With an ironic bow the younger man offered Marie his arm and,
without looking back, she let them lead her to the carriage.

Her arms were tortured when her wrists were tied behind her
back, and she shrank from the grey-green eyes as from a sudden
icy wave, recognizing the coachman who had driven her from
Versailles.

Her mother was already sitting in the carriage, quite still, as if she could disappear completely in her bashfulness and silence. Her long, dark dress coat hung open to reveal a pleated apron underneath. Marie was aware of a faint smell of oven black and wondered at the extraordinary, ageless little woman who rose at daybreak to clean the stove. For the first time it dawned on her that it was months since they had had a maid in the house.

On all sides the streets were grey and chilly. Their breath hung like steam between their lips. Marie had difficulty in keeping her balance as they turned the corner, but she swayed her body, trying to follow the movements of the carriage. She still felt no fear, only guilt towards her mother, and compassion for the old man crawling round the floor after her shoes.

She heard doors and windows slam, but did not look up, even when someone shouted. She waited until the carriage stopped and the man with the mocking green eyes helped her down.

Her movements were stiff and awkward as he pushed her into a room where she recognized the smell of damp and stone. She heard the key turn in the lock and saw him take a knife from his belt to cut the rope round her wrists. Her arms dropped to her sides and her hands, which she had almost forgotten, were heavy and red.

Still she did not look up. She saw only the short, smooth hands of a young man, and bowed her head as he stroked her hair like the feathers of a rare bird. Then he gathered it into his hand and pulled until her temples hurt and fear was a lump in her throat. She felt the knife touch her neck as with slow, clumsy movements he sawed off the thick bundle of hair.

As if he had been holding her suspended in the air, her body crumpled at the last cut, her head dangling like a withered flower on a stalk. She heard him lock the door behind him, leaving her tresses, dark and living, on the floor. She closed her eyes and waited.

He'll come back, she thought. He'll come again and perhaps he will tear the dress down over my shoulders and I shall wish my shoes were not too small and that I had large, flat feet. I shall mount the stairs like a cheap actress and people will gloat at my unsteady stumbling, heralding the long, plunging fall. For a moment all eyes will be on my little head with the ragged hair. I shall press my lips together and look out at the sky, which will be blue and stretched like thin silk and where, as Elizabeth believes, I may suddenly wake up again, in clear, pure air. And perhaps I shall be sick.

But why are my hands not shaking, like my uncle's when he brought the grey dress from the cupboard and grovelled for my shoes? It's as if I were already dead, only the cold of the walls reaches me. Perhaps I died on the day I left Elizabeth? She kissed me on the lips and then my uncle struck me on the mouth, my tears were a thin column of smoke in the night, scalding and soundless.

I hated my uncle's protection, the key that locked me in with the spinet and modelling tools; but I painted, modelled, found the right shades of colour and hair and learned to apply that fine, living glow to the skin so perfectly that they thought one scratch would make the wax bleed. Feelings and dreams were attached to those cool figures: perhaps our effigies sometimes suck the life out of people by turning them into heroes or rogues.

All the same, I wish I had had time to take my own likeness — it would make it easier to mount the steps!

Why was I already dreaming of steps and moors when I was a child? What of that dark woman who read my hand, mumbling of sorrow and fame and the hole in my lifeline? Is that my head, suddenly falling? If only it may be swift and wordless, without dragging me through interrogation — if only death is a fleeting image!

How am I to know if I am guilty or innocent? Two viewpoints, two lights shed on one human being: the prosecutor's and the defender's. Two stories. I cannot see my restricted little life in a distinct light, neither the rose-pink of the heroines nor the blue of the thieves. How am I to explain it — I, who was once a precocious child, am now an ignorant adult.

Marie frowned and pushed her fingers through her hair. Outside, the sky was silvery, the iron bars making a sharp, stern pattern on the window. Suddenly the door opened and the older man pushed her tool bag into the room, grinning jovially at her astonishment; but it was the young former coachman who led her out, further down the long corridor, to a large room with long benches and tables. She heard voices, laughter and the clatter of spoons, glass and bowls.

Through the smell of greasy soup and stale wine she found herself almost sneaking past the twenty or so women at the table, to reach the empty seat beside her mother.

Marie pressed her hand under the table. Her mother's face seemed both younger and less strained without the long plait which had always made a stiff black halo round her face. Nor did she seem particularly disturbed, eating the bread with hungry appreciation and tasting the luke-warm soup critically, perhaps contrasting it with the wholesome flavour of her own cooking.

With well-tended hands the young woman on Marie's other side broke the bread into small fragments with which she played abstractedly. Fresh as a spring flower, she smiled with carefully painted lips and eyes, and as if from a great distance Marie noticed that she herself was smiling again. Soon afterwards they introduced themselves politely.

Neither Marie Grosholtz nor Josephine Beauharnais had any real women friends. As children they had played and gone for walks with the girls their families thought suitable, behaving as politely and pleasantly as expected, but none of those friendships had lasted.

Perhaps it was not entirely Marie Grosholtz's fault that other women found her rather tiresomely reserved and ambitious. And perhaps it was wholly the fault of Josephine Beauharnais' sensual nature and the knowledge that she was a Creole that made people think her a little superficial, less than true, and much too flirtatious.

Work, for Marie Grosholtz, had taken the place which might have been filled by friendship with a grown woman. Men, for Josephine Beauharnais, had filled all her emotions. Even now, surrounded by women, she seemed to have stepped out of a coach after a romantic excursion and to be about to walk with small, rapid steps to her boudoir to perfume herself thoroughly and stroke a powder puff over her fine, salty skin. Her hands were small, almost stubby. Prison food had not yet tamed her body, her breasts still thrust against her neckline when she leaned forward, but her pretty, bright eyes held a desperate question.

Hopelessly cut off from everything, Marie and Josephine cast themselves into each other's arms with abandon, caressing each other's skin with dry, pouting lips in their longing for tenderness.

Marie thought what an enchanting model Josephine would be, although she was not in the least famous. 'Sit for me in peach and hyacinth blue,' she whispered.

Josephine thought what a wealth of charm had been wasted in Marie's light little figure. 'My treasure, you should never cry,' she whispered back, promising herself to introduce Marie to some men if they were set free. When they were set free.

Marie had certainly been a virgin far too long — an affair would make her blossom!

Josephine's shining hair and rounded body would entrance everyone — she would attract a large audience.

'My angel. Little hare. My love. My flower!' They drugged one another with words and plans, flowing out on each other's voices into the future and back into the past. They had to whisper for the sake of the others, but it made their relationship all the more intimate. They were loving and generous and like ideal friends they laughed and cried on each other's shoulders and promised one another the world.

When Marie woke up she hoped for a moment that it had all been a dream, but looking across the room with its narrow, battered beds, she knew where she was. She had never imagined a prison like this: it was more like a field hospital, or a poorhouse.

She looked for her mother's slender form, which had quite disappeared under the blanket. Further along the wall Josephine was tossing restlessly in her sleep and Marie sighed with despondency and longing at the thought that she had promised to make at least ten portraits of Josephine on the day they were released.

Josephine laughed, making her short curls dance, and dimples appeared at the corners of her mouth, but soon afterwards she cried and said her husband had already been executed.

Madame Grosholtz patted her hand and spoke sympathetically of grief, as if grief and gastronomy were her specialities. But it was not so much grief as fear of what would become of her and her children that was responsible for Josephine's tears.

Later in the day the two children arrived for a brief visit. The little girl was delicious, the very image of her mother. The boy had brought a sentimental lapdog, which Josephine lifted up. Her smooth fingers poked under the collar and found a coded note.

'King on trial — no carrots for love or money — your carriage and horses confiscated,' she translated in a whisper, two tears running down her cheeks. But in order not to distress her children she gave a big, animal snort and behaved cheerfully for the rest of the time. 'Snivelling sober,' she said, sipping with the air of a connoisseur some liqueur the children had brought in a scent bottle.

Marie looked at her hands, as if that were the only way to remember who she was. It was too long since she had worked, her nails had grown and when she scratched her head she found tiny eggs and grey lice with short, agitated legs. Holy Virgin, she thought, I must have been here more than five days. A louse takes five days to mature and a human being soon turns into an animal with a verminous coat and pointed claws.

Why has my uncle not obtained our release before this, with all his fine friends? He was talking about a foreign journey and boasting of his good German, but next morning he was an old, old man with trembling hands. He dressed me like a doll in this grey dress which now smells of sweat.

Does he no longer know that cool, handsome man, the one who should have been an actor instead of a politician — the way he wallowed in his own emotion before Marat's effigy! But only outwardly: inside, he was cold. Why is it never his head I have to model? Every time I waited in the Madeleine Cemetery I knew it would never be his face that I met.

Why, at least, does Curtius not take my mother away? Has he suddenly lost his power and the last remnants of decency? I ought to hate him, and I ought to hate those who brought us here — I wish I had a fine, sharp hatred and pride to turn against them. Instead, I sink deeper and deeper, but I am still alive and the lice thrive.

She heard light, rapid footsteps and thought that Josephine must also be awake. But instead she saw the young coachman coming towards her bed. He seemed greatly changed, yet that could only be because he now wore very thick-lensed glasses which were far too big, the gold rims more suitable for an older and much larger man. His eyes shrank into tiny green pinpoints behind them. In his hand he carried one of the pretty, woven baskets she had recently seen filled with eggs, cheese, vegetables or flowers.

He came right up to her and swung the basket before her face like a gift, while the smell of blood made her feel ill. He shunted her against the wall with the basket, brushing her throat with a soft gesture. Tears rose behind her eyes and her mouth filled with bile.

'Come, we've some work for you!'

In order not to have to submit to his chilly, appraising eyes, Marie stood up and followed him along the passage. He was suddenly moving very easily, his hand finding the keyhole at once as he locked her into the little room where her box of tools was waiting. No one had taken the trouble to sweep up her hair.

'You've done it before.' The green pinpoint eyes nailed her to the wall.

She bent reluctantly over the basket and a scream burst from her lips as she recognized the King's face.

Smiling, the former coachman removed his newly acquired glasses and his eyes took on a frighteningly distant look, which she found so shameless and provocative that he might as well have taken off all his clothes. But he left the room quickly and she heard him whistling in the passage. Perhaps he would leave this building altogether, go into the town. The sparrows twittered shrilly, piercing her through and through. Marie knelt down beside the basket, like someone brought to a sudden stop in the middle of a fall.

Water, she thought, surprised to want something that might keep her alive. Perhaps the room and the shorn hair had already altered her. Perhaps she could never again be that same young and charming Marie Grosholtz, but only a grey, anonymous being whose body had absorbed the morning mist until the cold had invaded her soul. And the shorn hair had given her the little sharp face of a jackal.

Slowly, as if to accustom her fingers to the work, she began to stir the plaster and then to smooth the sleek wax with her fingertips. She heard a faint crackling and saw the stove in the corner, containing far more water and bread than she needed. It was not long before the rich, satisfying smell of wax had almost soothed her.

It seemed only a few days since she had left Elizabeth. She saw the King and his sister walking along, with that peculiarly rolling gait which both knew to be slightly comical. She looked down again at the basket. Released from the weight of the body, his face was almost handsome, fit to be stamped on a coin, his features calm, his eyes closed in polite meditation. Blood on his cheeks, wine on his lips, and still a few shreds of meat between his teeth.

Marie observed without surprise that His Majesty must have eaten his last solitary meal with the same frank, hearty appetite as when he dined in public.

She imagined him in the middle of that great hall, leaning back a little and belching, heedless of the crowd on the balcony disguising their sniggers with coughs and sneezes behind inadequate handkerchiefs, while the Queen's shy, vulnerable glance sought the children and Elizabeth leaned forward to whisper: 'The meat — eat a little of the meat. Just cut off the fat ...'

But afterwards they threw off their obligations, Queen and children running down to the ponies and donkeys in their little enclosure, followed more slowly by Elizabeth and her brother.

Only now, it seemed to Marie, did she see his true face. She remembered how lively and interested he had been, as he sat reading with those round, gold-rimmed glasses on his nose, and she shaped the face easily, lightly, as if this were a living model whose most attractive and characteristic features she must emphasize.

'No need to make him better looking,' snarled the young man, returning to fetch her work.

In a sudden fit of rage, she advanced on him, straight-backed, and he grabbed her shoulders to push or shake her, but she stumbled, pulling him with her so that the gold glasses which she now recognized as the King's fell from his nose and the sparrows' high, strident voices shattered everything. His flesh was very warm and pure as she pulled him, or he crushed her, against the wall and she opened her mouth towards the shaking head that tasted of salt and sun-warmed stone and little rippling waves, and his hair was curly and prickled against her tongue.

He bumped into her instrument case and in revenge she sank her teeth into his throat, experiencing at the same time a desire to drown, to vanish altogether under his warm body. She felt herself sinking deep down under the water, consciousness deserting her, her breath rising and bursting into bubbles on the surface. She remembered all those she had despised for letting themselves fall, glide, float, as if love were no more than a breeze carrying them this way or that.

Her body let itself be blown away like a dandelion seed while with one part of her mind she was telling herself that it was only good sense that made her pull off her dress, so that that at least should not be damaged. And she thought of the moon-coloured carp in the pond and the feminine dance of the veiltail goldfish, their open pairing amongst reeds and ferns and his lips were coral-red fish swimming under her skin, while she kept her eyes shut so that her images should be left undisturbed.

His sighing and panting embarrassed her, as if he were trying to persuade her that she had done him harm, although it must be he who had injured her. She noticed his clumsiness as he gathered up the glasses, and wanted to laugh, to obliterate the whole episode. Instead, she got dressed with her back to him and lay down under the window, where the light fell sharply on her body.

She pressed herself close to the wall, opening her lips to the raw chill of the stones, the tears running down her nose, sliding over her temples and into her dark, dishevelled hair. But she did not notice. With her knees pulled up under her she deliberately bruised her hands against the stone while the cold entered her breasts. She was as cold as a statue, she would never again be able to force a word past her lips. If she opened her mouth, out would gush a thin, ice-cold stream of water, clear and transparent.

In a short, uneasy sleep she dreamed she was going to see M.

Voltaire, but all the clothes she could find were too tight. Her corset had no laces and was comically small, like a child's garment, and in all her cupboards she could find only one stocking. When she heard the key in the lock, she stayed where she was.

'You are free.'

For the first time she became aware of her coachman's, or lover's, ugly, southern French dialect, but he was probably just saying it to drive her mad and she did not even look up.

'You and your mother, you can go now. If we need you we know where you are.'

She suddenly found him monstrously formal, with his big glasses and his clean salt skin. She rose, as if the movement were an experiment, but her legs were as strong as a foal's, trembling a little but supporting her body as she followed him along the long, crooked passageways. For a moment she wished he would take her hand.

'You are from the country,' she said, about to tell him that she too came from a long way off and that in reality they were as helpless as two children brought into a strange world.

'We do not speak the same language,' he snarled in rude anger. 'You apparently have important friends.'

He walked faster, as if to shake her off as quickly as possible. Almost clinging to the bunch of keys, he pushed her into the arms of her mother, who was waiting, small and straight — she might have been at the dressmaker's or the corsetière's.

Marie suddenly felt weak and far away, as if she had long been forced to move without her shadow, and the two women clung to each other as they walked out into the street.

Every time they heard footsteps they jumped. Every time they saw someone they pressed back against the house walls. In one tree a black bundle hung like a shaggy clump of darkness. Marie was horrified to see a wolf-sized dog, hanging with its back legs stretched helplessly towards the pavement, its sharp teeth gleaming.

As they turned the corner into their own street two very young women walked towards them, the one tall and thin, the other short and evidently pregnant. Both had bare feet and barbaric gold ornaments shone on their toes and in their ears. They wore light dresses, cut very low and so thin that their nipples, navels and pudenda were clearly visible. The little one had curls like a savage, the taller had shaved herself almost bald, so that her scalp shone white through the short, henna-coloured stubble. The girls' faces were pale, brightened only by the rouge on their cheekbones, and round their white necks they had tied blood-red ribbons, so tightly that they cut into their skin like the collars of two lapdogs.

Both Marie and her mother uttered a little shriek, behind hands hastily raised to hold back the sound.

The two girls leaned against each other, giggling ecstatically.

Marie and her mother returned home to an empty house. They searched for some trace of Curtius: a used cup, a wine stain or an unmade bed. They peeped into his room, but the bed was tucked in and flat. Only his wigs were still hanging on the faceless wig-stands.

From then on they did not draw the curtains, seldom lit the candles and lived principally on wine from the cellar and withered potatoes. Sometimes they felt quite high-spirited, but the next moment they were scared at the sound of their own excited voices, or of footsteps. They quaked inwardly, their sleep fell apart in wretched fragments, their skin was dry and thin.

At last, on the seventh day, they heard Curtius' step on the stairs as he let himself in. Marie had imagined herself advancing towards her dear uncle, flinging truth after truth in his face and questioning him about his important political journey, but a meekness in his movements frightened her. Her uncle had become a little old man, his captain's eyes puzzled and lustreless.

For a moment the three stood close together, close enough to feel the warmth of each others' bodies. Then Curtius went to his room and the two women listened anxiously for snoring, a shout or footsteps, but there was silence. Later in the day Marie opened the door and saw her uncle lying with eyes as lifeless as a figure not yet properly lit, his hands clutching the hangings of the four-poster, tugging on them. Only the pillow held up his head and as though simply lying there were an effort, he pushed out his lips and groaned weakly, slowly and erratically steering the bed into an ice landscape which might crack at any moment. As Marie went over to the bed he let go of the hangings and touched her dress with a shy, reverent gesture, and she promised herself that the next day she would re-open Curtius' Waxwork Cabinet and undertake all the practical work herself.

Little by little the days became connected and commonplace — a string of dull little beads, all identical, and held together on a solid thread. Marie Grosholtz sat at the box office, neither making new portraits nor even rearranging the figures nor changing the lights. As far as possible she avoided visits and the news, shunning political pamphlets as if they contained an insidious poison.

With light soups and little glasses of chambré wine Curtius' strength gradually returned, until one day he again ordered the carriage for Ivry-sur-Seine.

Like three convalescents they tucked themselves under the driving rug and sipped the air expectantly, but their paradise had been transformed into a musty-smelling house, one or two preserve jars and two semi-wild hens which Marie captured only with difficulty. And even after several hours' boiling, the flesh was so tough that it could not be stripped off the bones.

'We shall not come here again,' muttered the disappointed Curtius.

'Our country place,' said Marie. 'We shall restore it.'

But her smile faded as at that very moment a fragment of molar tooth chipped off: a bad omen! She was no longer young.

They drove home the same evening, the grumble of the wheels a stab of pain in her jaw. She poked her tongue into the spot and tasted blood.

To dream of losing a tooth portended a death in the family, she remembered, but if it was real it didn't count. She leaned back. Fortunate that it was a molar — she could still smile! And that was all that really mattered where her teeth were concerned.

Nevertheless she smuggled a bottle of apple brandy in among the perfume flasks to deaden the pain. This must not become a habit, she thought, as the alcohol forced her into a heavy, rather rough sleep — but constantly waking before daylight was intolerable. Tonight she would sleep.

It was only five however when she thought she heard drums, coming closer and closer, like a thudding against her eyelids and temples. She kept her eyes shut and pulled her knees up, as if by making herself small she might vanish altogether in the depths of sleep. But the drums lifted her out again.

She remembered having drunk the strong wine in order to sleep, the glass was still on her dressing-table. But no one knew, no one was coming in, it must be this irritating thudding sound that was making her feel queasy.

She dreamed that two men, one young and one old, whose names she did not know, were standing on either side of the bed. They looked down at her as if at a doll, but when she tried to open her eyes there was only a clicking noise inside her head, her open lips held their fill of darkness; everything was at once obtrusive and very distant. She tried to rise, but her legs and arms, her whole body were heavy. At last she opened her eyes — and there really was a knocking, a thin, irritating little knocking with a ring or a stick, and a voice she seemed to know: 'Wake up, we are — we must—'

She rose slowly and went to the door and when she opened it David's head appeared, half concealed by the velvet collar.

'Come on, I've reserved window seats for us.'

'What do you mean?'

'I have hired a room looking onto the route. Aren't you coming?'

'I do not read the papers.'

'Have you no ambition? A queen on her way to the scaffold!' His eyes fell on the bottle. 'I did not think you had begun to drink. Are your hands steady?'

'Of course, but I don't want to go.' Her mouth felt as dry as ashes.

'Get your clothes on, the streets are full of people, we must hurry.'

'I'm not going with you.' She took hold of her hair, which just reached her earlobe.

'Have you turned soft? And who do you think got you out of prison?'

'My uncle.'

'You think so? He cannot even hold the whip over your back any more. You are not doing any work.'

Marie's hands had automatically fixed her shoe buckles, loops and ribbons. She combed back her hair and pulled the hood of her cape forward over her cheeks, trying to disappear inside it. Then she picked up her drawing things and followed him down to the sedan chair.

They moved as quickly and lightly as two children, or as two small jackals with silky pelts, and from his better side she found his profile quite soothing and dear. Nevertheless her teeth chattered in the clammy morning air and she pushed the rug aside to show how little she appreciated the invitation.

An old woman let them into her room and generously pointed to two hard chairs set by the window. She behaved as if she were selling tickets for a gala performance, but as soon as a couple of gold coins had been pressed into her brown-stained fingers, she smiled a contented, toothless smile like a satisfied baby. For a moment it seemed that she might speak, perhaps making them privy to her family circumstances or her thoughts about the performance, but David brushed her aside and she stood, mouse still, a step or two behind their chairs. Marie felt ice-cold and hollow, but she sat upright, her knees pressed together, her pencil already on the paper. Her face might have been made of white stone and if she closed her eyes she would see into that stone's cold white heart; and all light and gentle movements had been nothing but a dream.

They listened to the drums and the scattered cries, like birds of prey circling their game. It was eleven o'clock and still they had not spoken to each other.

'Do you know the charge on which she was condemned?' whispered David suddenly.

'Treason, I suppose,' said Marie in a small, indifferent voice.

'Incest with her son.'

'That's a lie!'

'Of course, but the truth is that the woman has been condemned.'

'Do you think you are talking about some floozie? She is a queen!'

'Are you insane? Someone might hear you — are you determined to ruin everything?'

The sounds were quite close now: creaking tumbril wheels, a single shouted insult — and fear, fear in soft grey feathers with silken feet clasped round her temples. If only she could shake it off, lean forward towards the window; but the fear pulled her back. She felt herself sinking with death on her back and it had a toothless smile and soft, dusty wings.

When she opened her eyes she was looking into the old, furrowed face, the mouth gaping slightly, and for a moment she thought the woman had dribbled or spat on her, but it was cheap lavender water that had been splashed on her temples and the old woman was still supporting her when she leaned forward to see David's drawing. Another stroke or two and then he smiled and straightened, satisfied.

On the sketchblock Marie saw a tumbril bearing a sharp, slight little woman in a thin morning-dress. Her hands were tied behind her back, her face turned to the light as if to lift herself above the street, the filth and all the inquisitive and hateful eyes. And perhaps only for a second she may have looked up at that little window, cleared of pot-plants, polished clean and with the curtains drawn right back, scanning her like a big, icy eye. And she closed her lips defiantly, as if over a tough piece of meat she had to swallow.

'You're lying,' whispered Marie.

'Ask the executioner, or go to the Madeleine Cemetery. But come now, I told the chair to wait.'

'I shall walk.'

'I would not advise you to walk, looking as you do.'

They rocked their way across the town, through air that seemed filled with thunder, and for a moment all was completely silent.

It was over now, thought Marie, and to forget David's sketch she herself began to draw trailing honeysuckle and holy candles, and the Queen dancing, turning graciously under the lights. Rooms like silk-lined jewel caskets close round the slender form, her hair set up with pearls, threatening to catch in the candelabra. She is shepherdess and bride, a white butterfly that might vanish at any moment. She must hold fast to her image in order not to disappear; the mirrors throw it back to her — the mirrors and the light.

She is a powerful woman, or a child spoiled by her environment, doomed to pleasure from cradle to grave. If she stoops for an egg or a pin, if she caresses a lamb or a child, even when she removes a louse from her round, white neck, the gesture must radiate happiness. And she dances with the chosen and play-acts for the chosen, she is a thousand shifting images until, stripped of everything, she looks within herself, with fine, crystal-clear eyes.

'Her eyes were not like that,' muttered the painter, seeing Marie's drawing. 'She looked more as if she were half-blind. You're lying—'

'A lie is only part of the truth.'

'You're just being sentimental — do you intend to exhibit her like that?'

'Naturally I shall exhibit neither her death-mask nor the King's. Their two children are still alive.'

'All those thieves and murderers you and your uncle exhibit may have children too.'

'That is quite a different matter.'

Marie dismounted from the sedan chair. hugging her drawings to her, and David followed, uninvited.

'This is a gift for you,' he said, laying a large package on the table. 'A costume I created myself.'

Marie opened the package and was astonished to find a smart, feathered hat and a dark blue, extravagantly folded cape, weighty as Elizabeth's home-made coats, but of a cut both elegant and uniform-like. 'Is this to be a new fashion for women?'

'For everyone: serving wenches, doctors, coachmen, peasants, hairdressers!'

'It is at all events suitable neither for peasants nor for hairdressers!'

'Of course it's suitable. Put it on when you go out.'

'I do not care for uniforms.'

'This is a democratic costume.'

'Clothes are never democratic. Some look better in them than others — and besides, dark blue is simply not my colour.'

'Do as you like, but stop running about in your old crinolines
— they are completely *passé*. Incidentally, we shall not see each
other for a time. I am rather busy.'

Without really wanting to, Marie put on the cape and hat and
went over to her uncle's Waxwork Cabinet. She turned up the
collar and noticed that the uniform-like cape made her stride
longer and firmer.

'What's this?' said Curtius. 'Have you enrolled yourself in
some corps or other?'

'It is the fashion,' said Marie, and the pretty white feather
stood straight up in the air.

'I do not care for it,' said the old man resentfully. 'Women
should be soft.'

And for the first time in her life Marie began to smile and not
long afterwards to laugh, openly and quite loudly, at her uncle.

Dear Jacques-Louis David,

Yesterday I wore the blue cape. I waited at the cemetery
for a long time to make Robespierre's death-mask. My
uncle had not the strength to accompany me. Altogether, I
have been greatly troubled for his health since that diplo-
matic journey, on which I believe he was poisoned — and I
also believe that he has the same idea himself. At all events
he has sent for the notary to write his testament, and moreover, it is the first time that he has allowed me to drive to
the cemetery alone.

The cart arrived at last — ah, Robespierre's handsome
head, which I had so much wished to model, before I knew
what it contained! If only he had not ruined it! Apparently
he attempted to commit suicide when he was arrested. Perhaps his hand shook, or he may have been prevented by
force from carrying out his intention, for the bullet had
bored itself into his jaw without killing him. And I am now
in possession of this heart-rendingly ugly mask, which I do
not know whether to place among heroes or criminals.

My uncle has not been himself since he saw it. He should
have avoided the sight, just as I avoided being faced with
poor Elizabeth's rigid features. From what I hear, she

seems to have made a calm and dignified death, although
the wind tore off her kerchief, and I know it must have
shamed her to meet her God with uncovered head.

As for myself, I seem to be meeting everything at a little
distance, as if I saw both myself and others through finely-
polished glass. That is the only way I can live.

I hope for other times.

Your friend,
Marie Grosholtz

In the streets all the crinolines collapsed like punctured silk bal-
loons. The powdered hair, the bulging breasts, the white hands
with their rosy nails vanished.

The *demi-mondaines* occupied the town, in dresses so thin that
they could be pulled through a ring, walking the streets almost
naked, with long, narrow boys' hands and light sandals, and
anyone who used to squeeze her foot into a tight shoe or had
bunions was laughed to scorn.

But Marie did not see the street, for she spent the whole day
sitting at the cash desk and in the evening she would steal off to
her uncle's room, listen to his wheezing breath, arrange his
clothes so that they were easy to put on and pull up the trodden
backs of his shoes.

But one day a light carriage stopped at the front entrance, and
Josephine Beauharnais — lovely, lively Josephine with glossy
lashes and hair in riotous curls above her hyacinth blue dress,
almost ran into the Waxwork Cabinet, and her voice was warm
and tender and lilting and just a trifle hoarse after celebrating her
freedom.

The two young women whirled about among the silent, important personages, never noticing that they were embracing under
the death-mask of Robespierre himself.

'I am free again!' cried Josephine.

'I shall work again!' Marie assured her.

And Josephine was a wonderful model, a series of living,
flickering images. Josephine with her short hair combed smooth
and cut provocatively high on the back of her neck. Josephine in

133

white, her neckline so deep that it made Marie blush, and Josephine with hair like a wildcat, in a fuzz of tiny little curls. She wore golden sandals and golden rings on all her toes and fortunately her figure had not been ruined, either by food or by corsets. She was still so shapely that she did not need to pull on that tiresome, skin-coloured underwear which gave only an illusion of nakedness. No, Josephine could be almost naked, and now that breasts had to be small and elegant, Josephine's breasts were smaller too. What had become of all those women's breasts and all that hair?

'Is this to be the new Sleeping Beauty?' asked Curtius, alarmed.

'Beauty awakened,' said Marie lightly, working on, but still remembering to straighten the backs of his shoes.

But one evening the long, wheezing breath stopped. Marie listened intently and touched her uncle's forehead. The cold shocked her fingertips: Curtius was dead, closed and cold. Perhaps there had been a moment when he spanned his breaking point, when all feeling and expression left his body at once — an unheard scream or prayer.

She seemed to be sinking deep, deep into a hole which she had always known was just under her feet, and the moon landscape of his temples was distant and unfathomable.

When Curtius' will was read, his pupil Marie Grosholtz found herself heir to a country house at Ivry-sur-Seine, bought rashly and dear, as well as to two houses in Paris, one modest and rented out, the other, on the Boulevard du Temple, luxuriously, almost splendidly equipped with furniture, paintings and mirrors. And this house was now inhabited by two unmarried women, together with a number of waxworks representing crowned heads, revolutionaries, heroes, murderers and robbers!

When Marie looked into the long hall of the Waxwork Cabinet, where the golden rows of mirrors cast a dazzling light over those prominent personalities, she felt giddily rich, but when she examined her accounts, her dear uncle's debts, the monthly sum for wages and all the bills which began to pour in, she was forced to recognize that she owed money.

For a moment she thought of Josephine's advice to marry

someone who understood business affairs, but what she could not manage alone she certainly could not manage with others. She straightened, clutching the funeral bouquet so hard that the bitter sap of the white chrysanthemums ran over her fingers.

'If only uncle had kept away from politics he would have been alive today,' she said, gently stroking her mother's hair.

'Curtius—' The reserved little woman was weeping aloud and bitterly — 'Curtius was your father, Marie!'

'But the soldier — the Swiss guard — the hero?' Marie dropped the big white bouquet onto the floor.

'The soldier was a brief affair, and a dream I built round myself. I was a maid with a prosperous young couple, and Curtius was a haggard student who ate the scraps in the kitchen.'

'Mother—' Marie stooped to gather up her flowers.

'I never went any further than the kitchen, but I let him know that you were the very image of him, and it was the image that interested him!'

CHAPTER SEVEN
A Quiet Life

1795

Spring, and the tender rosy foam of apple trees, dogs in mating mood, tugging at their leashes, the *modistes* showing the new, thin fabrics in ivory, rose and white — innocent bridal white. Parasols were flung out, the bold showed off the ragged fashion: costly materials ruthlessly ripped, riches revealed only to the initiated.

Marie owned two houses, a country place and a debt that kept her awake at night. She bought dresses.

'Just you,' said the *modiste*, when thin apricot chiffon glowed like the sun against Marie's bare skin. 'Exactly your colour — a colour for dark-haired women.'

And the light, white muslin: 'Exactly your style — cut for slender women, fortunately not inconvenienced by breasts!'

As if she could assume innocence and youth, Marie turned and twisted before the mirror.

'But am I not too old?' she whispered, thinking of her thirty-four years.

'Old!' The milliner's toe rings jingled with indignation and the silk quivered round her scrawny hips and pitifully pendulous breasts.

'I sell these dresses to women of sixty — it all depends on the mind! Take off your shoes, throw away your corset, pull the pins out of your hair — be fresh and romantic!'

'What about black?'

The woman shook her head, her near-sighted seamstress's eyes creasing with merriment.

'I sell black only to widows.'

Transformed and bewildered, Marie stepped into the street carrying light packages. The sparrows' twitter was irritatingly loud, lovers leaned against each other, reading the circus posters or day-dreaming before Philipstal's magic pictures. Withered bunches of violets floated in the gutter, their sweet, cloying scent blending with the smell of rotten fish heads. And the air was as soft as fur.

But Marie was in a hurry, determined to brush off the spring air and escape from the clinging couples. Nevertheless, she stopped suddenly, gasped for breath and almost dropped her packages.

A very old couple were crossing the street, holding hands, the man's stick groping over the cobbles as if expecting to find soft soil, the woman so short and round that her eyes almost vanished in plump folds. With great gentleness she supported her husband, who walked as mincingly as a clipped sparrow.

Marie felt an urge to run over and throw her arms round the gardener she had so recently seen walking across the Trianon lawns, watering the vegetables and handing over the most perfect of them to M. Léonard. But he would scarcely recognize her, he had aged and appeared almost blind: a reminder would only cause pain.

Hastily blinking back tears, she hurried on to Curtius' Waxwork Cabinet.

'If you do not learn to clean your shoes properly I shall be obliged to dismiss you,' she hissed at the young doorman.

With a deep sigh she sat down at the cash desk in her new, apricot-coloured dress, but when a couple with four children came in to buy tickets she relaxed into a smile and gave them a discount for the two youngest.

Shortly before closing time another visitor arrived, a young man who counted his coins out slowly — perhaps he was from the country and was afraid of being cheated! His hair was thick and blond, there was a tooth missing in his lower jaw, but his skin was so smooth and golden that it reminded her of a young deer.

Reverently he inspected the famous characters from a distance, as if it would be disrespectful to go too close, and she smiled involuntarily to see him so completely confused, bowing to personages whose faces she had discourteously massaged with oil and covered with a cold and not particularly agreeable mixture of plaster and water. And he bowed to her, too, when he was about to leave without even having seen everything.

Marie locked her cash box carefully and rose, reaching precisely to his armpit, and feeling light and feminine in her new spring dress. And since as usual she would be touring the whole gallery after closing time she asked the young man if she could show him all the things he had not yet seen.

She seemed to him to be asking for protection — a little woman, a delicate, apricot-coloured tropical bird, perhaps afraid to go round alone! He bent over her reassuringly, his breath a little sharp, and she smiled confidently up at him, for she always remembered to use a pleasant-smelling mouth rinse, or to suck peppermints.

How could he help seeing her as a golden bird, a spoiled princess? After all, the entrance to her house was a portal and inside it the light fell on people he had never met and whose names he could scarcely remember, yet she was critical, adjusting their hands, hair and clothing. And never, never had he seen anything so bewitchingly lovely as the Sleeping Beauty with her long auburn curls, the sweeping lashes, the foot arched towards the floor and the fine little hand with thin, slightly curved fingers — such an easy, graceful sleep.

Marie bit her lip and led him on to Marat, but that was a mistake, for the young man shrank back three paces when she told him how she had taken a cast both of him, bleeding into the bathtub, and of the tall, fair girl. She decided to miss out the murderers and the great thieves that evening. In any case, the hard blue light would drain the colour from her apricot silk.

Perhaps it was really the shock that made him stammer a little when he showed her the book in which he had written the address of a distant aunt who might be able to house him for a night or two.

No, she did not know that area, and besides, she was not particularly good at finding her way, but perhaps Philipstal would know. She blushed at this sudden inspiration, for what she really wanted was to show the young man the magic lantern pictures, knowing that the programme had recently been extended to include distant, exotic places, so lifelike that people who had been there swore they felt as if they were walking along the streets. And finally there were fireworks, in which both sun and rockets were produced by light and sound effects. If anything were to make him forget the painful Marat episode, it must be to stand in the midst of that firework display!

She must remember not to recount any more such things, or she would ruin everything. Everything, she thought, what everything? Then, throwing her shawl over her shoulders, she assured him that it was no trouble and they would not even have to buy tickets.

They saw temples and elephants and Roman fountains. In Venice the gondola carried them up the Grand Canal and the secret doors to all the palaces stood open.

Afterwards the dazzling lights and dull explosions of the fireworks made them quite dizzy, and the young man held Marie's arm protectively when they came out and was completely at a loss when the master of the magic lantern, Philipstal himself, bowed his tall, crumpled form over the girl, looking as if he were about to bite her glove. Fortunately he pulled himself together, simply depositing a damp kiss on the back of her hand. She enquired smilingly after Madame Philipstal's health, but evidently quite forgot to enquire for the aunt's address.

With sudden extravagance and gallantry the young man invited the rich young woman to cakes and wine and for the first time in her life Marie allowed herself to be escorted down her own street. The professional waiter cut through the snowy icing on the cake and poured wine into two tall glasses and when the door opened there was a faint, sweet smell of horses. The young man told her that he was an engineer from Macon, looking for work. He wanted to tell her that she resembled a porcelain figure, but he was wondering whether his hands could lie side by side on her back.

She sat with downcast eyes, noticing how small and frippery

the glass and the cake fork appeared in his hands and wondering
how often she really needed a man in her daily life. The workmen
simply bled her of money, because she was unable to assess the
price either of materials or of labour. Her eyes grew thoughtful
and troubled — how difficult it was for a woman on her own to
make herself respected! And with sudden, motherly concern she
asked if he had any lodging for the night other than the aunt
whom it would certainly be difficult to find in this confusing town,
and if he liked — she, Marie Grosholtz, had so much space, after
all. Beds, tables, chairs — whole rooms standing empty. It would
not be in the least inconvenient and in any case it was several
months since she and her mother had received guests.

There was an almost maternal softness in her eyes and young
François Tussaud from Macon simply could not resist her refined
little gestures and her remarkable blend of directness and
reserve.

Perhaps women in the big city were of quite a different breed
from those he had known, for only a quarter of an hour later he
found himself seated, and on a chair with four frail, curved legs at
that, taking soup. Fortunately his shirt was spotlessly clean and
his hair so thick and blond that it did not matter that his mother
had trimmed it slightly aslant at the back.

No doubt Mademoiselle's mother alarmed him, with her
silence and her big, hungry eyes. But he forgot all about her in
the liveliness of the young lady's face and the charming turn of
her hips as she took the linen from the cupboard, hesitating for a
moment between pink and cream. Unaware of her mother's disapproving look, he saw only Mademoiselle, carrying the starchy,
creamy linen to the guest-room with as much care and ceremony
as if it were an infant.

François Tussaud gazed at his feet for a long time before lifting
first the left and then the right into the wash-bowl. He sat on the
edge of the bed, his legs stretched out to dry, and lay down at last
with his hands on top of the quilt like a good child. He remembered stories about jolly farmers' lads who had suddenly woken
up in the beds of well-born ladies and scratched his thick, fair hair
thoughtfully. He remembered the Sleeping Beauty, with her
smooth eyelids and that slender foot stretched towards the floor

and for a moment he also saw a little face drained of colour and a body covered with sores—an ugliness as open and defenceless as a flower — and he shuddered at the thought of witches. Then he pulled the coverlet right up to his chin and imagined the fireworks and the young lady who moved, light as a bird, down the long, long hall with its paintings and mirrors in brilliant gold frames.

Marie Grosholtz looked at herself in the glass for a long time, seeing a narrow little face with large eyes and some very fine wrinkles. She pressed her nose right against the glass to see if there were any grey hairs, but no, her glossy curls were as dark as ever. There were only those very fine lines round her eyes and a little furrow above her nose . . . She smiled, ran her fingers through her hair and pulled the thin apricot dress right down over her shoulders. The glass was cold and smooth against her breasts. Parting her lips slightly she leaned back, so far that the image disappeared. Faintness overcame her.

At Ivry-sur-Seine the air was fine and quivering with sun and insects, the silhouette of a red kite sharply defined against the sky. The fieldmice hid in their tiny nests, the hares raced away and the red lily beetles ran casually up the long, smooth stems.

At Ivry-sur-Seine Marie wore a corset of very thin white lace, lifting her breasts which for the moment pointed upwards. One foot caressed the carpet idly while she leaned back, having carefully spread her dark hair over the pillow so that it lay round her face in abundant curls. She sighed and withdrew her foot to join the rest of her in bed and it seemed to her that she was floating in soft, luke-warm water while shoals of little coral fish floated past and into her. She leaned against François Tussaud's shoulder which was big, firm and comfortable, and followed her sigh with a smile so that he should not think her worried or dispirited. It had been a very light sigh, indicating that she was too fatigued to say: 'I love you', but that she would have no objection to his saying something of the kind.

When she closed her eyes his intensely blue gaze swam into her, his sensual lips, that moist, greedy exploration of his tongue in her mouth which she had remembered to rinse with peppermint. Their teeth were cliffs, his missing front tooth a particularly dramatic crag, and they sank down into underwater dreams. She had never seen the sea, but this was how she imagined it, these waves, these heavy, gentle movements.

François Tussaud looked at her, thinking it was remarkable that it had been so easy. Of course, he had heard that city women were fast, and she was certainly not like Blanche at home in Macon — stubborn Blanche, whom he had pursued for a whole winter without receiving more than a kiss or two, a slapped face and a basket of dirty clothes flung at his head.

Her shoulders fitted his hands exactly, he thought in astonishment, for he had believed that that question would never be answered.

'Is this yours as well?' he asked cautiously, looking up at the ceiling.

She nodded, thinking of Curtius' stiff, cold features and the big bundle of bills and instruments of debt, and the will, which must certainly be the most direct expression of love he had ever given. And she remembered his loneliness in the bed alcove.

'You are mine,' the young man tried out the words, still gazing at the ceiling, gripped by a sudden shyness and anxiety that this fairy tale might disappear.

'For ever,' she replied, quite matter-of-factly.

'We must be married.'

'Yes.'

'When?'

'As soon as possible.'

As if in confirmation, she offered him a box of candied fruit and a bottle of wine which she had providently and practically placed within reach.

Utterly captivated by the motherly and pragmatic in her nature, François Tussaud thought that if his existence were to turn out like this he would never have to get up again.

Blanche should see me now, he thought, a little spitefully, remembering her milky complexion and the heavy, braided hair which forced her to strut a little. Blanche would never have believed this: it would make her sorry — or perhaps not, after all . . .

'We shall be together always, the two of us,' he whispered, but it was himself he reassured.

'Till death us do part,' said Marie, cracking a chestnut between her teeth. 'The three of us — there is my mother, too.'

'Of course,' he said, both apologetic and generous. 'How could I forget her?'

And he thought how unbelievably marvellous it was that she was intelligent too, and wondered how much brain there could be under the dark curls, in that little head, every centimetre of which was brilliantly exploited.

'But the money—' she asked anxiously.

'Money—' he murmured. This must simply be a manifestation of female anxiety or nervousness! 'You really must not concern yourself with that.'

He did not hear her quick breath of relief and it did not even occur to him that a girl with three properties and mirrors in gold frames could have debts. He thought of the great hall, where he would now consort with the richest, the fairest and the most important people in the land — in wax, to be sure, but all the same!

'Do you think I shall be able to handle it?'

'You will learn.'

'And there is enough for a man to do?'

'More than you know: repairs, lights, signboards, supervision — masses of practical things.'

'Or I could sit at the cash desk.'

'At the cash desk, my love? That is my place!'

Marie and Tussaud. Tussaud and Marie. Tussaud. She had given him her little pearl-embroidered purse. They visited shops and the contents of the purse were converted into a gold watch, a silk shirt, coat and breeches and a pair of shiny, narrow shoes.

Marie was rejuvenated, with a blue scarf round her waist and a childish bonnet from whose shadow she could not see where she was going. She had to turn from side to side, feeling light-headed and coquettish.

Marie and François bought two gold rings to go to their own wedding. They exchanged pecked kisses and in the mirror they saw themselves like a couple made in marzipan on top of a cake with shiny white icing. When they went out into the street they seemed to feel the stiffly whipped cream about their feet.

'Dearest,' murmured Tussaud, at the vision of himself as master, 'you know, I am only twenty-six.'

'Beloved,' whispered Marie, 'do you know that I am thirty-four?'

For a moment he gave the young woman with the fine wrinkles round her eyes a shocked look. Then he pulled himself together. 'Just the right age!'

No, François Tussaud was no longer looking for work or women. He had got his feet under his own table, by marrying into three properties, and one of them in the country at that. He proudly displayed his vegetables, his chickens and his smart hunting-dogs. Of course the house needed some improvements here and there — he pictured terraces, summerhouses and possible extensions. And he might cultivate something or other — his grandfather cultivated vines. Cultivation! That was in the blood, and it was much more sound and natural than all the knowledge he had worked to acquire. At Ivry-sur-Seine he felt alive, whereas Paris sapped his soul.

Moreover, he was waited on. His mother-in-law, who would not come to the wedding, made the food — fine, elegant dishes, as if they simply could not be good enough. True, she frowned when she saw him slicing garlic over his cabbage, but she said nothing.

Unfortunately there were times when he was obliged to go to Paris because his wife demanded it. He must play a part in the business, she said, sounding just a trifle impatient. One day she suggested that he should take over the management of the whole lower floor.

'Am I supposed to go round in the cellar with all those thieves and murderers?'

'You could sit at a mahogany desk.'

'In that blue light?'

'Of course.'

'Well, but it makes everyone look like a criminal!'

'Naturally the person in charge of the department must also resemble a criminal!'

'Never,' he protested, 'never in my life!'

The sharp little furrow between her brows deepened.

That same evening he was lying in her girlish bed, protecting her from the feeling that the door might open and someone might come in and carry her off.

But suddenly she sat up.

'Money! I cannot work when I have debts: it traps my thoughts and I can think of nothing else.'

'Sell the chairs or some of the paintings and those big mirrors.' For a moment he thought she was going to hammer his chest with her clenched fists, but she thought better of it and beat on the coverlet instead.

'I shall sell none of Curtius' things! In any case, one never receives the proper sum when one is obliged to sell.'

She ostentatiously turned her back on him and stared at the wall.

But at Ivry-sur-Seine she was sensible and mild again. They lay in the four-poster bed, his warm, heavy breath making her forget Curtius' debts and the large stack of unpaid bills. She slid her hands over the back of his neck, as if he were a big, harmless dog.

He stretched and looked at the stars with a satisfied expression, and he watched the sun rising with the same expression of satisfaction, of someone who has finally found his place in life.

Only her energy was disturbing, the nervous energy which made her leap out of bed and splash ice-cold, rose-scented water on her face and under her arms — the way she moved her feet, as if she would prefer to run but was obliged to walk for the sake of decency.

But one day that lightness was transformed into languor, the cabbage smell from the kitchen made nausea rise in her throat; the herbs, the rose-bushes, even the bottle of smelling-salts revolted her. She was dizzy and when she moved she seemed to feel the curve of the earth beneath her feet. Under the currant bushes the chickens tripped charmingly along on their tiny little legs and she saw everything as a good omen.

*

Pregnancy pushed Marie Tussaud's feet out sideways, her stomach protruded, she dragged herself about with the ponderousness of an elephant, so she thought, but without its dignity and charm. The hired carriage drove her between the country house and the town house and all the time she felt she was going the wrong way.

Her skin stretched and even the touch of her skirt became an insect-like irritation. Images fluttered past instead of fixing themselves in her mind. She felt locked within the frame of her body, its fluids, nerves and senses affecting the sureness of her hands and eyes.

In Paris she was working on a portrait of Josephine Bonaparte, for Josephine too had married and was suddenly the town's most important and elegant lady, swathed in simple classical garments and with a frontlet to prevent her hair from bothering her when she moved with her quick, free grace, as if her reception room and boudoir were a gymnastics hall.

Josephine too was pregnant, but only just. She could still bend easily, her eyes shone and her skin was delicate and matt, whereas Marie's eyes were red with sleeplessness and her cheeks flushed with effort. But Josephine's fruitfulness was actually only a little padding, because it was now so modern to be pregnant—it looked healthy, beguiling and positive, and besides, it would be immensely practical to have an heir.

Charming Josephine sighed glumly.

Why Napoleon, of all people? thought Marie: a soldier, and interested in politics into the bargain. A folk hero — much too insecure! She really deserved something better.

'You should have married a businessman, as I said.' Josephine gave her friend a look of slight reproach.

Marie pursed her lips, as if she simply had to concentrate to make the narrow frontlet appear both sporting and piquant for Josephine's new personality. But her words lingered, long after they had kissed one another goodbye.

A businessman — or a man with money. Perhaps I shall have to sell something after all. We have no cradle yet and I cannot even take one from the Waxwork Cabinet: we have never exhibited babies! Clothes, equipment — my mother is sewing swaddling clothes and dresses. She says nothing, but she hopes it will be a girl, though I would rather have a boy. His life would be much easier. Perhaps I shall have to sell after all.

Tussaud does not understand me — he thought he was marrying a golden bird. Perhaps he wants to strip me of my feathers.

'Sell,' he says, 'just sell!'

He does not understand that one cannot sell oneself out of debt. It is humiliating, and people will talk if they see silver candlesticks and mirrors carried out of the house. It would only make us poorer. We must work ourselves out of debt, that is the only way. Besides, one receives nothing for furniture and mirrors if one is forced to sell: one has to be arrogant and have no reason whatever to part with them, to be willing to wait for payment until one has found the right purchaser.

Tussaud can build a bridge or a terrace and perhaps he can also conduct water to the vegetable bed, but when he sees what is in my cash box he wants wine, meat and comfortable shoes — he never thinks of investment, and so I am obliged to hide the money from him. But wherever I put it, I seem to have a tender, vulnerable place on my body. Sometimes I put it under my mattress and the money and my weight make me push him away.

Marie looked at her accounts again, the bills from tailors, dressmakers and wig-makers, all to maintain the exhibition. Doctor's bills, wages for cleaners and attendants. Despite the hopelessness of the accounts, she would fall asleep over them, waking up with stiff neck and shoulders to order the carriage back to Ivry-sur-Seine.

But at night sleep was a deep, soft hole, too narrow for her pregnant body to sink into. She stretched out her body, throwing wide her arms, hovering above sleep. She pushed a pillow under her stomach and pulled up her knees, kneeling, entreating the sleep that would not receive her. Her brain was forced to work on: something new! She must think of something new, entertaining, attractive or scandalous. Napoleon — perhaps Napoleon, while he was popular, but she would have to wait until the baby was born. Perhaps Josephine had been lucky after all. And Philipstal: she had recently seen Philipstal in a spanking new costume, proud and elegant. And herself — she almost blushed with shame for her worn shoes and the big, dark blue cape. Everyone else succeeded, only she did not. Old Philipstal with his magic lantern theatre, patent leather shoes, silk waistcoat, vulgarly resplendent. He had been travelling to England. Was that where his money came from? Curtius would have known; while he lived everything was quite different — might he really have been her father? But he had left. You cannot leave a child. You can die, but you cannot leave it, you are bound. Bound.

She looked at the man at her side, his heavy sleep, his breath warm and sweet with wine — that everlasting heavy sleep! He never remembered what he had dreamed, or at least he never told her. His mouth was open in sleep, quite different from Curtius' firm, decisive lips. François Tussaud was superficial — a child, she thought. What she needed was a protector, and what she had was a child, soon to be two children. Only six months ago his youth had drawn her as the moon draws the tides; her feelings were great, round waves reaching out for him. And now, suddenly, that had gone — had it been merely something she had wished, something she imagined?

The morning sun and the yellow silk canopy of the bed gilded his face like an ikon. Marie, her eyes dark-ringed, frowned and got up, making an unnecessary clatter with the wash-bowl.

She prowled round the kitchen, taking from the larder a lemon which she sniffed for a long time before cutting it into quarters and sinking her teeth in the sour, juicy fruit.

She went into the Tussaud family's handsome, newly de-signed garden, where the morning air was flinty and raw and she was struck by the scent of fresh wood from the newly-built terrace and pagoda-like summerhouse. Her hands stroked her thin white negligée. At the entrance two red hounds slept cosily in separate kennels with little spires.

The hole, she thought — a green hole in my lifeline, the fine, cool scent of wild roses and the world divided up in fields, yellow, green, grey-green, swelling or meagre. Work: fields filled with corn, vines, justice — square, although the earth is round.

Was it not here you had wanted to wake up, when death was near you everywhere; when you touched it, sometimes caressed it, and longed for your hands too to be suddenly still, for your body to stretch out and become immovable?

That suffering and unpredictability had gone. You could go into the kitchen and cut the white bread in thick slices and if the bread was dry, you could throw it away. The red kite hovered over bright, pretty fields, the swallow and the mouse cheeped, only your lips were closed. You looked out over fields of corn, vines and olives, the sky stretched above them, a vault, a whole heaven, the air pure; and the cicadas' untuned instruments, innocent, not like the music to which you once danced.

Your red house shoes, Marie. They are not blood in the grass, they are light, velvet shoes, but you are moving too fast, your feet like the flight of two red carnivorous beetles. Iris and lily grow in your garden, their sweetness making you desperate, like the perfume you poured over your breasts; the smell of a thousand *cabinets de toilette* which engulfed you when you left your carriage, or were carried along, enveloped in scent.

A pregnant woman should be like a closed flower, but suddenly you shun even the scent of flowers. And you are as stiff as a thistle.

The dogs suddenly woke up and bayed, and glancing at her watch she remembered that she had ordered the carriage for seven o'clock.

'It would be better for you to drink milk,' said her mother, looking at the lemon peel. 'You do not look well.'

'I am happier than I have ever been,' said Marie obstinately.

'A pity one cannot see it.'

For a moment she thought of waking her husband, but she let him sleep. He was no real help over practical things and she had no use for his ideas: having an orchestra to play dance music in the long hall on Sundays, or making the Sleeping Beauty breathe by means of a rubber hose and a little inflatable cushion.

Typical, thought Marie, nothing but expense and machines, musicians and breasts, but once the birth is over things will be different. Her own breasts were heavy and though she wiped her forehead, small drops of sweat stood on her temples as she walked out to the carriage.

As usual she fell into a light sleep and was deeply embarrassed that the coachman should have seen her with closed eyes and open mouth when he held the door for her. When he reached his arm right into the carriage to help her she got up quickly, swayed for a moment, caught her heel on the step and landed in a long, flying fall on hands and knees at the very feet of the young doorman whose shoes still needed a polish. But she could scarcely reproach him, since he helped her up and made the coachman drive off for a doctor.

'What made her think of going to the city in this condition anyway?' she heard the doctor ask the young man and she decided to dismiss them both as soon as she could get up, but the pain from her grazed legs seemed to enter into her and fill her entire body.

'Not now,' she whispered, 'it can't happen now!'

'You are thirty-five years old,' said the doctor, 'do you not think it is high time you gave birth to your first child?'

For a moment she thought of the cradle which had not been bought and of the sum she would have to pay this man, who seemed filled with restless energy.

He rummaged in drawers, found sheets, loosened her clothing and all the while he actually drank her wine. She felt lonely, and angry with this charlatan who was beginning to cover her with sheets as if to conjure the child out of her body before an invisible audience.

He should have been a smith, she thought, with his hairy hands, and she hated her body which had failed her. Her senses floated lightly, in a long, fainting descent, until the pain overpowered her. Her heart was a trapeze artist, swinging in a blood-red shirt towards a thin, icy heaven, her genitals a spaniel pup with port-wine eyes and torn belly. She clamped her teeth on the pain, which splintered like glass, and it was not until she saw the baby that the tears ran down her cheeks.

A little phantom being, she was, with dark, wet hair and long lashes. The baby opened eyes of a dizzying blue depth, as if from another world, and Marie scarcely dared to touch the veins in her temples and the soft, purplish feet.

When her mother and husband arrived at last they seemed almost like overbearing strangers, their hands too big and clumsy to touch this dream-child. But very quietly and gently, almost indifferent to her business affairs, she had herself driven back to the country three days later so that her angel could wake to pure, clear air and the sight of flowers and leaves.

Time after time the baby fell asleep at her breast and she could not bear to awaken this creature who seemed incapable of protesting or crying. She could not imagine a more beautiful being and it was as if the baby's angelic patience entered into her. It was impossible to picture this child growing teeth or using ordinary speech, and at times both women knelt by the cradle, fairy godmothers, fending off the whole world.

Sometimes she would remember the fat, well-nourished infants with dimples and round cheeks whom she had helped Elizabeth to model, but she soon pushed them away. Her child was far more perfect and exquisite. When the little one was asleep on the terrace she would doze by her side, but she never fell asleep completely; she kept all her attention on this delicate little daughter, so that she would not disappear or turn into a doll. A fairy tale princess who could not be awakened even with a kiss! And yet the child was withering away between her hands like a flower from a far, exotic country.

'But you can sustain another pregnancy,' said the doctor.

She laced in the waist of her dress and her breasts, the child's death an ice-cold landscape within her, too painful to be touched by words. When she held her hands before her face it seemed to her that the child was still present in her body smell.

But one day she used perfume again, one day she sat at the admission desk again, very upright in a high-collared grey dress. The sun shone down through the yellow silk canopy, gilding François Tussaud's face, and she wrote to Josephine's husband requesting permission to make a full-size likeness of him, to be exhibited in the middle of the great hall in a clear, flattering light. One day her sense of smell was as sharp as a deer's again and the earth so round under her feet that she almost stumbled walking across the grass. Once again a foetus turned her body into a palace of frail flesh. Her eyes followed the red kite. She sympathized with the mouse. She moved like a gentle, clumsy angel.

Mother, father, child. The poplars bowed in the wind and again and again Marie and François Tussaud bowed over the cradle, humbled by the sight of their child Joseph, so perfect and so healthy.

Baby Joseph held on. He held on with his feet, his hands and his mouth as if he were constantly in mid-fall and had to stop himself. His screams were demanding and assured, his pulse alive and strong. Marie stroked his hair, the fontanel so vulnerable — the night like a fragile egg, a floating tiredness that stayed with her all day long.

'Let me grow old,' she begged, 'let me see him grow up, protect him and never leave him until he is adult, safe, secure.'

She pictured herself teaching him the names of flowers, leaves, butterflies and trees. Table, chair and spoon were far too earthy, she thought, although he was just as happy to follow the progress of the silver spoon to his mouth as the swinging branches of the dove tree.

This was no dream-child, but a child of this world, already grabbing at flies in the cradle with aggressive fists and deep growls and Marie shivered to think what would happen if he put them in his mouth.

One day his features gathered themselves into an irresistible smile. The dog's wagging tail sent him into hearty, almost hysterical chuckles. He cried for three nights to produce one snow-white tooth and Marie forgot her whole Waxwork Cabinet for that new creation.

'You're spoiling him,' said her mother. 'Crying strengthens the lungs.'

But Marie turned her back defiantly on the heartless grandmother. Never should Joseph lie in bed feeling himself abandoned, fearing that someone had gone away and he himself was about to vanish — never! She would protect him against anything, everything, and especially against loneliness.

He could scarcely crawl when she found him in the flowerbeds, busy filling his mouth with earth, manure and pebbles, and the pretty white teeth bit her fingers hard when she tried to scrape out the mess.

Joseph was the centre of his mother's, father's and grandmother's worlds and Marie felt both tenderness and pride when she saw her two men disappearing among the fruit bushes to build a secret den.

One day she drove back to Paris with François and Joseph, the child enjoying the rolling of the carriage, his nose pressed to the glass, absorbing every possible impression.

'He will make roads and build bridges,' dreamed François Tussaud.

'He will be something special,' said Marie.

Quite unimpressed, the two-year-old Joseph wandered down the long hall with its gilt-framed mirrors, passing by princesses, revolutionaries, heroes and villains. Only the shepherdess's little white lamb held him fascinated, as he patted its woolly coat, while Marie at last taught her husband how to place lights.

Their beloved child played with wax and coloured chalks, with earth and stone and with the red hounds. When they went to the city he was so alert and well-dressed that people could not help turning to look at him, quite in love with his liveliness, his big dark eyes and the fine, bird-like profile emerging gradually from the baby fat.

'He's bringing us luck,' smiled Marie when she opened the cash box. The long-awaited letter from Josephine arrived at last, announcing that her husband would set aside half an hour at six o'clock the following Friday morning.

'Do the rich rise so early?' mutttered François Tussaud, watching his wife packing the bag, and the carriage woke both dogs and mice when Marie walked across the grass, wrapped close in the old dark blue cape against the chill of dawn.

But in front of the Tuileries she smoothed her best summer dress and her hair, looked in the mirror and pinched her cheeks in order to appear healthy and unabashed. She walked, straight-backed, across the garden, which was charming and bright, with its fountain-fed roses and bathing sparrows. When the guard led her up the steps she held her letter before her rather stiffly, like a weapon, and it was not until she was in the middle of the hall that she realized she must have been walking on tiptoe all the way, either to muffle the sound of her footsteps or to take up more space in this gigantic room, whose coldness brought her arms out in goose-pimples.

At last Josephine entered the hall, accompanied by another woman. Her negligée, light as down, and her casually arranged short hairstyle were a delightful challenge to the stiff splendour of the hall, her curves seemed to mock all the pillars and despite the cold she appeared as warm and at ease as if her body had a climate of its own. Nevertheless, Marie was disappointed, for Josephine looked at her a little guardedly, as at someone who had recklessly squandered her opportunities.

But Marie had little time to wonder, for just then her model came in, his faced framed by the uniform collar, his boot heels scraping the floor, his eyes manic with the brilliance of insomnia.

Josephine's husband did not actually have the world's most interesting face, thought Marie, when the First Consul was kind enough to sit down and ask her to be quick. While her hands carried out the familiar movements she was surprised to hear the two lightly-clad women talking in high, excited voices about regiments, battalions, boots, straps and horses as if their well-rehearsed dialogue could keep him in his chair.

He seemed restless however, and fatigue or nervousness brought a little muscle by his eye into twitching life.

'Don't be nervous, the process is uncomfortable but harmless.'

'Me, nervous!' He sprang to his feet. 'I would not be nervous if you were to surround my head with loaded pistols!'

For a moment she was afraid he was going to rush from the room, but as luck would have it he sat down again quite calmly. The two pretty women were silent, the only sound was of the First Consul's breathing, two hot little airstreams hissing through the straws, and when Marie took the mask from his face she saw that Josephine was obviously troubled and anxious. When she forgot to smile there were thin lines round her mouth, and her eyes were both strained and tired. But once again the smooth fingers closed about her wrist and she felt Josephine's breath on her cheek, her voice lowered to a mysterious whisper.

'Be careful with his head, Marie — he only did it for my sake!'

And she decided to retouch the portrait a little and make Josephine's husband not only impressive but also uncommonly handsome.

Brilliant, as if caught in a sudden movement, and dauntless, though his head was surrounded by loaded pistols; that was the young Napoleon, when he took the place of the shepherdess in the Waxwork Cabinet. The sun shone on all his uniform buttons, making his face lively and energetic. Marie Tussaud added Napoleon Bonaparte to the signboard at the entrance — a seductive name.

'We shall soon be out of debt!' Her voice was as bright as the chink of money.

'Let's go to Ivry-sur-Seine.'

François sounded tired and impatient.

'Not yet.'

'Joseph needs the country air.'

'Joseph does well in the city. Tomorrow, perhaps. I have a meeting today.'

'With whom?'

'Philipstal.'

'That old fool!'

'He is industrious and helpful.'

'Joseph wants to go back to the dogs and his grandmother.'

'Philipstal wants me to go to London with him. London is teeming with emigrants.'

'And so?'

'They will value Curtius' and my work — perhaps I shall be rich!'

'We have all we need.'

'Please do not keep interrupting me just now.'

'Joseph, Joseph! Come, we're going home. Your mother is working.'

'You do not understand.'

'Come, Joseph. We understand that you do not wish to be disturbed.'

Marie got up to follow them, but before she had slammed the

cash box shut and locked it carefully, the carriage was rolling away. She pressed her forehead to the glass and saw it swinging round the corner. Then she bathed her face in cold, scented water, put on her hat and pushed her hands deep inside the muff so that no one should see them shaking. In the mirror she appeared cool and presentable and when she walked up the stairs in Philipstal's house she was quite calm and hopeful.

The widower, who had apparently got hold of a young house-keeper, made her feel secure and light-hearted again. His hands were laden with rings, but his figure was still slim, his eyes as velvet soft and brown as when she was a child. It struck her that he must be the same age as Curtius when he died, but wealth had made him look much younger.

Philipstal's voice was as gentle and engaging as a seducer's: England, Scotland, Ireland! — he placed them gaily-wrapped at her feet and she allowed herself to be carried away over the rocking waves. Her wax figures would be exhibited in theatres and charming salons, and she had a clear picture of the living coming face to face with their dead acquaintances.

'But,' she asked meekly, 'is it not a little unsuitable?'

'Unsuitable, child? — I have invested in an Egyptian mummy and I make a ghost walk out of a mirror in three dimensions. The people love it, they scream! You can make them experience the Revolution, the death-masks will make them shudder even while they rejoice to be alive. Moreover, you will be famous!'

'My little boy—'

'We'll take him with us.'

'But my husband—'

'Your husband does not understand you. We go next summer.'

'I may be with child again.'

'Everything is possible, I'm telling you, everything, in London.'

Philipstal picked up a tiny package, a silk handkerchief folded round three very large, white fingerstalls.

She frowned in annoyance at the idea of wearing them at the cash desk. How could he misjudge her size so grossly?

'Sheepgut, Marie. If Tussaud uses them you will not be with child.'

'Yes, but—'

'You can get everything in London.'

Blushing, Marie stuffed the silk handkerchief and the three white fingerstalls right inside her muff.

On the way home she poked her fingers into the handkerchief and felt the waxy smoothness inside. Sheepgut! How was she to tell him? And her journey . . .

At supper they bent over their dishes in haste, burning their lips on the steaming hot soup. Only the child's little voice made holes in the silence. All three of them looked at Joseph, who smacked at the food so that it scattered across the table, excited by all the attention, and hurt when, instead of laughing, they took the plate away from him.

'My angel, my treasure, my little lion!' Marie smothered him with endearments so that the scorching fumes of silence should not penetrate his sleep, and the voyage over the water was no longer a choice or a decision, nor some old prediction she could laugh at. It was even now in her body, like a pattern etched in stone, and she had already, somehow, told her husband about the parting and the miraculous effects of sheepgut.

Under the gold silk canopy he reached out a hand to her and soon afterwards an intimately demanding foot.

'Why?' she thought, pretending to be asleep. Was it love or hate? His skin always felt warm, alive and young.

Since the child had left her body and the milk was no longer staining her dresses, her breasts had grown slack. Her stomach drew in, flat as a boy's and her legs, still thin, no longer had the litheness of a young deer. A little awkward stiffness had settled on her movements.

She sighed, knowing he knew the sigh was one of chilly resignation rather than desire. His skin smelled faintly of alcohol and sweat and she thought experimentally of the sea she had never seen, of woods and plains and of the young red-headed housekeeper with her moist eyes and lips. Her own eyes felt dry and burning.

'Marie, what are you thinking about?'

'Landscapes, faces.'

She opened her eyes suddenly.

'François, I do not want any more children!'

'Children — one does not always have children — isn't it *gratis*?'

'*Gratis!* Nothing is *gratis*. Everything for which I have not paid cash I have paid off in interest and interest on interest.' And with a quick, triumphant movement she put Philipstal's little packet before him. 'You use these.'

'What's that?' He regarded the three wax-white sheaths with revulsion.

'You put them on, and we avoid children.'

'It's unnatural.'

'It's unnatural to want it several times a week. I'm tired.'

'It's love!'

'It has nothing whatever to do with love. It does not even have anything to do with me. It's lust — lust, pure and simple.'

'Love and lust go together.'

'Love and security go together.'

'If you love, you want children, a whole nestful. I'm not using that unnatural muck. Where did you get it from?'

'That is not your concern.'

'A brothel?'

'Philipstal, if you really must know.'

'Philipstal — so it's he who is your lover! That is why you must always go into town.'

'Philipstal could be my father.'

'Yes, why not? Your lover and your father.'

'You're insane.'

'Yes, you make me insane!'

'Dearest, there has never been anyone but you.'

He flung himself heavily on the mattress as he turned over and soon afterwards his body was shut off in sleep, like a big onion in its many skins. The impenetrability of sleep was filled with enmity, the yellow canopy was the colour of sulphur and hatred, and Marie wept bitterly to think that she was not yet old enough to be unable to conceive.

Then she dreamed she was sailing in a very narrow boat, almost a gondola. The water below was quite clear and she suddenly saw herself sailing over bodies lying motionless on the bottom — beautiful, smooth bodies without a blemish, no sign of decay. The sun shone through the water onto calmly sleeping faces.

Your forty-second year, and the hair snaps between the teeth of the comb. Your forty-second year, breasts which are no longer firm, the hole in the lifeline. You see it on your open palm like the pattern in a stone.

Once you believed that it would be a whirlpool, a plunge between life and death, but it is a green hole, the bolthole of Ivry-sur-Seine. The yellow light falls through the canopy. The heads of a husband and two sons, round and soft: Joseph aged four, little François nearly two: children more beautiful than anything else, formed of your flesh and your heavy, dreaming blood.

Your hands stroke their cheeks and bodies. Your hands shaped neither their heads nor the strong, eager grasp of baby fingers; those were shaped by the deep, glowing cavern under your heart. Your husband's seed and his refusal to use sheepgut shaped them, the weight of your body shaped them, your husband's broad, handsome face shaped the baby's touching profile: the Tussaud line of coppersmiths, farmers and housewives. Joseph has your nose and your eyes, your mother's slenderness, and perhaps his obstinacy from Curtius, or the hero with the silver plate in his temple — the Captain of the National Guard or the Swiss Guard officer. A family tree which does not help you to fall asleep.

The bread baskets at Ivry-sur-Seine are round and soft. You take the knife and cut the loaf in thick white slices and lay them on the dish. When it is dry you throw it out, for there will be fresh bread tomorrow; your mother will bake, or you will. The smooth, white dough sliding between your fingers, the smell of security.

But sometimes your hand stops as you cut. Sometimes your hand shakes as you throw out the dry crusts. You say you are afraid of rats — why should you be afraid of rats? Afraid of the wind, of withered leaves that blow against the panes, afraid of storms, of lightning striking. Your hands shake like birds pursued by a cat, cutting the bread askew, dropping the salt.

Could you be going insane? Insane. The word comes like the irritating buzz of a fly, a word like *gratis*. *Gratis*. Tormenting, seething words. And you see yourself from without, from your husband's standpoint, from your own standpoint, buzzing, whining, insane. Is a fly insane?

The children have bowed your body, the sun has burned the waxen tenderness of your arms, but the disquiet is still there. The soft grass, buttercups and blue orchids sway by the roadside; the pale irises and the thistles stand erect.

The children swing on the apple tree bough, the shadows of the leaves falling on their faces.

You pickle yellow plums, bursting with juice.

Under your skin a brittleness, as if you yourself might break and the wind might scatter you over the landscape in a thousand fragments.

You can shut out the sun in the west-facing room, where only the bed's yellow canopy gives light. That fine crawling on the back of the neck, from lust or fear. Tussaud's lips heavy with apple wine. Love! A piece of sausage skin is enough to make short work of his passion.

To explain: dearest, I have simply no talent for happiness, not in this way. I cannot play, only work.

Or: our marriage is a mistake, but we are both blameless. I wanted a friend, a support, perhaps another Curtius, but I wanted to be his equal.

Or: money. Money! When I have none I think of nothing else, it stultifies my brain. I freeze, my feet grow heavy, I am afraid Joseph and little François may ask me for something I cannot give, and afraid that you will suddenly invest in something or other without asking first. Money is freedom: I must go to Paris and work, or else I shall go to London with Philipstal and grow rich. After that — after that we shall be very happy.

Lies, Marie Tussaud.

Pushing the hair from her forehead, she smoothed her apron and went out to the children in the garden, but soon afterwards her mother's crackling voice was calling them in to supper.

François at once made himself as soft as a chick in her arms, but Joseph pouted and said he didn't want to wash or eat.

'Neither do I,' said Marie sharply. 'It is something we have to do.' All the same, she promised him plums with cream.

At the table she watched her mother's timid movements, proffering, urging, and that submissive look at Tussaud, always afraid lest the food be not sufficiently hot, sufficiently tender, sufficiently seasoned. All that sentiment over the cooking pots, all those efforts, just to eat, and her patient tempting of little François: 'A little bit for Papa, a little bit for Maman, a little bit for Joseph, a bit for doggy and a little bit for Grand'maman,' while Joseph, who could not bear meatballs and cabbage, messed about with his food, quite indifferent to his grandmother's reproachful eyes.

Marie rose suddenly and shook him hard: 'The aristocrats put up with it, the revolutionaries put up with it, and you, you spoiled brat — you just mess it about!'

Joseph turned a reproachful, adult stare on her and François Tussaud brushed his forehead with an irritated movement, as if a fly had landed there.

'What have aristocratic and revolutionary eating habits to do with us?'

'Do you think my mother should give herself all this trouble for nothing?'

'Nobody asks her to. And no one asks you to interfere.'

'Perhaps I am superfluous. Joseph—' She tried to hold her elder son's eyes, 'Tomorrow we go to Paris.'

He will never forgive me, she thought, watching him stuff his mouth with a mixture of tears and cabbage.

But next morning when the carriage stopped at the door he was singing with anticipation. Marie smoothed his hair while he waved to his father, who had not yet risen, and to his grandmother, who would not leave the kitchen.

'We're going back to Paris, Joseph.'

'To play with wax!'

'First I must talk to a man, and then I shall work.'

'Washing the floor, that's nice work for girls!'

'Joseph, I can never do all I would like I am so tired.'

'Do you want to sleep?'

'You watch the road, Joseph. When I was your age I travelled a very long way with Grand'maman, further than you can imagine, over mountains and frontiers, up hill and down dale!'

'Shall we travel too?'

'Perhaps. It depends on the man I'm going to see, the one with the magic lantern.'

'I can't bear ghosts. I like ladies with fine clothes and breasts much better!'

'My own, promise me to be sweet!'

So Joseph bowed, as well-behaved as an angel, to Philipstal, who regretted that he could not invite them in because his house-keeper had just left. suddenly it seemed to Marie that there was something hard and untrustworthy in his eyes — impertinent eyes, she thought, eyes that undress you in a second.

But when they were sitting in the restaurant he was once again the old Philipstal she had known since she was a little girl. They sat at the very table where she and a young man from Macon had once eaten cake and drunk sweet wine and she was already ex-cited, almost intoxicated by the sounds, smells and voices of the city.

Philipstal ordered the tastiest food and wine, and fruit juice for the child. He pampered him, enquiring if he would prefer ice cream or cake.

'Fruit,' muttered Joseph, simultaneously overwhelmed and perverse.

Marie patted her pretty, discomfited child and ate lamb. The smell of horses and dung came in through the door and in the mirror her eyes were larger, her nose longer, while her slimness made her almost girlish. Her eyes moved on, resting on a very young couple who had been served, the girl's hands fussing over the dishes of meat and vegetables as though she would really have preferred to prepare them herself. The light gave her face a delicate pink tinge, as she took care to put the best pieces on the gawky young man's plate. He poured the wine with restraint, a little less for her than for himself.

A grey-suited man clasped the waiter's wrist as he passed, the waiter brushed his shoulder in a very slight, unobtrusive caress and the gentleman was served with more wine.

'Beautiful woman!' the waiter whispered to Marie, to her suprise, since she was neither beautiful nor thinking of tipping him. Then she concentrated on Philipstal's plans again.

'Only a month,' he said, 'and we shall be going.'

'A month to pack and prepare my family?'

'A month is quite sufficient for packing. If you take thirty figures you can pack one a day!'

'And you?'

'I shall travel with my old exhibition, my mummy, my ghost and my landscapes. I may restore the fireworks as well and, of course, I shall be helping you. I will reserve places on the boat, carriages and labour for the loading. Dearest, you will be famous!'

'And the money?'

'We will draw up a contract.'

'Maman,' Joseph tugged at her hand, 'can't we go home soon?'

'Hush, Joseph, Maman is working.'

Philipstal ordered sorbet and gave the impatient child a shining silver coin from England.

'What can I buy with it?' asked the boy practically.

'Wait till we are over there.' The old man smiled affectionately and praised Joseph's business sense — and the sorbet was a dream: small, cool waves tasting of raspberry, lemon and champagne, slipping over his tongue.

'Now, the coast,' said Philipstal. 'When you arrive at Dover the cliffs are as white as a cake — only bigger.'

Then, with a sudden movement, he grabbed at his pocket and Marie's cheeks burned when he jumped up, shouting to the whole restaurant: 'My purse, my purse has been stolen! And the bank is closed!'

She took her little pearl-embroidered purse from her bag.

'I hope you will allow me—'

'It goes against the grain, child!'

'It is only a loan. You can pay me back in London.'

She slid the little purse under the table into a pair of experienced hands weighed down with gold rings.

In the mirror she saw the waiter's smirk.

'Maman,' said Joseph, as soon as they were alone in the street, 'could we not buy something to take home to Papa and Grand'maman and François?'

'My treasure, you know we cannot.'

'Maman, you drank wine with him.'

'It was necessary.'

'How could you talk to him? Did you not see he was wearing patent leather shoes?'

'It was necessary — I did not look at his shoes.'

'Maman, I have a headache. I feel as if some big horns were growing out just here—' He clenched his small fists and held them to his forehead. 'Like antlers.'

'Antlers! My own, where do you learn these words?'

She kissed him and tried to swing him round but he pulled away.

'Joseph, we're going in a big ship. When we come home again we shall be rich.'

'And we'll buy presents for home?'

'Of course, everything, we shall buy all sorts of lovely things!'

Tussaud. Tussaud. Marie Tussaud. François Tussaud. Joseph Tussaud. The rolling wheels repeated the name.

Tussaud.

We shall bring London home as a present.

But not sheepgut.

Beloved, we shall begin from the beginning.

Parting is renewal.

I am going for your sake.

For our sake, Tussaud.

Only you mean anything, nothing else matters.

Tussaud — till death us do part!

Waves like silk, a coast like white cake.

I will make you rich, François.

You shall sit at the box office, impressive in your smart suit and patent leather shoes.

You shall manage everything as long as I am away.

The doorman — remember he must be well-groomed!

Please don't be jealous.

I am not going for my own enjoyment.

I am going for your sake, to make money.

Dear mother, you did the very same.

Do you remember the woman who told my fortune?

The voyage over the water is inescapable.

'Sorrow,' she said, 'and fame.'
And I was indifferent to the sorrow, if only I could be famous!
Am I in my senses?
Not very much more sensible than I was then!
I must get out of this hole.
The bolthole that shuts me in and drives me mad.
I have made my decision, Tussaud!

However, it was not Marie who gave her husband the surprising news, but Joseph who ran to his father and little brother with the silver coin in his hand.

Before she had paid the coachman she saw her husband turn on his heel and make for the inn, followed by the two handsome dogs. A little *distraite*, she scolded the surprised Joseph for running without thinking of his clothes and pushed him quite urgently ahead of her into the kitchen.

'I am leaving in a month,' she said, trying to make her voice light.

'And the children?' For once her mother let go of the cooking spoon and turned her back on the stove.

'I shall take Joseph with me and leave François with you and my husband.'

'Are you sure this is right?'

'Yes.'

'Then let us hope so,' said her mother, turning her sad, reproachful eyes on the cooking pot.

And Marie remembered her as a young woman, with a voice that was light and sparkling with expectancy, when without being over particular about the truth she made little Marie a party to her disappointments, anxieties and dreams. But what had become of that woman, who flung wash-bowls, stepped undaunted across horse dung, braced her hands against an overturned coach, and said: 'Do not wait, Marie, never wait for anything at all!'

Was the journey only a dream, or a brief transit between self-effacing waiting and self-effacing anonymity?

If she went back to the kitchen and faced her mother at this very moment, would she simply be silent, or try to explain everything away with another layer of pretence? As if in all her life she had

committed only one tiny little sin, which she must always nurse by
making herself unapproachable, brushing away all traces of her
own movement, drowning herself in duties. Her mother's fate
filled her with a despondency which made it no easier to meet the
husband suddenly returning from the inn.

'And all this means nothing?'

He looked round the room and down at his polished shoes, as if
that would describe the whole of their marriage and that fine sensation of walking in whipped cream when they had bought the
rings. And for a moment she thought he was like a child, hiding his
vulnerability in defiance.

'François, everything is yours while I am away. The cash box,
the exhibition halls, the houses, everything! I beg you only to take
care of François and my mother until I come back.'

'Do you think you can simply discard us and then come back?'

'I have told you, you mean everything.'

'Then what is it you lack?'

'Security. You have simply never given me any kind of security.
When we were expecting our first child there was no money for the
cot or even the doctor. I had to do everything myself.'

'You said nothing about it then.'

'No.'

She turned her back on him, as if it were imperative for her to
know precisely how much linen there was in the drawers and how
many petticoats and stockings she should take with her.

For a moment he was dumbstruck. Her slim back and the quick
little hands, the scent of rose water and the clear, defiant
voice made him remember the rather old-maidish girl with the
shining dark curls, and he dreamed of seeing her, a little plumper,
surrounded by children in a garden just as beautiful as the one that
surrounded them now, and protected by imposing pedigree dogs.
Fruit trees, their branches heavy with fruit, would cast fine
shadows on her face; children would arrive with the seasons. In
summer they would walk under the dense branches of the trees; in
winter they would sit by the hearth, drinking home-made wine.
Every morning he would go to work, to return home to the delicate, unskilled creature who was in need of his protection. And
every year there would be a new baby, little boys with fair hair and

strong hands and legs, and little girls with white bows in their plaits and bright, dark eyes.

'Marie, sell your house in town, sell Curtius' Waxwork Cabinet and the paintings and mirrors! Sell the whole of that collection of criminals and heroes to people who want them. I will look for work!'

The words surprised even him, and he saw Marie stiffen as if an icy wave had poured over her, almost bowling her over. She let go of the bundle of clothes and stood with her feet buried in white and cream petticoats.

'You know I cannot!' Her voice was very dry. 'I could not live without working.'

'Then find a nice little studio where people will come to have their portraits made for payment.'

'I am leaving. And afterwards we shall begin again from the beginning.'

The word 'leaving' hung in the air, buzzing like an insect.

It could not be made light of or brushed away: it determined their movements. They said it, or avoided saying it, but even little François learned the word.

Leaving made Marie see her mother as a frail old woman with shoulder-blades that poked out under her shawl like wings and hands that shook when she fed François, and she imagined how greatly the little boy would change, even in a few months. He would have more teeth, his face would thin down, his hair darken, the dimples in his hands disappear. And his laugh, even his laugh would change, and perhaps he would cry and bite the sides of the bed and his father would not hear him and his grandmother would say that crying strengthens the lungs.

On those days she hoped that Philipstal would cancel the journey, that war would break out, that the frontiers would be closed, that Philipstal might be ill or that she herself would be struck by illness or break a bone.

Once again husband and wife drove to Paris, sitting in the carriage like two travellers, their voices cool and soberly friendly, as they discussed how François Tussaud was to organize the box office money, pay the wages, move topical figures into the light and withdraw the less interesting — and above all, note the public's reaction.

Marie Tussaud packed. The beautiful Queen Marie Antoinette, King Louis XVI and their two children, the Sleeping Beauty, Jeanne the old coquette, Marat, Voltaire, Robespierre, Josephine, Napoleon, the Shepherdess, who now had a new lamb. Both aristocrats and revolutionaries, the living and the dead lost their heads, which were carefully packed in a wooden box with fine wood shavings and kapok. She smoothed the costumes and packed them up, trying to include the right colours of silk and wool, buttons and ribbons in case anything was damaged en route, as well as her wax, modelling tools, eyes and hair.

The luggage of the thirty wax figures became more and more extensive, hopeless, unmanageable, and Philipstal had made himself invisible, while François Tussaud sat at the cash desk in his elegant suit, complaining that the town sapped his energy.

But at last everything was packed. Joseph's clothes, her own dresses, hats and cloaks occupied so little space. For the last time she took an evening walk along the pretty terrace where the scent of late roses hung in air that was still delicate and soft as feathers. She picked redcurrants, setting her teeth in the acid fruit, like the very first time she had come to Ivry-sur-Seine and the hens tiptoed in and out of her skirts. She longed to stay there for ever. Tomorrow was a salt, flinty wine: she drank and grew thirstier still.

And once again Marie's and François' bodies were soft and yielding: 'For ever and ever,' she whispered as they met, and: 'Forbid me to leave, forbid me to sail!' But that she only breathed out in a sigh, like little bursting bubbles.

For a moment she saw his face above her as if transfused with light and hated herself for not asking him to take care. Then she closed her eyes again, fearful at the thought that they would soon be far, far away from each other.

In a short, uneasy sleep she dreamed she was going on board a great ship which lay unusually high in the water. She felt a light, rocking motion and suddenly realized that she was sailing, and alone. The ship must have pulled itself loose.

To her relief she discovered that she was sailing on the Lake of Zurich: she could see the mountains quite clearly, and people standing on the shore. One man waved, a young man, and without her doing anything at all the ship slid towards him. He scrambled on board and handed her a piece of canvas, which she held fast. When he lowered her down she noticed the blood running from her palms and felt an overpowering fear of being unable to hold on and of not knowing where she was going.

Then she woke up and listened to the heavy, peaceful breathing at her side and the children, who drew breath so lightly. And in the next room her mother snored with a gasping, bronchitic sound.

She gave up trying to sleep, and tried instead to absorb the sounds of her family before putting on the grey, high-necked travelling costume at dawn. She woke Joseph, shushing him as she splashed cold water over his eyes, and he was immediately lively and cheerful.

She kissed her mother and little François, but tiptoed about, taking care not to slam the doors in order not to wake her husband.

Then she took Joseph's hand and went out to the familiar carriage, the little boy turning to wave again and again.

Marie Tussaud was stepping out of a picture into which she knew she could never return and suddenly she longed to be held back, but there were no footsteps behind her, not a sound.

Do not turn back, Marie! If you do, you will turn into salt, or tears. Forsake this picture, forsake your husband, forsake this house, forsake your child, your mother, your shadow!

Not until she was sitting in the carriage with the door carefully closed did she see her mother standing with the little one in her arms. She was moving his hand and up and down, making him wave and gurgle and she saw her husband running across the grass and turning down to Joseph's den, which lay like a deserted nest.

She was about to step out of the carriage, but at that moment the whip hissed through the air, her hand flew to her mouth, the carriage set off and she waved and waved with Joseph, feeling a little faint and very light. And outside, freedom beckoned.

CHAPTER EIGHT

London 1802

At the Customs my crates were opened. I had hoped to avoid this, with Philipstal's help, but since he had made himself invisible I had to explain as best I might what I was bringing into the country.

The first crate contained hats and wigs and they looked in some surprise at Joseph and me, as if our modest appearance were not altogether in tune with all these curls, buckles, bows and feathers.

The next crate unfortunately proved to contain Robespierre's death-mask, more alarming than ever without a wig.

The poor Customs official, who had been somewhat over-bearing until then, leaped back with an exclamation, dropping his hammer and pliers.

When I tried to take his arm to show him that the lifeless face was only made of wax, he pulled away, his whole face distorted with fear, as if he had met a ghost.

After that no more crates were opened and all in all that was quite a good beginning, although I was sorry for the poor man.

In fact, the whole journey had been quite other than I had expected.

If the sea is supposed to be like silk, this sea was silk being rudely torn up for flounces and ruches; and if the coast is supposed to be like white cake, then this was a large superfluous cake, offered when one's stomach had already contracted in spasms.

My bunk was narrow and I squeezed against the wall to make room for Joseph, feeling as if I had a thin steel rod in my back. But I thought only of my figures, now pitching and tossing in their packing cases, and how I did hope that no dirt nor even the slightest drop of salt water should enter and ruin irreplaceable silks and velvets; yet I feared for the slender fingers and fine noses.

But Joseph was completely unaffected by the sea. Every day he found new friends and every night he slept peacefully. My dear one, once I believed that you would show me the whole world and that I would see everything with your eyes. Now I am seeing everything like a child again: the sea, the steep cliffs, the soft hills, the sheep and the big grey dogs with their undulating run. All the things that make Joseph laugh!

Now I am living in a city again and the very air excites me: the street hawkers' cry, the mussels, fish, chestnuts, muffins and pieces of coconut — all are eaten in the street, with lightning speed and no formality. Joseph and I love that. These burning hot, light meals are more delicious than the food one eats in restaurants, where one must sit and work one's way through a whole menu. No, Joseph and I eat as we walk, and sometimes as we run. No fat accumulates and the restaurants make no money out of us!

We have rented a modest room with a double bed, a table, two chairs and a cupboard. That is sufficient. We are there only when we sleep and in fact we are both fully engaged in preparing the opening of Curtius' Waxwork Cabinet. As I expected, there are masses of broken fingers. matted hair, creases that must be removed and tears which must be repaired and concealed as far as possible. Joseph, who used to regard such things as a game, is now aware that this is really work.

Yesterday Philipstal suddenly appeared and asked if I would be ready at the agreed time.

'Of course,' I replied, after spitting out the pins. 'There will be nothing to criticize, not a single fold, not a single hair!'

He asked if I would hire an assistant and I told him that I had a brilliant assistant in my son. Then he was out of the door again. Waiting in the cab was a red-haired girl whom he had already pursued on the boat. The one practical thing that man has done is to hire the Lyceum Theatre — and claim the best rooms for himself.

*

Dear one, I hope you are diligent. I promise to return prosperous, but I do not think I will put my money in a bank. I will sew it in a belt so that I can always feel the cool weight of gold pieces and if anyone tries to steal it, it will be over my dead body.

I know you are taking good care of our son, but look to my mother as well. Joseph and I send you a thousand kisses and love

Thine for ever
Marie Tussaud

P.S. Simply in order that the red-haired girl shall have something to do, Philipstal has hit upon the idea of her selling tickets for my exhibition as well as his own!

At last! We are ready, although of course I miss my uncle's great hall, the mirrors and paintings which cast a glow of wealth and life over every face. But Curtius' and my figures are also effective in these humbler surroundings and when Joseph and I walked round among them it was almost like being at home again.

Joseph and I celebrated. For the first time we permitted ourselves to walk quite slowly through the town, looking at the shops. Joseph fell in love with a little wooden sword and I saw a pair of black gloves and a shawl of light, soft wool which will be charming for my mother. We made our purchases and went to a respectable hostelry to eat.

We were in our best clothes, but apparently we did not diffuse any particular smell of money. The waiters kept us waiting for an age, while I clung to my little bag and my purse. It was so humiliating that in defiance I chose one of the dearest dishes, a fish swimming round in a mysterious mishmash of shellfish and sauce.

When we had paid and could go at last, two shining carriages stopped right across the street. Three men carried small fragile furnishings into one of the carriages — a bureau, a toilet table and a little tea table, together with some porcelain and silver. The men were extremely well dressed but their strained faces showed that none of them could be the owner of all this grandeur.

Quite close to the carriages a woman and a little girl were

walking. Their dresses were made of heavy blue silk, with lace insertions. The woman walked gingerly in her high, dainty shoes, the little girl's stockings were snowy white and in her shining blonde hair there were plaited ribbons of white silk. Both carried lace-edged parasols.

They were like delicate beings from another time, two fine marionettes momentarily come to life. Their feet moved in the direction of the palace, as if that were the only natural way.

Joseph's eyes followed them for a long time as he clutched his cheap wooden sword and he even spoke of them before he fell asleep. He was sorry for them, he said.

'Why?'

'People of that sort are for putting on exhibit. They simply cannot be living rightly!'

I froze and pulled the shawl round my shoulders. The black, lined gloves smelled of cold stoves and oven black — it must be the colour. I began to cry, but fortunately Joseph was sleeping soundly.

The names of the famous Curtius and the wax figures were written on the noticeboard in elegant letters, and at ten o'clock Marie Tussaud was sitting at a little round table, tearing a corner off the visitors' tickets.

There was some pushing and struggling, and a crowd of emigrants, dressed as if they were still at Court, launched into a breathless race to reach the royal family as quickly as possible.

One woman cast herself sobbing into her friend's arms and the friend began to cry as well. Others joined in, until there was a large, surging group of men and women embracing one another, carried away by grief and emotion. In the midst of them Marie recognized the well-to-do lady from the hostelry with her little girl clinging to her dress.

Even the Comte d'Artois with his family and retainers went past Marie's little table. The footman handed her the thick stack of tickets and she covertly watched the Count. Trouble had visibly marred his features, but he still exhibited the same self-assurance and elegance as when he had stood on the stage in that *lait-de-puce* satin costume, courting pretty young Rosina, who was so obviously in love that her radiant eyes, her blushes and the little excited leaps of her voice reached to the backmost row, while the helpless hands had continually to caress the air.

But Marie was unable to see the Count's face when he reached the wax figures which so precisely resembled his brother and sister-in-law, for in front of Marat a woman had fainted and had to be carried out while her husband demanded a refund for their tickets.

There were constant alarmed outbursts from in front of the death-masks, and pale, elegant women produced snuff, smelling-salts and candied sweets to give themselves strength, whispering that this was too much, they must go out, they needed air. But none of them went out into the air; on the contrary, they drew closer and closer to those heads which they claimed they simply could not bear to see.

The men touched the wax masks slyly as they supported their loud, fainting wives and refined, anaemic daughters, growing steadily paler and more listless. Only the corset bones seemed to hold them up, and certainly did them no good. But these delicate creatures lifted their veils and gazed with large, perhaps near-sighted eyes, absorbing everything and regardless of mothers, fathers or sweethearts trying to hold them back. Elegant young gentlemen leaned thankfully on their canes and even in the thickest press everyone retained gloves and hats. It was unbearably hot and the small leaves of paper grew damp between Marie's fingers as she calculated that at least ten pounds must have come into the box office.

In the middle of the hall everyone stopped, almost dazzled by the clear, sharp morning light falling on Josephine and Napoleon. The young men straightened, observing that this war hero scarcely came up to their shoulders, but the women saw only Josephine, a charming classical gown clinging to her body, so simple and light that she, the First Consul's lady, might just as well have been naked. And her hair was held in place by that coquettishly practical frontlet; the curls stayed where they should, impeding neither her view nor her concentration.

'I might have my hair cut like that!' said a girl whose fine features were almost smothered in a golden mane of only partially tamed corkscrew curls.

'If you dare—!' Her father banged his walking stick on the floor.

'A woman's glory is her hair,' her mother firmly drew the foolish child away from the pernicious French influence.

'But what are those clothes she is wearing?'

'It must be a nightgown.'

'But he is in uniform!'

'Perhaps he has come home unexpectedly.'

'Then he might just as well be in a nightshirt.'

'One does not think of generals in nightshirts — nightshirts are something one irons!'

The couple led their golden-blonde treasure away between them, but she looked back once more.

'I think she is dressed for battledore and shuttlecock.'

'It is improper.' The outraged father looked back several times; apparently it was essential for him to memorize the lightly-clad curves of the First Consul's wife.

It was almost eleven that night before the last visitors had seen everything. Marie rose, stiff all over, and woke Joseph, who had fallen asleep under the table. The scraps of paper she had torn off the tickets entirely filled her cash box and most of her bag.

She walked through her exhibition premises, carefully extinguishing all the lights. She knocked hard on the door to Philipstal's magic lantern theatre, but it was closed and dark.

So she locked the heavy doors of the Lyceum Theatre, pushing against them and shaking them a little, as she imagined a thief might do.

'Are we going to be rich, Maman?' mumbled Joseph, leaning close to her in the cab.

'I believe so, my treasure.' She stroked the back of his neck and pulled the rug right up to his chin.

Marie had counted all her ticket corners and tied them in a big, pink bundle. She had asked the landlady to sit with Joseph until she returned and if necessary to give him his breakfast when he woke up. That day she would remember to close the exhibition at tea time and allow an interval of about an hour, or at least send

Joseph home for tea. The landlady was glad to look after him —
Joseph Tussaud, a wonderful child! He already spoke English
better than his mother, and he was not yet five. She would buy the
pistol that went with the sword, and new clothes as well for both of
them.

Those colours again: ivory, oyster blue and apricot, with low,
low necklines, almost like the dresses in Paris.

But my arms are no longer young, the skin on my neck is
growing slack and shall I not grow broad round the bottom, sitting
still so long every day? But one can try, one can always try!

Marie twisted and turned before the mirror, and before a
woman with heavy gold rings on her fingers and honey blonde hair
that was dark at the roots.

The thin, apricot-coloured material was like a ray of sunshine in
the dim fitting room.

'But is it not too *outré*? Should I not be more discreet?'

The honey blonde began to speak French.

'I tell you, Madame, no one can resist that colour, everyone is
mad about the dresses! I dare not sell them any more — or else I
shall have to move to a better district. Do you know what happened yesterday? Two young gentlemen came in straight off the
street — such a shock!'

'Did they mean to steal your money?'

'Not at all. They undressed completely, in front of this very
mirror, tried on the skin-coloured underclothes and my silk
dresses and asked if I could cut the neckline less low, so that one
could not see the hair on their chests! One of them had a neat leg,
ankles as slender as a woman's. I thought I must be going mad!'

'Did they buy anything?'

'What do you expect? I am a respectable woman! I refused to
sell them anything at all.'

'What a shame. I will take the apricot.'

In the street Marie recognized a young couple who had visited
the exhibition.

The gentleman removed his hat and swung it in a great arc and
the young lady's lips seemed to shape 'Congratulations!'

Marie was still smiling when she turned the corner and saw a tall,
dark figure on the other side of the road: Philipstal. She was about

to cross over, but the man's impenetrable anger shut her out; he
turned to the wall to avoid her greeting and her eyes, as if she had
injured him. She could not understand it, there must be some
mistake! When she met him in an hour's time she would find that it
had been a mistake. The man she had seen must be someone else,
wearing the same clothes and with the same body, and exactly the
same profile, and if it really was Philipstal, his rage must be meant
for someone else, not for her. For the red-haired girl, perhaps.
One defiant glance and he had turned away, vulnerable as François Tussaud when she told him she would be leaving. But she had
not spoken to Philipstal of leaving. She had not, and she would not
fail him.

At home — she was surprised to find herself already calling the
rented room 'home' — Joseph was sitting up in bed eating his
breakfast. The landlady's heavy, housewifely figure, with solid
hips and long, English legs like posts and the child's confiding
English chatter momentarily damped her spirits.

Not until the landlady had gone did Joseph speak French again,
and Marie hugged him and put the parcel containing the pistol in
front of him. Then she unpacked her new dress, feeling the gauzy
material light and living against her skin as she slipped it on and
climbed onto a stool to see her reflection from shoulders to hips.
Her neck muscles were taut as a tightrope dancer's and her skin
not very smooth.

'Maman,' came Joseph's voice behind her, 'are you going out
like that?' And before she could answer he continued: 'You will be
a disgrace to the whole family!'

My love,
    Philipstal is a monster. He is a mean parasite and I do not
know how I could have signed that contract. He takes half
my receipts and makes me pay all expenses. According to
the contract I am bound to travel to Scotland with him in the
spring. His magic equipment consists of a few lights, some
mirrors and pictures, whereas I have to transport thirty
full-length figures.
    I do not yet know what the freight will cost, but it may even
exceed my paltry fifty per cent. I have spoken to a solicitor

and received nothing from him but a bill. He supports
Philipstal, who claims that he offers me practical help and
protection, but how much can a single woman pay for
those? Moreover, I would much prefer to take charge of
my own affairs. My figures are what people come to see,
not his cheap illusions, which please only children. I must
part company with him, free myself, even if I have to pay
my way out.

Nevertheless I am happy to be travelling. It is, after
all, far more important to be recognized here than at
home, where I always felt I was under Curtius'
protection.

Every day I hope that you are all well and that you
remember to move the up-to-the-minute figures into the
light. I know you take good care of little François, but
look after my mother, too! Do not give me cause to reproach you.

How Joseph and I long to be with you now and
embrace you!

But depend on me, I shall not come home until my
purse is full. What I would like is to come home to you
dressed in gold pieces from top to bottom, and only you
would be allowed to take them off.

Forgive this scratchy, uncontrollable pen.

Many loving greetings to you all.

Joseph and Marie Tussaud

I saw Philipstal kiss the red-haired girl's white neck and felt a
tug of longing. It was not Philipstal's narrow lips I longed for;
it was a great, painful yearning, which I also feel sometimes
when I see spouses whose hands are at peace with one
another, without great expectation or surprise.

Their security, when they walk down the street together —
if only I could drink it!

A pinch of snuff, a glass of port wine.

Joseph is asleep.

Holy Virgin, do not let the wine turn my nose red, do not

let my teeth rot. And do not let my husband's and my last embrace
have consequences, although I enjoyed it!

The season will end soon and there are now so few visitors that we
have had to reduce the prices. Those who come are mainly
children and they are like a different race, sinewy, hard-working
and hollow-cheeked. Boys not much older than Joseph put their
own money on the table and are a prey to spirits, snuff and tobacco.
Joseph's admiring eyes terrify me and I try to keep him as far away
from them as possible.

The children always spend hours in front of the death-masks
and the murder of Marat, as if the horrors absorb them until they
disappear into these frightening tableaux and have to cling to each
other or dig their nails into their palms in order to return to reality.

Terror should be forbidden to children — they will see those
faces again at night, the darkness high-lighting the images. But it
would be foolish of me to lose customers, when one considers that
executions are always accounted both entertaining and
educational.

These little ones are greatly in need of education, especially the
boys. Yesterday two were looking at the Sleeping Beauty.

'Must be pretty nice to be the man there!' said one.

Later they spent a long time in front of Josephine, loudly
discussing what she must be like to go to bed with, without paying
the least regard to the husband I have modelled at her side.

Fortunately I did not understand all their racy talk. Above all I
must keep my son from that sort!

Money! When I have none, it dominates my thoughts. I walk down
a street and when a man or woman passes me I instantly add up the
value of their clothes. Each individual represents a quite
astonishing sum, even the humblest, but I include everything: I
imagine the under-garments, the contents of a bag and the soles of
the shoes.

I add myself up in the same way — and Joseph. My greatest fear
is bankruptcy and the debtors' prison. Philipstal feels precisely the
same fear, which is why he clings to me like a burr. He says the
journey to Edinburgh is already paid for and one day very soon I

shall get my money, but I shall not believe it until it is in my hands. He promises, promises, promises. He says we must stay together and support each other — how I hate his hypocrisy! Moreover, he cannot conceal his jealousy and says I am taking his customers, as if it were my fault!

The reason why Joseph and I did not starve long ago is my private commissions. Just now I am modelling a portrait of the Duchess of York, who would like me to make her still pretty features ten years younger; and an exceedingly well-to-do, childless lady has written inviting me to model a sweet, sleeping boy.

Fortunately Philipstal knows nothing of this, or it would be just like him to demand fifty per cent of my sleeping Joseph!

I have one reason to welcome leaving London: my landlady's daughter is engaged and is visited every evening by her intended.

If the landlady had not always been so kind to us both I would demand that the young people did it more quietly on account of my work and my child's sleep.

The exhibition has closed at last. The last days produced little. We pack, pack and pack, Joseph and I. Oh, all those fragile fingers, all the noses which the sea may break again!

While the landlady baked cakes with Joseph — for the last time — I was delivering 'The Sleeping Child'. My customer proved to be an elegant woman of about thirty years. She kissed the thick dark hair, the temples, fingertips and sweet, half-open lips ecstatically, not knowing it was my Joseph she was covering with kisses and soft rugs. Perhaps this copy of my son will receive far more security and far more tender kisses and caresses than I ever had time for.

I walked part of the way home and for once it was almost quiet in the town. The afternoon hung like cotton wool between the houses and the lights in the shops were already lit.

I stopped at a bookseller's. I did not understand the titles but some drawings were on display, drawings of martyrs with flaming hair, rent clothes and bodies stretched in agony — only one of them appeared worldly: a young woman in a dress so light that it seemed a part of her own delicate skin. She was kneeling, her skirt

flowing out over her feet and covering most of the floor. Her
waist was tiny, her unkempt hair hung over her slender
shoulders — perhaps she had not had time to attend to it, or
perhaps she knew it would be no use. Her hands hung limply
down, as if she had given up wringing them in despair or clas-
ping them in prayer. Her features were so regular that her face
would have seemed characterless had not her eyes, her half-
open lips and the appealing inclination of her body expressed a
total resignation to fear and anticipation. These emotions,
which seemed to permeate the young woman's skin, dress and
hair, were directed towards a dark, upright silhouette: a man,
perhaps a lover, perhaps an enemy, perhaps moving towards
the woman, perhaps away.

Out there in the street in the afternoon, a sudden longing,
which I should only feel under a silk canopy yellow as
sunshine, or sulphur, an overwhelming desire, a lust without
object which may even show through my clothes, my movements. I wanted to go in and buy the drawing, that little
martyr in her rather old-fashioned dress, but what should I
say? That I thought it expressive, a little work of art? Any
shop assistant would see through me!

No, I must go, go home quickly. My temples are damp even
through the veil and my hands — into the muff, deep inside
the muff! A little smelling-salts, a little snuff. Joseph shall
never see pictures of that kind — and yet, ten minutes later I
stop, turn on my heel and go back.

I have only to walk nonchalantly into the shop and point to
the light that glows over the little drawing as if over a reli-
quary. A martyr, in almost modern dress, with strait-laced
figure and pious little breasts. I do not know her story —
perhaps her slim, anonymous body rests under some church
vault or other, cool, sheltered and chaste.

My feet move lightly, brushing the ground — of what should
I be ashamed? And for whose sake, the painter's or the
owner's?

Cool jasmine water on my wrists and heart, beating expectantly. I want to buy that lust, experience it again and again.

But there is a gap in the display. All the other martyrs are in their places, fighting wild-haired lions, with savagely dilated eyes. Only she is not there.

Her image is still behind my eyes, but I do not know if it is disappointment or relief that makes my body suddenly so heavy.

Now everything is packed and the journey to Edinburgh will carry me still further away from my dear ones, little François, my mother, my husband.

I must be a bad mother! Only an unnatural woman would leave a two-year-old child. I have not loved him enough, there was no joy in my blood. It was as if a strange being had invaded my body to suck me dry, taking possession of every single cell — and then I longed for him to finish quickly with my breasts.

But now every time I see one of those touching, toothless smiles or a little pair of boots, my whole body is filled with longing and I wish I still carried him under my heart, that I had never let him out.

I dream that Tussaud beats him. He comes wobbling towards me on his strong little legs and I want to pick him up and kiss him, his eyes shining with tears, his little lips agape with astonishment and injustice, and I long to plunge a knife into Tussaud. In sleep I lift my arms, my own whimpering awakens me. Not even Joseph's peaceful breathing is enough to make my body relax. François, my darling child — but I did not want him. He was the result of Tussaud's heavy body and his aversion to sheepgut — and how could I manage two children here?

But no woman deserts her child. Even when I was going to Paris I felt it was wrong, though I felt relief and happiness at the same time, a pure and simple selfish gladness at being able to concentrate again, have ideas and move quickly and lightly.

I told myself it was for the children's sake I did it, so that they should have food, clothes, shoes, dogs and money for piano lessons and good teachers.

But what happiness can my younger son have from my trying to make my fortune in Edinburgh?

CHAPTER NINE
Edinburgh 1803

My dear one,

Once again the sea, and once again broken noses and fingers, yet the journey was relatively smooth. Here in Edinburgh I know that Joseph and I shall be happy. This is no small town, in fact it is quite fashionable. My landlady speaks fluent French and in the evening I sometimes hear her sing in French at the piano. Our son will soon have forgotten his French, but it will come back again. When the sun shines we can see snow-covered mountain tops from our window, and the spring air is so light and fresh.

Otherwise we made a poor start, for Philipstal had paid for neither the journey nor the freight. Had I not been able to borrow money we should have lost everything. I have no illusions about that man!

But I have rented premises for my exhibition, far finer and also more reasonable than in London. The advance public interest is promising. I hope here to be able to buy myself out of my contract, although I do not fully understand why it should be necessary. All the solicitors seem to support my incompetent and untrustworthy partner, who will not arrive for a week or two with his lantern slides and other cheap effects. In fact I do much better without him. but perhaps men make laws for each others' advantage. Forgive me, I meant nothing personal!

We would be very happy if you would let us know how things are at home, first and foremost as regards your

health, but also our economic situation. You can do just as
you like with our exhibition, now that I am no longer there
to scold you.

Joseph looks forward to seeing his little brother again
and to teaching him English, and he has even begun to
read. He is an industrious and interested pupil to whom
everything comes easily. One of our friends has also begun
to give him free piano lessons.

You ask if I can speak English.

I speak precisely the amount of English needed for my
work. I still pronounce neither town nor street names
correctly and you know that I have no sense of locality, yet
we always arrive punctually and I have learned my
numbers. So much for my English!

Joseph and I miss you and kiss you all and impatiently
await your news. You cannot possibly have less time than I.
Take care of our child and my mother. Perhaps you could
help her a little in the kitchen now and then.

Many loving greetings,

Joseph and your wife Marie Tussaud

I must always think of the future and I take pains to keep up.
Who knows? Perhaps this journey will turn out to be longer than
we thought.

Today a young robber and murderer was hanged. His accom-
plices are still in prison and I applied to take casts of their faces.

Permission was not hard to find and while Joseph was occupied
with his books I walked to the gaol.

First I visited the man who had planned the murder. He
behaved with extraordinary amiability towards me, as if hoping
that this impression of his fine, depraved features might act in his
defence. He even essayed a smile when I rubbed the oil on his
face. While the plaster was drying I noticed that despite his youth
he was almost bald and his poor nails were bitten down to the
flesh. When I left he opened his mouth as if to say something and
a shudder ran right through his body.

Out in the yard lay the corpse of the actual murderer and even now one could see that he had been unbelievably strong. with his broad shoulders and short legs. But when I took the hood off his head, despite the ugly, distorted expression, he had the face of a hurt child, a child with lips and eyes open in astonishment at having been punished for no reason. And I saw this sturdy, sore and primitive child being enticed into criminality and murder by promises of affection and reward. Just one quite simple grip, eyes closed, those short, strong hands used quickly, accurately, and everything would be within reach. The soft beds, steaming stews, tender steaks, clean clothes, glossy expensive shoes, wine, beer and pomade that women like. Otherwise, nothing — nothing but toil and hunger and rejection.

When I left a big dog came towards me, a terrifying beast, large as a small lion, with massive feet and shiny black jaws. If it had not been so imperative for me to get the two plaster casts home safely I should have broken into a run, but I controlled myself and put out my free hand to soothe the animal. Its warm breath blew right up my sleeve!

One of the guards told me that this was the murderer's dog, which in response to his earnest pleading he had been allowed to keep in the cell where it had both eaten of his food and relieved itself.

I looked round for a carriage but there was none, and it was impossible to shake the beast off. If I started running, it could easily overtake me on its long, muscular legs. I did not dare to show my fear and I prayed that the animal would not be able to smell it, as I clutched my bag close to me, looking down now and then at the long head, tongue lolling between a fearful set of teeth, and watchful, bloodshot eyes.

I had no time to close my door before it had pushed its way in and I uttered a scream when I saw it loping over to Joseph, who flung his arms round it protectively, if you please, and called it his little puppy!

The animal began to wag its tail, lick Joseph's face and push its great heavy head against his shoulder and from its movements I could see that this clumsy, homeless monster was not even a full-grown dog.

Naturally I dared not say where I had found it and the boy

thought it a miracle or a gift. It ran round our room like a
lumbering lion. It wagged its tail and swept the tea cups off the
table. In the morning its excrement was on the floor and the
smell of dog here is so dreadful that I cannot understand why
we have not yet been given notice.

The worst thing is that I cannot work. Every time I take out
the masks of its master and his dubious friends it lies before me
with a watchful, melancholy look in its eyes or runs off,
growling, with my modelling tools and puts its great rough paws
round my neck when I struggle to wrench them out of its
mouth.

Sometimes Joseph falls asleep on the floor with it, the dog
stretching out luxuriously and laying its loving head against
him. Its yellow coat shines like honey in the sun and its face is
remarkably full of character, with that black, velvety mask. The
lashes shine like silk and its nose is like wet paint. I simply do
not know where it can go when we have to travel again and
sometimes I hope it may run away or come to a sudden, painless
end. But I know it will not.

Today I witnessed something that really shocked me.

In the solicitor's waiting room sat a youngish woman, crying
inconsolably. One could see from her clothes that she had left
the house in great haste: a pair of expensive French boots,
imperfect stockings, a fur cape over a silk dress, and finally a
summer hat flopping on her tousled hair. Her handkerchief was
wringing wet.

I assumed that her situation was acute and permitted myself
to ask if I could help, but she told me she regarded her fate as
hopeless. Five years ago her husband had left her in extreme
want, and without a word. In that time she had earned enough
to furnish her simple needs and had of course not the slightest
desire to meet him again, when suddenly he arrived on her
doorstep without a penny in his pocket.

She let him in and served supper and wine and they had quite
a friendly conversation, until the moment when he threw her
out.

I thought her case must be simple. However she had earned

the money it was hers and a couple of strong constables could easily put him into the street.

No, she explained with a fresh storm of tears, the law was on his side.

The laws must be insane! How shall I ever sever myself from Philipstal? What will happen to Joseph and me, if both Philipstal and Tussaud can claim everything without lifting a finger? Husband, companion — I no longer trust anyone.

I am afraid.

Joseph, his thin bird voice — as soon as he is not near me I grow nervous. Any loud sound is a cry of help from Joseph. If anything should happen to him I do not know what I would do. If any injury came to him I would commit murder. If Joseph should die I would throw myself in the sea.

What thoughts!

Outside the birds are singing loud and shrill, it is spring and the sky is as innocently blue as a child's shirt that has been washed too often.

Joseph and the dog come running up, the dog, with its lion's gallop and swinging ears, turning and stopping to wait for Joseph. His boots hamper him and he has taken them off, his face is hot and shining. He has picked three anemones. I put the flowers in water. When they fade I shall press them at the bottom of the cash box to bring us luck.

I must try not to spoil Joseph with too much attention, but show him that I depend on him — my indispensable darling.

Everything is ready now, each figure stands in the proper light, there is not a fold to be smoothed, not a hair out of place. Still Philipstal has not arrived, but I am fully determined to open tomorrow despite everything, even despite the letter from home.

We rejoiced when we saw the envelope, but the contents were the worst imaginable. I am still concealing them from Joseph, he is too young to understand.

My dear wife,

Here at Ivry-sur-Seine all is well. We are glad to hear that you and Joseph are in good health. As regards your

partner I have never had a high opinion of him and do not
consider him suitable company.

When you went, you left me as guardian to an infant and
an old woman, not a light task. The domestic drudgery is
quite incompatible with managing and arranging exhibi-
tions in your and your uncle's Waxwork Cabinet. I therefore
deemed it wisest to sell the house on the Boulevard du
Temple. Fortunately I found a buyer who was prepared to
take over figures, furniture and mirrors and this advantage-
ous sale ensures us a fixed annuity. I hope you will think I
have made the right dispositions.

François, your mother and I send many loving greetings
to Joseph and you and hope to see you again soon.

Your François Tussaud

He has sold my home, Curtius' famous Waxwork Cabinet, the
only place in the world where I belong! For the sake of a fixed
annuity, he has betrayed my uncle's work, the gilded hall, the
cellar with the blue light. It would have been easier had the house
been burned to the ground; that at least I could have understood.

Now I can never return to Paris. I would feel like a prisoner in a
cage of debt, no matter how many pounds' weight of gold I
brought with me. The thought fills me with shame.

I have often been able to drag myself away from pain and
experience everything at a distance, as if seeing both myself and
others through freshly polished glass. Only when something has
shaken me have I been torn from that distance, and the glass was
broken.

This is a blow: splintered glass, ice in my bones.

Joseph had smuggled the dog into bed with him into the
bargain — the smell woke me up. And when I was scolding
over the filth, the beast picked up our one pot plant in its mouth,
shook it so that the earth spattered over the floor and disappeared, with Joseph behind him.

Cleaning, rose water — waking up in filth and appearing
presentable.

My son stinks of dog. I wonder if this acrid animal stench will

come through my perfume! I am so afraid that we shall be given
notice.

I opened up and sat at the cash desk myself. People poured in,
the crowd and the admiration were almost greater than on the
first day in London. Joseph was very happy and charmed everyone. I would like to model him exactly as he looked today, his
cheeks bright with excitement, and that engaging, candid smile.

I was smiling too, remembering how pleased and proud I had
been at the opening in London and trying to recall those feelings,
bring them to the surface and make them reach right out to my
fingertips and my smiling, grateful, politely conversing lips.

A gentleman invited me to show the exhibition in Dublin.

With pleasure, anywhere in the world — Dublin, that must be
a long way. Yes, thank you!

But my body weighed me down, I had to pull myself up by the
hair in order not to sink into a hopelessly indifferent torpor.

If the sale of my home had been a revenge directly aimed at me
I could have understood and perhaps forgiven, but in reality
Tussaud simply does not want me back.

Free, free at last! I have bought myself free of Philipstal with
almost the whole of my Scottish capital — a grievous sum, but
better than being his slave, perhaps for the rest of my life. Joseph
is singing with glee — and yet, when I saw that tall, dark figure
turn on its heel and disappear without a word, as if I had
wounded and offended him, I felt for a moment very dismal and
discouraged.

The frontiers will probably be closed now: everyone fears
Napoleon and people flock to the hall to see him. Let us hope it
will be the same in Dublin!

Departure precisely as bad as I had expected. When Joseph
realized we could not take the puppy, he cast himself sobbing
round its neck. 'My Papa, Grand'mère, François and now my
little puppy,' he whimpered, and the animal licked his cheeks
and looked at him with an expression so deeply troubled that one
would have thought it understood.

I know that I have not only taken my son away from our family, but our itinerant life will also make it almost impossible for him to form genuine friendships. For a moment I truly wished we could take the puppy with us, but with such a travelling companion we would never obtain lodgings nor work undisturbed. When I think of everything it has already ruined!

To comfort Joseph I promised that he should be here when we returned and I went to the landlady, told her of the child's grief and paid her to feed the creature out of doors for six months. Before the end of that time I would be in touch with her.

The pretty, well-groomed woman took the money sympathetically and then remarked, still smiling and quite casually, that if the animal became a nuisance I must agree that she should let her husband shoot it. That nice lion-like coat would not be lost, however; she had long thought how stylish and exotic it would look before the hearth.

What am I to think of this highly cultivated woman, who both speaks and sings French!

I could not ask for my money back, but we shall never cross her threshold again. How Joseph would suffer if he were to see his four-legged playmate laid flat before the fire!

My dear one,

Joseph and I are now quite free. We have nothing to do with Philipstal's cheap exhibition: my figures do not belong in a circus, everyone respects me here. Our son no longer speaks a word of French and everyone believes him to be the son of an English gentleman. I am unhappy that I cannot give my younger son the same opportunities.

We have decided to go on touring. I have so many offers that we can look forward cheerfully to the future. There is no way back. I am not frightened of anything now, Monsieur Tussaud.

But I beg you, take good care of our little son and let me never repent having left my mother in your care.

Loving greetings to her and little François from
Joseph and Marie Tussaud

In London again. We are living in a respectable house and manage very well with a single room. Joseph reads fluently and easily and passes his time playing the piano. I shall stay long enough in each town for him to keep up his accomplishments. Three towns in a year will surely be convenient.

I intend to write to the Comte d'Artois and ask if I may open my next exhibition under his protection. The Duchess of York has already permitted me to use her coat of arms on my new black lacquered carriage — two gold escutcheons on the sides, that will look splendid!

Joseph's figure will stand at the entrance, smilingly bidding everyone welcome. He himself is very proud of this portrait! And I shall sit at the cash desk, discreetly and elegantly dressed in dull silk with a little lace. Otherwise I know quite well what the reaction would be in the provincial towns — those transparent materials, clinging casually to the body, light and almost skin-coloured. But I desire above all to be a lady, both for my son's sake and in order that my own person shall not distract one whit of attention from my figures.

One of the main attractions will be the two young Scottish murderers.

In a side alley as narrow as a rock cleft the rather elegant Hare tempts his simple friend Burke by showing him the sum of money of which he robbed his first victim.

Hare's face shines, pale and tense in the darkness, the fair hair clinging to his forehead. He attempts a smile, leaning persuasively towards Burke. The street lamp casts a blueish, glimmering light over the gold coins he holds in his hands, invitingly generous, yet the fingers with their bitten nails are crooked with fear lest he should drop one.

Burke's heavy, childlike features reveal his fear, but there is also ferocity there, his whole body drawn towards the shining gold, his shoulders, arms and short legs tense. He cannot have enough of gazing at the money Hare has suddenly conjured into the light, and he remembers all the stories he has heard of poor young men who by sheer chance gain the world's wealth and fortune. One can go close in under the street lamp and see that the gold coins on top are genuine.

The greed, fear and mutual attraction of these two men are among the horrors.

But in the middle of the largest hall, in the most dazzling light, Josephine will be crowned Empress.

David was kind enough to send me one of his sketches of Napoleon's coronation and I could tell from his short, arrogant letter that he himself has become a very important gentleman. Perhaps I might have envied him, had I experienced his success close at hand, but now, across frontiers, seas and mountains, we shall perhaps be expressing the very same thing.

Charming Josephine is kneeling and a murmur goes through the assembly at the sight of her modish, ultra-short hair, in contrast to the ermine cloak and golden crown which the Emperor presses down over her brow and temples. Everything about them radiates splendour, not extravagant or luxurious, but solidly powerful. But not even ermine, silk and velvet can conceal Josephine's provocative body and although she kneels and bows her head to the gold and to the broad little figure of the Emperor, she is far from the image of a saint.

These two tableaux, I believe, must occupy the greater part of my posters and programme. The printing costs will be covered by advertisements from London's leading cosmetic houses.

'A Cream that makes the Skin smooth and young. With constant use Wrinkles, Freckles, Moles, Pockmarks, Birthmarks and all other embarrassing Blemishes are removed.'

'This simple but effective Powder gives a softness to the texture of the Skin unparalleled in the annals of Art and consequently enhances the value of the rich donation of nature.'

'An entirely new description of Artificial Teeth, which so perfectly resemble the natural Teeth as not to be distinguished from the originals by the closest observer. They will never change Colour or Decay and will be found very superior to any Teeth ever before used.'

Such was the illusion of eternally radiant, frozen beauty, as if beauty were something inorganic, totally unconnected with birth, life or death!

But I believe that this well-established firm, which works so solemnly on dreams and illusions, will put me in a position to

print my name on the front in dull gold: Marie Tussaud. For I
have realized that over here I am far better known than dear,
widely celebrated Curtius.

In fact, I am already so prosperous that I can no longer carry all
my capital on my body. If I did, I would appear to be in an
interesting condition!

I could buy diamonds, gold, antiquities or furs, but I shall
never put my money into anything like that. To me money means
freedom to work and live and therefore I invest it only in materials, carriages and lighting.

Joseph's and my needs are few. In fact we need money only
when we entertain, and I feel secure in the knowledge that we
shall be travelling together. His light, musical voice lends itself at
once to the dialect and melodies of the language, while I follow
behind, breathless and stuttering.

CHAPTER TEN
Birmingham 1810

Joseph and I have now been nomads for eight years. The constant uprooting has become a habit, in no way a reminder of that first, weighty step I took into the carriage when I drove away from Ivry-sur-Seine.

When I look at my face I see no great change. The features have become a little sharper, the nose seems longer still, the chin more determined. My eyes have lost a little of their shine, but I still see everything clearly.

Joseph has long since grown out of his portrait. He has lost that aura of childhood, the engaging smile and graceful movements, and the light, intimate melody of his speech has been replaced by loud, rising notes and sudden drops. With angular movements, faster than he can control, he is tearing himself away from me. My caresses are left hanging in the air.

Yesterday he suddenly disappeared in his best suit, with a sharp smell of cheap eau-de-Cologne from neck and armpits. He came home long after dark, bruised and dirty, his trousers in shreds.

I gave a shriek of fright and tried to draw him to me, but he shook off my arms and went to his room, silent and reserved. I heard him brushing and rubbing at his trousers, complaining of the damage, and later tossing and turning in bed, and I was afraid he had been involved in a fight.

Today I learned what had happened. A man came to see us with his daughter, a girl perhaps a year older than Joseph and certainly taller and more developed. Those long, English legs in white lace stockings, and fair corkscrew curls round her ears. Her eyes were tearful, yet there was a certain pride in her demeanour.

The man declared that this dear child had played the injured innocent the night before and locked herself in her room. Both he and his wife had begged her in vain to open the door, especially as they could hear two voices from inside, and one seemed to be a boy's or a young man's.

Her father had therefore positioned himself outside his daughter's window with the family dog while his wife waited outside the locked door, and after darkness had fallen a boy came tumbling out of the window right onto the roses and herbaceous plants. The dog had grabbed hold of his trousers but he was very nimble and had escaped.

My heart was in my throat and I quite forgot to demand payment for the trousers, as I promised the man I would pay for the damage my son had done to his garden.

'We are leaving tomorrow in any case,' I said, 'so you can be quite at ease.'

'I shall wait for him for ever!' exclaimed the little lady ardently, and instantly received a cuff from her father. She gazed at him with such passion and defiance that I was even inclined to like her, although of course it was all the fault of her lace stockings and corkscrew curls. Had anything happened to Joseph I do not know if I would have strangled the man or the dog.

Today I saw my son and the girl walking by the river, arm in arm, like a little married couple. He came home a quarter of an hour after the time we should have left. How I longed to shake him, hit him — he *must* be punctual! How else am I to manage? How am I to make him understand that it is absolutely essential for him always to be punctual?

Sheffield, Leeds, Bradford, Appleby, Carlisle, Newcastle, Glasgow, Edinburgh. I bring them the latest novelties: the dazzling, scandalous Mary Anne Clarke, the Duke of York's mistress. My Chamber of Horrors would even venture to recommend the fearful sight of William Corder, with the stabbed, shot and strangled body of his victim, Maria Marten, in an exact copy of the interior of the infamous Red Barn. People with weak nerves should not expose themselves to this sight.

Novelties of this kind must come out as fast as possible, otherwise all the work is in vain.

Even if I am sometimes tired to the marrow of my bones, I have worked at my drawing board and with my modelling tools evening after evening and night after night, the whole time, to renew my exhibition.

The shepherdess with the lamb, the beautiful Sleeping Princess, the royal family, the dying Socrates with his hemlock juice, the dying Cleopatra with her poisonous asp, even Marat expiring in his bath and Robespierre's death-mask — all these have gradually become things of the past. There must always be a new crime, a new scandal, a new exclusive marriage or divorce, a piquant love affair, a general's defeat or a young prima donna's mysterious death, and above all we must be first with the news. We must be quick and accurate.

Sometimes I wish I could stay in one place and not have to pack up all those fragile figures and their wardrobes time after time. Travelling, sometimes in intolerable heat, sometimes fearful lest the horses may slip on icy roads, or of being shaken and flung to and fro by the waves, knowing that every time a crate moves it means an irreplaceable loss or hours of extra work!

Little by little I begin to dislike both sleeping and waking at chance inns, with all their noise, dogs, horses in the stables, coaches in preparation. And I look at my watch again and again, its ticking like little drops of metal seeping into me, making me wide awake and tense. Joseph sleeps, but I hear the cats, the drunkards, the maids dragging themselves about, drunk too, but with sleep, or merry parties arriving late at night. And the bugs do not always leave us in peace.

Only when I am sitting in the coach again does my head drop forward, and before I sleep I dream of a permanent place, a quiet, ordinary life, in which the morning light always comes in at the same window, and Joseph's books can stay in the bookcase, and my dresses hang in a cupboard like other people's clothes, and my bottles stand on the same dressing table. My figures no longer having to be dressed and undressed and divided up into all those vulnerable parts, my heroes and heroines standing in one great hall with mirrors in golden frames, the ceiling gilded over, the light like liquid gold over faces and clothes.

In a dark, sinister room, just as large, but damp and uncomfortable and with an untreated stone floor so that every step echoes — there I have my criminals, their faces long since in another world. They are stiff, primitive masks, instilling a fear we do not fully understand — and perhaps that is why it cannot be shaken off.

Again and again I see that gilded hall and I seem to hear music, but I know I am dreaming. It was I who made the choice, for both Joseph and myself.

I am always having to begin again from the beginning, and yet when I drive into a town and find the right premises for an exhibition and one or two rooms for Joseph and me, there is at once an excitement, a kind of prickling pleasure and anticipation — that little tremor under the skin that I felt for Astley's smart horses, which both danced the minuet and took the Bastille, standing on their back legs.

For that feeling I have renounced a husband, my mother and that late-born son — a cavity in my soul.

If Joseph disappoints me I am lost.

My life is all fragments and small, sharp splinters. How long can I live like this?

CHAPTER ELEVEN
Liverpool 1822

François

There was a storm last night. The sea was a welter of foam and along the shore the trees bent like feathers. Fortunately we were not at sea ourselves, but I dreamed I was standing in the middle of Curtius' great hall when suddenly the large crystal chandelier fell and the splinters filled the hall so that I felt them under my feet, in my hands and in my mouth.

Footmen with wet brooms swept the splendid chandelier into little heaps. I felt embarrassed at spitting out splinters while they were watching, so I swallowed some down and the sight of my palms depressed me utterly. When am I going to stop dreaming about the golden hall of my childhood?

I left a message for Joseph that I would take a little walk round the town before we opened. He of course was asleep, although he has already been married for a whole month to Elizabeth, his little girl from Birmingham, so proud of her new silk dresses. She chooses the newly fashionable colours, startling and immodest, which never float, but keep one's body earthbound.

All the same, Joseph and Elizabeth are a handsome pair: he, slim and distinguished in his dark suit and she radiant in cyclamen, canary yellow and reseda green. For the time being she no doubt regards these constant departures as a kind of honeymoon. Twenty-two years old and breakfast in bed every day. I hope Joseph has chosen the right one, after all!

The shops are not yet open, the city is remarkably bare, like a great machine soon to be set in motion. Only a few people in working clothes hurry by along streets which the wind has filled with paper, broken glass, tiles and whole branches. The butcher's boy is sweeping with a big, dripping wet broom he can scarcely guide. He has only one shoe.

Recently my exhibition was criticized for not showing models of the weavers in their miserable working conditions and social want, but which should I choose, among all those thin, anonymous figures that hurry past morning after morning? And how many people and how many looms would create the illusion of a factory? How am I supposed to show their poor food and brief sleep in bare, unheated rooms? And who would come to see them, when they have only to take a walk in London, Glasgow or here in Liverpool?

No, I must turn back, I am freezing. There is no reason to look in the shops, either. Elizabeth Babbington's — now Elizabeth Tussaud's — colours are in all the dress shops and it will become a problem on the day when I can no longer obtain the right materials when costumes have to be renewed.

It is of no importance to me personally. Only twice in my life have I bought peach, apricot and white — when I was married and when I was free. There is no reason to think of it again. I am sixty-one and I dress in thick, black silk like a prosperous widow. This old woman's costume gives me a kind of independence. There is no need for me to adapt to the changing fashions and it matters not whether my feet are large or small, my breasts slack, my waist slender, as long as my sight survives. I can scarcely read the paper without spectacles, but I see faces and figures clearly. There is no cause for concern! I will turn round, go straight home and drink some chocolate.

But a silhouette appears: ten paces — seven paces away stands a young man. There is something about his bearing, a hesitancy, an uncertainty, betraying the stranger come to town.

As he buys a newspaper I catch a glimpse of his profile, his way of saying thank you, of counting his money. He moves with obvious uncertainty in a town that is just waking up. He does not seem to have had much sleep — perhaps he has just landed and was at sea in the storm.

To judge by his clothes and bearing he is not a sailor, and that

French accent carried on the wind, sweet as the scent of a white lily — why am I following him? It is like entering a dream whose colours and movements are already familiar. There is a likeness: he reminds me of a young man I once met, terribly young, in search of some aunt or other, a distant, almost unknown aunt. Perhaps she did not exist at all, she was only an illusion.

Later I was to show him other illusions, the gilded hall and all Philipstal's pictures. Philipstal the traitor, who turned towards the wall when he met me in the street, but needed my money. Tussaud — the scoundrel, who ruined everything. The grey and yellow colours of resentment, the sulphur yellow of the canopy — forget them, forget them! Go home and drink some chocolate.

But the young man's figure draws my old woman's body through the city, round corners, along alleyways, for I must see his face. Perhaps I am growing senile: old people often think they recognize acquaintances in total strangers. No, I am not yet as old as that! I must come closer to him, touch his sleeve with a light gesture of entreaty, just to see his face. Perhaps he will brush my hand away like a fly.

No, he turns his face towards me — and François, my beloved son, looks down at me. He has my eyes and the over-long nose, and my hands. We are reunited at last!

With tears and embraces on an ice-cold morning in Liverpool we cling to each other as if the wind might tear us apart, our exclamations fluttering like blue ribbons in the air. Without daring to hope, I have been waiting almost twenty years for this moment.

He asks what I am doing in the street so early in the morning.

'I knew you would come — I dreamed a happy dream!'

'How could you recognize me?'

'I would have known you among thousands, François, wherever I had met you — even had it been in India!'

My sons — two tall young men, one already married: Joseph and François. They shall never lack for anything, I shall work to the end of my days for their sakes — and for my own. For if I owned my childhood's gilded hall or even a whole palace in London, I would still have to go on recording the images and faces that I see.

We woke Joseph, leaving Elizabeth to sleep, and despite the long parting and widely different upbringing it was quite obvious that Joseph and François were of the same flesh and blood.

Fortunately François was sensitive enough not to mention his father more than was really necessary. When Joseph enquired, he said only that Tussaud was in good health and his economic situation satisfactory.

My beloved mother has recently died, peacefully, in her sleep. For François she filled a mother's place and was making grand, complicated dishes and washing and ironing on the day before she died, as if dying were something commonplace. And I still have a soft, pretty shawl in a drawer and a pair of black gloves with a musty smell.

When I had pulled myself together I questioned François about his education and position. He said he was a merchant, but there was a hesitation and an insincerity in his reply that told me more clearly than words that he was either lying or had gone bankrupt.

'Dealing in what?'

'In billiards.'

For a moment I was really afraid that my poor boy might be a cheat, or even a professional billiards player.

The word alone conjured up the sound of those ivory balls striking each other, drily and precisely, on those nights when Tussaud did not go to bed but drank with his friends or on his own.

It brought tears to my eyes, but I pretended they were tears of happiness and when I pressed the boy further it turned out that he had fortunately only done some occasional work, producing billiard balls and tables. I kissed him, pleased that he could carve both ivory and wood: a craft is more than enough, he need never bother with business.

He plays the violin, too. Joseph sat down at the piano and their music mingled and flowed towards me and although I am not particularly musical, it was like an act of love, at once tender and abstract. Later Elizabeth woke up and joined in on her harp.

We spent the whole day together, all so happy and light-hearted. That sudden meeting was a miracle.

'I knew you at once. I would have recognized you anywhere.'
'Even on the moon!' 'In a crowd of thousands.' We kept repeating our assurances to each other.

François was full of admiration when he toured the exhibition
and saw Joseph's and my work and the few figures left over that
were made by Curtius.

He produced good ideas at once, suggesting a little air cushion
on the Sleeping Princess's stomach to give the impression that
this celestial beauty was truly alive. And among the aristocratic
portraits he suggested that dance music should be played on
Sunday afternoons. The effect, he said, would be that at any
moment the figures would lift their arms and begin to dance a
rather stiff but delightful minuet.

Only one little blemish on my happiness. That evening, when
we had eaten, my son François went to his lodgings. Although
Joseph and I tried to persuade him to stay, he said he had no wish
to be a burden to us — a burden to his mother! I am afraid that he
does after all cherish some resentment towards me and is punish-
ing me by not wishing to sleep under the same roof. And yet I
would so gladly have paid my landlady for an extra bed.

'François,' I said, 'it was Napoleon who separated your father
and me, it was the war that closed the frontiers. Otherwise I
would have come back.'

He nodded and touched my cheek, but the gesture was hesitant and resigned and he might just as well have told me that it had
really been possible to return for years now.

Perhaps Tussaud told him about the sheepgut, or he remembers some tiny, chance movement — my hand brushing him
away.

There is a parting between us, a whole landscape of tears and
salt, far too painful to be entered into.

And when my rediscovered son left me, I felt for a moment
that he was just some young man I had met, not particularly well
educated, not particularly gifted.

What would he tell Joseph about Tussaud? And how much has
Joseph told him about me?

Our stories will throw different lights on the same facts. Even
in my greatest happiness there is a drop of gall.

My three children lay in my fate and my body like patterns in a stone. Joseph is my child, François is Tussaud's child, and that baby girl, too delicate for this world, like porcelain — perhaps she was everything I had to combat in myself.

Perhaps the children were already thin lines drawn in the childish hand the gypsy read.

Travelling across the water — once an enigma, then imperative and clear. But when I left I felt that it was I who had decided.

If only I knew what has brought François to me!

CHAPTER TWELVE
London 1841

Tussaud

Just what one might expect of Tussaud: a letter proposing that we open a theatre together! Word of my good fortune has reached Paris and once again he is hoping to receive something *gratis*.

It is a polite, almost friendly letter. He still has the gift of the gab and behaves as if we were friends, as if I had not given him to understand once and for all that it is over. It is all over, no longer do either our bodies or our finances have any connection with each other.

It brings everything back like a wound that starts to bleed again. Although our life together was short I know that both French and English law would support Tussaud. I remember all too well that young woman in the solicitor's office, her torn stockings and her tears.

Tussaud sold my home in Paris — does he now want to put me out of my golden hall in London?

I was much too shaken to guide a pen and although I have never spent a single day in bed, I lay down and asked Joseph to write to Tussaud.

My son's reply was brief and comprehensive — and as cold as I could wish. He simply wrote that we had never received anything at all for our maintenance and therefore regarded all links as broken.

This unambiguous reply reassured me so much that the very next day I was at the box office, enjoying the sight of the premises we have now owned for seven years.

Although I do not care for the responsibilities of a house-holder, I am thankful that our nomadic existence is over. Only now do I realize how much those twenty years of never-ending departures and difficult travel have tired me. That is not something I can expect of my sons, now they are both married and have children.

As long as we constantly renew our show there is a huge audience here in London and people pour in as they did to Curtius' Waxwork Cabinet in the old days. The sight of the great hall always makes me happy.

My son Francis, as we now call him, has not only learned to make billiard balls, he is a real artist in his field.

'Mirrors and gold,' he murmured, when he had looked round the big empty hall for a while, and he built Byzantine pillars and decorations as light and airy as Venetian lace. He gilded the entire ceiling and a golden light sweeter than maple syrup sets the customers' faces aglow. It is a dream world of mirrors and lace which for the moment obliterates all divisions.

The light falls on the weavers and the slim, graceful figures of the little milliners as they go right up to Queen Victoria — first to see her coronation and then to observe the sweet, romantic moment when the Prince Consort slips the ring onto her straight little finger.

She is wearing her wonderful bridal robe created by Miss Bidney, so flattering with its train and veil that the quite commonplace, stiff little Queen is transformed into a beauty. The admiration and dreams of the young girls cling to her silken hem, especially now, because as the years pass she can be viewed both here and in her real, harmonious family life with Prince Albert and their lovely children — how difficult it is, though, to make those children really captivating! I wonder if she will give birth again soon?

It seems that people of very high rank can make some kind of contact with their inferiors only by marrying, giving birth or dying. Poor Josephine, unable to bear children, was encouraged even by her best friends to die, for a divorced Emperor is a dubious commodity. But as a widower he would be enveloped in tenderness and sympathy.

We have unfortunately been obliged to move Josephine's charming figure. At the time of the divorce she had to take a less striking position and now she would be quite unsuitable in the dim little room where the dying Napoleon breathes his last on his field cot. What incredible good fortune that we were able to purchase the very bed! Almost every day one of his old soldiers arrives and conducts long conservations with his vanquished, dying commander. Sometimes I hear him crying, but at other times he seems excited and full of spirit. He always stands very upright and at a fitting distance between the pillars and the golden eagles. Only once did I see him straighten the bedcover a little. I am immoderately fond of this old man, who makes me feel that my work is important, and I gladly allow him to visit without paying, although in former times I measured my success in money.

I wish he would come now, because today I really have not the heart to go down to the cellar to ensure that the light still falls correctly on Hare's cat-like face, and to see if Maria Marten's corpse still makes people take a step backwards, while the hair on the back of their necks rises like the fur of a wild animal.

I prefer to remain in the gilded hall, where I feel as safe as a queen bee in her hive. I shall always remember the moment when we had completely finished arranging the place, when there was not a fold or a hair to be changed on the figures and light shone from the windows and the chandeliers. I felt as if at any moment I might float away like an elegant golden insect, seeing all the images at once, bright and clear-cut. I stood between my two sons and all the wounds and flaws were healed like plant stalks in a luxuriant green summer. The air felt clear and flinty, my daughters-in-law's hair smelled of roses and narcissi and my grandchildren were prettier than angels.

On that day I knew nothing of the letter which would take both my sons to Paris. If only I had answered Tussaud myself without saying a word to Joseph! But that is what comes of a moment's weakness.

Perhaps my sons have been in secret correspondence with their father? They said they would negotiate with Tussaud, but what is there to negotiate? To be of assistance to him, they said,

as if I were not in greater need of assistance now that we have
engaged musicians to play every evening, and I cannot even hear
if they play a false note.

Joseph and Francis even spoke of family feeling and the bond
of blood and all that kind of outworn cant, as if they were not two
respectable fathers of families but a pair of snotty little boys
coming when their father called.

I have some understanding for Francis, but Joseph — why
should he go to Paris? His place is here. He cannot even speak a
word of French. 'My childhood, my roots,' he says — that I
should hear that from him! How it wounded me. I made him
swear not to see his father but to negotiate in writing only and I
would have gone down on my knees to him if it helped.

My heart was ready to break when I saw my two boys go out to
the carriage in their frock coats and with their tall hats and
full beards and big, expensive cases. Fortunately both have
children and must return, but I shall not know a moment's peace
until they are at my side again.

Joseph's Elizabeth cried, Francis' Rebecca cried and their
children shouted about the toys they wanted brought back.
There are gilt fittings on Francis' case — he carries his wealth so
innocently, visible to all.

He showed me a nightgown and some underclothing he had
bought for his Rebecca. She is welcome to them — that girl, with
breasts like the figurehead on a galleon, inquisitive as a puppy
and, apparently at least, as bashful and inexperienced as a nun.
But underclothing like this! One would think their bedroom was
a circus ring — it must certainly be his father's influence!

If only I knew what Tussaud really wants, if only I could have
warned my sons. Let us hope this journey does not end by costing
us too much, both in emotion and in money. When I consider
how Tussaud turned my head I am afraid, remembering that
both in Paris and at Ivry-sur-Seine I sought and wrought for him
and became soft, shunning conflict. And now — now my poor
boys, with their full beards and heavy cases, will face him with far
less experience than I. If only he does not persuade them to stay,
or come here himself with his theatre. Am I, at my age, to be
dependent on a man and have problems with actors into the

bargain? As if that were not enough, Francis has engaged the French Crown Prince himself to play the violin in our orchestra — if it really is he, for I am beginning to have my doubts.

We employed him because of his moving story and the unusual charm of his slightly feminine manner and slim body. And of course he does play the violin with a fine and soulful tone. I had expected problems least of all with him, but now he keeps asking for higher wages because he can only drink French cognac and a particularly expensive Burgundy. Moreover, he claims his right to weep on his mother's lap. I do not know if the tears are genuine but the blots on my wax figure's silk dress are authentic at all events.

I have difficulty in recognizing that pretty little boy in him, the child who played with Elizabeth in the garden and was later misled into giving evidence against his mother. But when he is drunk I have at least to pretend I believe in the story of his unhappy fate and improbable flight.

He claims to remember everything, including his wet-nurse's breasts, smelling of vintage wine and chicken. She used to slap him round the head with them to make him go to sleep quickly, and when the crazy woman dropped off at last his fat baby hands would reach for the bottle and hold it between his toothless gums, the wine giving him that safe, heavy baby sleep which made his cheeks grow pink.

He loves to tell such stories, but if one questions him more closely about precise events he bursts into tears and declares that such memories are far too painful and that moreover numerous shocks have caused him to suffer from loss of memory.

Regarding the adventurous flight to England through thick woods and broad landscapes, everything had taken place in pitch darkness and everyone had been masked, therefore neither his forests nor his people had names. He does, however, claim to possess two visible pieces of evidence: one that he lived with a peacock because on a sudden impulse he had taken a peacock's egg from the Trianon, hatched it out in prison and brought the chick with him on his flight. Everyone complained about the hoarse, plaintive cry of this now fully-grown bird which mingled at night with the complaint of the violin. He had himself photographed with it again and again, the apparently besotted peacock unfolding its magnificent tail round his hips, and in no time at all the photographer produced a picture which was a definite likeness, though the bird was a blur.

Photographs are like a kind of magic, which frightens me. Darkness and light and those rays which extract a superficial little image from one.

Perhaps the soul also becomes flat and pitted like a piece of blotting paper. It seems to me that the Crown Prince, that soft, vain man, absorbs stories all the time, identifying himself with palaces, prisons and forests, but flickering imprecisely among stories of light and shade, vapid changing images — likenesses, but never accurate, as wax is.

The other proof of his origins is less aesthetic. For a small fee he will gladly roll up his trouser leg and show a somewhat slovenly tattoo of a lily. He says it was done by the Pope himself, but I greatly doubt that the Pope concerns himself with such matters — and so imperfectly, into the bargain!

I do not think it fitting that almost every evening he rolls his trouser leg up and down and bursts into tears and I have no desire to see him ruining our good name. Also I have remarked that the other musicians are becoming quite dissatisfied with this person, whoever he is. What *is* the masculine of prima donna?

How I hope that Joseph and Francis will return home soon and tell me what to do, and how I hope they do not bring Tussaud and his actors, or perhaps a whole circus, with them. Nothing that man did would surprise me.

Nothing in my life has frightened me as much as this completely unnecessary journey.

Joseph, Francis, I can no longer fight alone.

CHAPTER THIRTEEN

London 1850

Marie
This pain and itching in my body, as if there were rats and mice inside it — I know what these long, hoarse breaths mean: death is sitting inside me, ready to break through, held back only by the thin body, fragile as an egg.

I am moving closer to Curtius, who was perhaps my father, perhaps my uncle. It is really of no importance, for he shaped me and determined my movements as if I were one of his own figures, with a cool little head, a steel wire down my back and a slim body made of kid and kapok — his living doll, his obedient puppet.

And I am moving closer to my mother, who for almost a lifetime behaved like a saint, all for the sake of one little lie. And Elizabeth, whose death-mask I avoided making, as if in that way I could avoid coming too close to death. I was still young then.

Now I know that I shall soon be leaving my grandchildren, although their secure, shining faces bind me to life. Francis and Rebecca have a new baby every year — they want a whole nestful. Joseph with his three children is more sensible.

That boy disappointed me only once. That was when he, a mature gentleman of good reputation, travelled to Paris and knelt in his long frock coat by a little hole in the wall to catch a glimpse of his father. Since then he has described Tussaud as a charming old man and cannot understand how I could have feared him — and yet he had promised me so faithfully to negotiate in writing and never to meet him again! Like two little boys, he and Francis bored a hole in the wall the size of a finger, according to their account, and without Tussaud suspecting anything.

But if I know him, he knew all about it! He probably made the hole a little bigger himself, so that Joseph could see him clearly as he sat talking so cosily with his dear Francis — and in an armchair that Joseph claimed to remember from his childhood, with a coverlet embroidered by my mother.

So much to see through such a little hole! No, Tussaud undoubtedly helped in order the better to pose, the old fox. Moreover he was not ashamed to bore a hole in the wall that had belonged to Curtius; the only part of my inheritance he has not laid waste is still that modest little property which gives him a roof over his head.

I wish Joseph had never referred to it. I can imagine the beating of his heart and his flushed cheeks under his beard as he knelt before that hole. Has he no shame? My Joseph! When I think of all we did together!

Since then he has even sent money to his 'poor old father'. But there was no question of a theatre — and yet still the very thought of it makes me shudder.

When my grandchildren ask me to tell stories it is always about the time when Joseph and I crossed the sea and journeyed up hill and down dale.

These spoiled, pretty children have their own rooms, in homes with linen cupboards, stacks of porcelain in glass-fronted cabinets and expensive clothes in the wardrobe. Even Francis' dog has a room of its own.

I tell them about the days when we lived in any rooms that came to hand, those little rooms, painted brown, green, rust-red and a simple white. Walls against which I was always picturing little Francis and my mother before my eyes. The children seem to want me to tell it as a distressing tale, now fortunately over and done with, and I assure them that those days will not return, they can stay in their silk-curtained rooms with their dolls and toy soldiers, their dog baskets, tea sets, Sunday joints and fragrant linen.

But in reality it was not at all an unhappy time. I was perfectly at home in those occasional rooms, which asked nothing of me and were simply a resting place for the night. The wind howled or the sun shone and Joseph and I were content as long as we had a table, two chairs and a bed. We saw the poplars bending in the wind and in summer we walked on heather-covered banks where the air was hot and heavy with honey.

I concentrated on my tableaux and it was no sacrifice, there was nothing heroic about it. If I had had a great, luxurious house like my daughters-in-law or just an ordinary establishment, it would have torn me apart. I wanted no more than the necessities.

It occurs to me that Tussaud extended the house at Ivry-sur-Seine almost without my being aware. All I noticed were the expenses and the disturbance the labourers brought with them.

Tussaud was always making sketches of possible extensions and of garden designs which would be more handsome and more luxurious. I was *distraite* and only a little impressed. Perhaps I hurt him.

He had friends at the inn, but I saw only the people whose likenesses I needed for the exhibition. Tussaud played the piano, the violin and billiards. He sang and kept dogs. One day he said he had engaged a man to work in the garden; in fact he had so many leisure pursuits that he was obliged to employ people to carry them out. But I — I felt free only when I was working. At that time I gave it no thought, I simply opened my purse with a slightly irritated and perhaps close-fisted gesture.

Even now I live modestly, having all that a woman approaching ninety could need: a bed, a table, a chair, a little snuff, a glass of port wine, a little perfume and a close-stool.

My cheeks are hollow now and unfortunately my sight is no longer very sharp. I bump the glass with my nose when I am searching for my mother's face, but it is more often Curtius' face that suddenly appears, small and concentrated, as it was when my fingertips found him cold. There is no reason to struggle. It is the same with my eyeglasses, which both incommode and assist me.

I remember the old, bird-like women, pale-skinned, bodies smelling like foul water. Their clear, glassy eyes allowed every impression to flow by, or tied them hopelessly to something in the past: perhaps a simple splash of light in the dark — white, like the hectically shining petals of the chrysanthemums after the stalk has been stripped of leaves.

The thought of those eyes terrifies me, like sharp colours and photographs, and I walk across to the great, gilded hall. At the top of the stairs I meet the wax figure I made of myself.

Marie Tussaud looks out over the hall, her eyes alert and very clear, as if perceiving a connection in her portraits. She is a landlady, inspecting her guests, self-assured in her black silk dress, too old to dance the minuet but young enough to count the money. Perhaps she smiles, but even in the smile she keeps a little distance and even in the light she seems to be a little detached.

Inside her is the old woman who avoids pale colours, the little girl, like a piece of bric-a-brac, bobbing confusedly to her reflection in the glass. The slim, cloaked young woman waiting at the Madeleine Cemetery, slowly growing accustomed to the cold; kneeling, she bowed her head and stopped in mid-fall. The jackal girl, the woman who left her bolthole at Ivry-sur-Seine without looking back, and perhaps above all, an arrogant little girl is there, the stubborn child who stretched her ankle under the table to dance her way to fame, so eager, and so indifferent to sorrow.

I do not know how much I decided for myself. It often seems to me that events poured over me like waves. Perhaps there are things I should have done differently, but I have no regrets; although I often lie awake at night.

There is one dream that pursues me: I am walking along the narrow alleys of my childhood home town, following a child, a boy I think. His legs are thin, his body so meagre that all his movements are sharp and graceless. I talk and talk, to hold him back, only to see his face, but my voice is outside myself. At last he turns his head and his face is a glossy white plane, transparent and quite devoid of features.

When I wake up I feel my body is as fragile as a bird's egg, or a thread of blue silk, but there is no real fear. I fear only the pure angels.